Mary Lavin was born of Iris
Massachusetts, in 1912. She mov
living first in Athenry, County (
1930 she entered University Coll
her doctorate when she wrot
Holland'. By 1942, eleven of he
periodicals as the London *Good H* ~~~~
and *Harper's Bazaar,* and a collection of her short stories won the
Jamis Tait Black Memorial Prize. She continued writing up to the
early eighties, producing some nineteen collections of short
stories and contributing regularly to the *New Yorker.* She was
awarded a Guggenheim fellowship in 1959 and 1961, and she
received the Katherine Mansfield Prize in 1961, and she was
granted an honorary doctorate at UCD in 1968. In 1992 she was
elected 'Saoi' by Aosdána, an affiliation of Irish artists for
outstanding achievement in literature. Mary Lavin died in
Dublin in March 1996.

Evelyn Conlon is a short story writer and novelist and has been
described as 'one of Ireland's major, truly creative writers.' She
was born in1952 in County Monaghan.

MARY LAVIN

tales from Bective Bridge

**TOWN
HOUSE**

Published in 1996 by
Town House and Country House
Trinity House
Charleston Road
Ranelagh, Dublin 6
Ireland

British Library Cataloguing in Publication Data. A
catalogue record for this book is available from the
British Library.

ISBN: 1-86059-041-1

Cover illustration: *Seated Female Nude* by Mainie Jellett,
Private Collection, Dublin, by kind permission of The
Jellett Trust. We are indebted to Bruce Arnold, author of
Mainie Jellett and the Modern Movement in Ireland, for help
with the cover illustration.

Cover design by Wendy Williams
Typeset by Typeform Repro Ltd. Dublin
Printed in Ireland by ColourBooks Ltd.

Contents

New Introduction

In 1943 when this collection was last published, the preface was written by Lord Dunsany, a man older than Mary Lavin. Now so many years later, as I write, the difference in approach has nothing to do with age or gender but rather with what has happened since. Lord Dunsany was introducing a new writer, was signalling the depth and unusualness of her work, was painting us a promise to come, whereas now we can see this collection as only part of a consistently interesting lifetime's work. A writer is judged not by the normal forgiving mechanisms used to judge life, but by an exacting, strict and merciless standard, that should remain fairly consistent but which of course is affected by all sorts of extraneous factors. But the important point is that between 1943 and now, Mary Lavin did do the work, and did take on the task of being a writer, so when reading Lord Dunsany's preface today we can feel a glee born from the fulfilment of the promise for which he could only have hoped. Because this is the year of Mary Lavin's death we are re-looking at her work, bookshelves are being peered through, as we try to find old collections. I am remembering the first of her stories that I read. It has always been my great bone of contention that I was not taught her work at school, because although I did eventually find her, I missed reading her at the right time. Young femalehood in Ireland in the sixties would have been greatly illuminated by the voice that examined the wars of relationships rather than those of countries. The men had gone realistic, were concerned with old suspicions, still had the sounds of guns ringing in their ears. I knew the work of her male colleagues, of course, and would have been able to put them in a better context if I'd had this writer to flash past them.

The first story I came across was the first in this collection. 'Lilacs' is an extraordinary story about the way that love can survive among cow dung. We can look at it in many ways, including the differences between the two daughters, and the differences between them and their mother. We can look at it as the story of a love that has a certain amount of cantankerousness attached to it, but one that survives, despite that large mound of cow dung that is outside the door. It would be unfair not to mention that Frank O'Connor was also aware of the differences between himself, his male colleagues and Mary Lavin. In the book *The Lonely Voice,* a study of the short story, he says 'So an Irishman, reading the stories of Mary Lavin, is actually more at a loss than a foreigner would be. His not-so-distant political revolution, seen through her eyes, practically disappears from view. She has written only one story about it – 'The Patriot Son' – and from a patriotic point of view that is more than enough.' He complains that the point of view is 'perhaps too exclusively feminine, for as the story unfolds, a man may be excused for thinking that the mammy's boy is a far better type than the revolutionary, Mongon, and might even feel inclined to pity any matriarch who in future tried to bully him. But here at least the Irishman is on familiar ground, the ground of O'Flaherty and O'Casey. It is only when he turns to the other stories that he gets the real shock, for, though names, details, dialogue all seem of unimpeachable accuracy, he might as well be reading Turgenev or Leskov for the first time, overwhelmed by the material unfamiliarity of the whole background, versts, shubas, roubles and patronymics.'

Without endangering her distance from such feeble criticism, Mary Lavin wryly teases about these differences in 'A Story with a Pattern', published in *In a Café.* A man has been introduced to a writer, says that he is glad to meet her, and tells her that he has read a number of her stories and that he wants to tell her what he thinks of them. He does say that she has talent, and wonders if she knows it, but then he suggests that she take up writing seriously. The writer goes on to ask 'which of the stories did you like best ?' 'He looked at me. I beg your pardon, he said, did I say I liked them? I thought they were written with a good style, and I thought you brought the people in them to life, but I don't think I remember saying that I liked them.' The man continues, and tells her that her stories would never appeal to men because after a man had read a page or two, he would throw them aside because 'a man wants something with a bit of substance to it, if you know what I mean? A man wants something a bit more thick, if you understand.' At the end of the discussion, during which he has told her a story that he wants her to write, she asks again if he will not now admit that her very argument was indeed relevant to the short story but he concludes with 'please don't start that nonsense again,' and casually walks away.

Mary Lavin was writing in a time in which, as Tillie Olsen says in *Silences*, no list of writers admitted more than one woman for every twelve men. It was also a time in which it was extremely rare for a woman with three children (indeed in her case, she reared the children for a number of years on her own), to get any work done, never mind as much as she did. But of course she had another twist to this. She said in an interiew with RTE that women writers only wrote what they had to, whereas male writers, being minded continuously by either a wife or a secretary wrote far too much. She implied that consequently the work was of a more consistent calibre. She believed that she gained enormously from her responsibilities. This is indeed an extraordinarily encouraging thing for a writer of her stature to say.

One of the great characteristics of these stories is Mary Lavin's capacity to almost shrug off the drama of the situation, as it appears and then to draw us into another completely different drama. While on one hand 'The Green Grave and the Black Grave' is about the island woman versus the inland woman, about the holding down of love-talk, and the terrible things that the sea will do; on the other hand it is actually about the passing of responsibility from a father to a son. It could be read as a direction on how to knock at a door in the middle of the night when you have bad news. 'Keep your strength for the loud knocking you'll have to give on the wooden door, said Tadg Mor.'

Time and death are recurring themes of the work. She said that once when she saw her father sunbathing with other fathers, she realised how much older he was than the others, and at that moment became very involved in the notion of the passing of time. But this is a rather simplistic and overly modest view of how she deals with the essence of time. Of course, 'Lilacs' is also about death as well as love. It is not just about bossyboots Kate and dithering, dreamy, crying, fainting Stacy. It is about what these two daughters and this mother will do when their father and husband has died. It rests well on the icon of the 'nice cup of tea', a repeated consolation through many of Mary Lavin's stories. One cannot imagine a cup of tea being served with such dignity and such importance until one has finished this book and seen it appearing over and over again. The sense of eroticism plays a strong role in much of her work. When Ros is remembering the Phelim of her youth, she lists his physical attributes, and then remarks that 'that was the time he led her in a piece off the road when they

were coming from Mass one Sunday.' That memory takes its place
among the finest love sentences of literature because of its shy, covert
conveyance of shimmering sexuality. We become, as in all of Mary
Lavin's stories, implicated in the arguments of the protagonists. We
are never allowed to forget the menace of mourning that is waiting to
crop up in all its full-voiced wailing at the drop of certain words; in
this story the word is usually 'dung'. As in other stories, the getting old
is not sentimental, it may be a little poignant, but mostly it is matter-
of-fact and almost defiant.

Reading a collection of Mary Lavin can take a long time. The
reader needs to take breathers, because quite often, days after reading
the story, you realise that your original view was in fact only a minor
part of what was going on. Quite like a play in which the action takes
place before you, but the nuances take place later. Mary Lavin would
not, of course, have been dealing with the issues of morality, for
example God's law versus the Church law, that a writer might be
examining today, but interestingly there are moments of premonition
in which she hints at themes that will be dealt with many years later.
In the story 'Sarah' there is an extraordinarily brash and total lack of
trust in men. Whereas the woman, Sarah, is no doubt the fallen person,
it is understood that other women with sons or newly-married men
will simply have to make sure that their men don't go near her.
Somehow we are made to have sympathy with Sarah and not to trust
these sons or these newly-married men. By the end of the story,
sympathy for Sarah is complete, and not just because of the two
ludramauns of brothers that she lives with.

Mary Lavin seems to enjoy defining class. In 'Love is for Lovers',
she directs us exactly to everybody's place by showing us the way that
they are paid and then leads us into the great tension of the woman
battling to get the man to marry her, and he battling with the idea of
fantasy and the notion of ageing. She puts us on guard with her usual
strange wit. In this case, the woman is a regular scatterbrain, widow
and all though she is; the idea obviously being that widows should
certainly not be scatterbrains, that somehow or another widowhood
should have put upon them a seriousness that they might not have had
before.

In 'Say Could that Lad be I?' Mary Lavin watches herself writing,
in much the same way that Grace Paley watches herself in the story

called 'Debts'. Because of this confident self-consciousness the story becomes a much more modern one than the theme would suggest. This sort of examination of the role of the writer became a profound part of re-appraisal, particularly in the Black American short story of the 1960s and 1970s, and although Mary Lavin was not quite approaching that principle, she was writing again in that way which has two levels of significance, one obvious and the other less clear, even if implied.

While reading a 'A Fable' one wonders what exactly the fable is. Is there a twist? Should you record your feelings, your conjectures, shoud you indeed take bets? Unlike Austin Clarke's 'planter's daughter', who is loved and adored because of her beauty, the perfection of this woman gets on the nerves of the neighbours. And it is not until such time as she can be brought to some sort of level with them that people can begin to relate to her properly. The story is not just about beauty, it is about taking each person down that peg or two to make them fit into not just the social and class hierarchy but the hierarchy that deals with the look of the individual. And yet the author is sympathetic in some ways, because although as they 'put their arms into the outheld shrouds' they may not have learned what we have learned in the story, and somehow we do not blame them. But if the people in this story are unknowing to themselves, Miss Holland on the other hand knows herself and what her limits are. She knows what she doesn't know. She is bereft of certain kinds of knowledge, like what a living wage might be, how to give a tip, how to have a conversation, how to startle, and even worse, how to hate people. Miss Holland has reached a terrible paralysis, a crux in her life that the ignorance of this world has forced upon her. This same ignorance has affected Manny Ryan in 'At Sallygap'. We could say that he too has reached a state of paralysis. Here Mary Lavin poignantly contrasts city and country, and also compares life on this island to the wondrous beauties and excitements of Paris, where Manny could have gone, with his fiddle, if only he had not been moved by the sight of the woman who was waving goodbye to him. All the psychology books and political textbooks in the world could not describe so well the chasm of difference now existing between these same two people, both disappointed in their marriage. Dangerous lurking desires are hinted at on the part of the wife, and the resolutions of their differences come from a darker age.

In the concluding story in this collection, Mary Lavin takes a jump from that personal terrible world of the married couple who didn't have the wherewithal to deal with their own darkness, and moves instead to the world of 'The Dead Soldier'. This is not just a story about war and the futility of war, it is about the way that women approach war, the way women approach the death that happens during war. The mother spends her time thinking of her son, and cannot understand how anybody would not remember every single thing about him. 'If you were his mother you'd remember every single look he ever had on his face from the day he was born to the last day you looked at him.' The woman is portrayed, in a sense, as an innocent against the landscape of such a massive war. But by her insistence on common decency we are again back at the argument about Mary Lavin and the public world, and how that public world was viewed through the private ruminations of each of the stories, as opposed to the stories written by her male counterparts that were informed continuously by the backdrop of the sounds of war.

In the broad map of human relationships given to us in this collection, Mary Lavin colours some of the geography in stark shades. And there is a justice about the overall picture. At a time when publishers are failing to give the form the serious attention it deserves, it is appropriate to remember how scathing she could be about those who thought the short story inferior to the novel. 'Non-creative people' she called them, who thought that the short story was practice for the novel, mere five-finger exercises. Alertness and sensitivity are required of the reader here, precisely because these works are more difficult and startling than the longer form could ever be. The stories are subversive, dangerous even, in the way that human relationships, devoid of sincerity or morality, can themselves be. These complete pictures are not tales or anecdotes, they are instead fully-fledged, shocking reminders of how life is and has always been. Mary Lavin cuts her stories out of a kind of memory seldom represented by her colleagues. Short stories are also photography, and in this case well served, because the human behind the camera was blessed with good eyes and a second sight. First time readers are in for a startling, sometimes almost Gothic treat, and old friends will welcome the chance to read this fine collection again.

Evelyn Conlon
November 1996

Author's Introduction

Once in a while a book comes out under a lucky star. *Tales from Bective Bridge* was lucky in its day. The stories in it were accepted one after the other as they were written, by magazines of repute – *The London Mercury*, *The Dublin Magazine* and similar publications. They were quickly collected in book form, for which Lord Dunsany wrote a preface. The book was awarded The James Tait Black Memorial Prize, reviewers were unanimously kind to it, and it became a Readers' Union choice which made it a commercial as well as a literary success.

But all that was long ago and at the time I had no real ambition to be a writer. In my school days I had taken great pride in my essays, and always got high marks for them. This was not as creditable as it may seem, because I spent an excessive amount of time planning them and an inordinate amount of time in the writing of them. I also neglected other subjects. Predictably perhaps, then and later in University College, Dublin, people thought that I would become a writer. I had no such intention. Looking back I think it may have been vanity that held me back from attempting something at which I feared I might not succeed. Then one day, more or less by chance, I tried my hand at a story. To my surprise imaginative writing came easy to me, far easier than the composing of those school essays.

No manuscripts of those early stories are in existence today, but I am fairly certain that there would not have been more than one version of each story, with few corrections and no revisions. I do not think it entered my head that I could, or should, try to make them better. Now more than thirty years later, their flaws bear witness to my carelessness. Nevertheless, for a while I disported myself turning out other stories. Fortunately, before too long I saw, by comparison with the work of writers I admired, that my imagination was running away with me. I wholeheartedly believed – as I do to this day – in the power of the imagination to arrive at truth, but I did not know that the imagination cannot be trusted unless it is fully disciplined. When it is so disciplined, its blinding light shuts out all that is irrelevant.

It was probably then that I began to do several drafts of a story, probing deeper each time into the heart and mind of the characters. At this point also I stopped worrying about style because I was beginning to see that in a short story the way a thing is said has to be an integral part of what is being said, but that if I took care with the latter, the former took care of itself.

It was not, however, until I realised that in solving the problems I posed for my fictitious characters, I was in fact solving problems that had preoccupied me, myself, since I was very young, that I entered fully and irrevocably into the profession of writing, than which I believe there is probably no calling more difficult to follow to its end.

Here I should say that through the years since 1942 as the stories appeared again in anthologies, and particularly when they appeared in school and college texts, I got the chance to correct the most glaring of their errors in grammar and syntax. Sometimes also I was able to put right parts of a story where my imagination had not been properly under control. Sean O'Faolain, that master of the short story in theory and in practice, once said 'to rewrite years after is a kind of forgery.' This is something I have never been able to acccept. With W B Yeats I would reply

> The friends who have it I do wrong
> Whenever I remake a song,
> Should know what issue is at stake:
> It is myself that I remake.

Wrongly or rightly, I have tried at one time or another to re-edit all these stories. With regard to 'Miss Holland' and 'Love is for Lovers' I found I could only tidy them up as if they were the work of a student submitted to me in a creative writing class. 'A Fable', however, defied even my most frantic efforts to reshape it: every time I touched a line, the whole story seemed to fall to bits. I wasted a great deal of time and energy on it before putting my pride in my pocket and facing the fact that I would have to let it appear here in its original form.

It would not be fitting to end this note without paying tribute to Lord Dunsany. Although my initial gratitude must go to the editors who took my first stories, James Scott Moncrieff and Seamus O'Sullivan – particularly the latter, for it was in *The Dublin Magazine* that Dunsany first read my work – I nevertheless owe an immense debt to Dunsany for his constant encouragement, but most of all for his friendship and that of his wife Beatrice.

In his preface to *Tales from Bective Bridge,* here reprinted, a mistake was made which I would like to correct. Dunsany had selected for special praise a story called 'The Nun's Mother', which, for some reason, the publisher decided to drop from the collection at the last moment. Without reference to Dunsany the praise intended for 'The Nun's Mother' was inexplicably transferred to 'The Green Grave and the Black Grave'. This was all the more distressing because 'The Green Grave and the Black Grave' was a story Dunsany did not even like; he thought it was written in imitation of Synge. This was not the case. The repetitive style was simply an attempt to create echoes of waves breaking on a shore.

When I was young my gratitude to Dunsany was overshadowed by my embarrassment at the extravagance of the praise he had given me. Now, when that Preface as well as the stories it introduced belongs to the past, I am able to be wholly grateful to him. Only an extraordinarily generous mind could make the mistake of attributing more merit than it deserved to the work of a young and unknown writer.

Mary Lavin

Preface

I have had the good fortune to have many stories and poems sent to me by young writers. In nearly all of them the ardours of youth showed flashes, some rarely, some frequently, but in only two of them have I felt sure that I was reading the work of a master. And these two great writers, as I believe them to be, both wrote to me by a strange coincidence from the same bank of the same river, the left bank of the Boyne. One of these writers was Francis Ledwidge, who unhappily lived too short a time to do much more than show promise of the great bulk of fine work of which I am sure he was capable. But, although he has not a very large number of readers, that early promise of his has received recognition by lovers of poetry, both in his own country and at the ends of the earth.

I have now the pleasure of introducing another fine writer, Miss Mary Lavin; very different from Francis Ledwidge, except for the same piercing eye, which to Ledwidge revealed the minutest details of Irish hedgerows, with all their flowers and birds, and to Mary Lavin the hearts of women and children and men. Indeed, when I once asked her to meet one or two writers in my house, and when one of them, a professor from Trinity College, afterwards read the only story of hers that as yet had been printed, he realised rather uncomfortably that those searching eyes must have gone right through him; it was rather as though he had come with his pockets full of all sorts of collected objects, and perhaps had a broken rib long ago mended, and had afterwards learned that he had been all the while exposed to the action of X-rays.

I am afraid that there is a tendency among writers, when at last any recognition comes to them, rather to regret the arrival of any new competitor, or at least to expect that competitor shall spend as many weary years on the road to recognition as they were forced to spend themselves. But for my part it is not the writing that so much attracts me, nor the recognition that it may be given at last, but the intrinsic thing, the glittering idea that the writing may make visible. If this glittering idea is seen by myself, I have had all the hard work of hewing it out of the cliffs of dreamland; but if somebody else will lay an idea before me, shining from the page of a book, without my having to toil at it, I feel that I, and everybody else, are very lucky to have it shown to us.

When Ledwidge first brought his work to me I gave him a very little advice, which he immediately profited by, as people do not usually profit by advice. The best thing I did for him was to lend him a copy of Keats; and the great speed with which he seemed to absorb it, and slightly to flavour his work with it, gave me some insight into his enormous powers, which were unhappily never developed. But my first impression when Mary Lavin sent me some of her work, an impression that I have never altered, was that I had no advice whatever to give her about literature; so I have only helped her with her punctuation, which was bad, and with her hyphens, about which she shares the complete ignorance that in the fourth decade of the twentieth century appears to afflict nearly everybody who writes. Only in these trivial matters do I feel I know anything more about writing than Mary Lavin.

I have never had much to do with the classifying of writers, my attitude towards art having always been that of a child to a butterfly rather than that of an entomologist, that is to say, a greater interest in its flashing beauty than in its Latin name; so that others will classify Mary Lavin's work, if it is necessary for it to be classified. To me she seems reminiscent of the Russians more than of any other school of writers and, with the exception of the gigantic Tolstoy, her searching insight into the human heart and vivid appreciation of the beauty of the fields are worthy in my opinion to be mentioned beside their work. Often, as I read one of her tales, I find myself using superlatives, and then wondering if such praise must not necessarily be mistaken, when applied to the work of a young and quite unknown writer. And yet are not such doubts as these utterly wrong-minded? For if there is no intrinsic thing in any art whatever, irrespective of its date or the name or age of the writer, how then can there be anything in good work at all? How, if we cannot recognise great work when we come across it unexpectedly, have we any right to say that even Shelley or Keats wrote well? Should we not rather say in that case: 'I have been told they wrote well'? I know people who can never tell a beautiful piece of silverwork or furniture until they have first found out the date of it. If it is over a hundred years old they think it is bound to be good, and if it is made in this century they think it is bound to be bad. Often they are right in both cases, but they have no judgment whatever and, though they are quick to find out the date of a Chippendale chair or the hallmark of a piece of old silver, and will praise their beauty immediately after doing so, nevertheless the emotions that should respond to beauty can only be awakened in them by the aid of a catalogue. That is a very sorry state to be in. Let us therefore always praise intrinsic beauty whenever we see it, without concerning ourselves with irrelevancies, such as the age or name of Mary Lavin, or how on earth she came by her astonishing insight.

But read these stories for yourselves, and see if again and again you do not find sentences which, if they had been translated from the Russian, would make you say that they do indeed show us that those writers understood life. I am reluctant to quote, because anything I would quote lies before you in this book, and because there are quotations which I might make from those tales which would seem to prove my point with almost unnecessary violence. But I suggest that a page should be taken at random from 'The Green Grave and the Black Grave' and compared with a random page of any novelist of the present century, to see which page evokes the vividest pictures. I am not, by the way, challenging comparison with Kipling, as he was rather a writer of the last century, which saw his greatest work. After all, writing a story is a matter of acquiring the reader's interest, and holding it while you tell the story, and making him see what happened. Words that do not make us see what happened are rather like false bank notes: offer them in exchange for thought and they are rejected by the mind as spurious. Many yards of such words are often to be met with, but I do not think that one finds Mary Lavin ever wasting a word.

She tells the stories of quite ordinary lives, the stories of people who many might suppose have no story in all their experience; and when she tells these stories there may be some whose ears, attuned to the modern thriller, may suppose that they are not stories at all. The pivot of one of them, for instance, is where a fly thrown out of a cup of tea, 'and celebrating his release a little too soon by sitting on a blade of grass rubbing his hands,' is killed by a small dog. It may seem too tiny a thing to notice, and the man's life, which turns in another direction from that moment, may seem tiny and unimportant too, to any who may not reflect how hard it is for any of us to say what is important and what is not. Browning speaks of the gnats:

> . . . that carry aloft
> The sound they have nursed, so sweet and pure,
> Out of a myriad noises soft,
> Into a tone that can endure
> Amid the noise of a July moon,

and many an ear must miss that tone, and many may miss the work of Mary Lavin. The bold plots and the startling events of the modern thriller are to these tales what a great factory is to the works of a gold watch. Those looking for great engines running at full blast might overlook the delicacy of the machinery of such a watch.

Years hence this preface of mine will seem quite unnecessary. It is only the unimportant circumstance that I was born in the last century, and she in this and that after twenty or thirty years of writing I have a few readers, whereas she at present has none, which accounts for my writing a preface for her instead of asking her to do the same for me. I do not write it because I think there is anything whatever that I can teach her about literature. I merely stand, as it were, at the portals of this book to point within to what you may find for yourselves, and to recommend you to look for it.

Lord Dunsany

Lilacs

'That dunghill isn't doing anyone any harm, and it's not going out of where it is as long as I'm in this house,' Phelim Mulloy said to his wife Ros, but he threw an angry look at his elder daughter Kate who was standing by the kitchen window with her back turned to them both.

'Oh Phelim,' Ros said softly. 'If only it could be moved somewhere else besides under the window of the room where we eat our bit of food.'

'Didn't you just say a minute ago people can smell it from the other end of the town? If that's the case I don't see what would be the good in shifting it from one side of the yard to the other.'

Kate could stand no more. 'What I don't see is the need in us dealing in dung at all!'

'There you are! What did I tell you!' Phelim said, 'I knew all along that was what was in the back of your minds, both of you! And the one inside there too,' he added, nodding his head at the closed door of one of the rooms off the kitchen. 'All you want, the three of you, is to get rid of the dung altogether. Why on earth can't women speak out – and say what they mean. That's a thing always puzzled me.'

'Leave Stacy out of this, Phelim,' said Ros, but she spoke quietly. 'Stacy has one of her headaches.'

'I know she has,' said Phelim. 'And I know something else. I know I'm supposed to think it's the smell of the dung gave it to her. Isn't that so?'

'Ah Phelim, that's not what I meant at all. I only thought you might wake her with your shouting. She could be asleep.'

'Asleep is it? It's a real miracle any of you can get a wink of sleep, day or night, with the smell of that poor harmless heap of dung out there, that's bringing good money to this house week after week.' He had lowered his voice, but when he turned and looked at Kate it rose again without his noticing. 'It paid for your education at a fancy boarding school – and for your sister's too. It paid for your notions of learning to play the piano, *and* the violin, both of which instruments are rotting away inside in the parlour and not a squeak of a tune ever I heard out of the one or the other of them since the day they came into the house.'

'We may as well spare our breath, Mother,' Kate said. 'He won't give in, now or ever. That's my belief.'

'That's the truest word that's ever come out of your mouth,' Phelim said to her, and stomping across the kitchen he opened the door that led into the yard and went out, leaving the door wide open. Immediately the faint odour of stale manure that hung in the air was enriched by a smell from a load of hot steaming manure that had just been tipped into a huge dunghill from a farm cart that was the first of a line of carts waiting their turn to unload. Ros sighed and went to close the door, but Kate got ahead of her and banged it shut, before going back to the window and taking up her stand there. After a nervous glance at the door of the bedroom that her daughters shared, Ros, too, went over to the window and both women stared out.

An empty cart was clattering out of the yard and Phelim was leading in another from which, as it went over the spud-stone of the gate, a clod or two of dung fell out on the cobbles. The dunghill was nearly filled, and liquid from it was running down the sides of the trough to form pools through which Phelim waded unconcernedly as he forked back the stuff on top to make room for more.

'That's the last load,' Ros said.

'For this week, you mean,' Kate said. 'Your trouble is you're too soft with him, Mother. You'll have to be harder on him. You'll have to keep at him night and day. That is to say if you care anything at all about me and Stacy.'

'Ah Kate. Can't you see there's no use? Can't you see he's set in his ways?'

'All I can see is the way we're being disgraced,' Kate said angrily. 'Last night, at the concert in the Parish Hall, just before the curtain went up I heard the wife of that man who bought the bakehouse telling the person beside her that they couldn't open a window since they came here with a queer smell that was coming from somewhere, and asking the other person if she knew what it would be. I nearly died of shame, Mother. I really did. I couldn't catch what answer she got, but after the first item was over, and I could glance back, I saw it was Mamie Murtagh she was sitting beside. And you can guess what that one would be likely to have said! My whole pleasure in the evening was spoiled.'

'You take things too much to heart, Kate,' Ros said sadly. 'There's Stacy inside there, and it's my belief she wouldn't mind us dealing in dung at all if it wasn't for the smell of it. Only the other day she was remarking that if he'd even clear a small space under the windows we might plant something there that would smell nice. "Just think, Mother," she said. "Just think if it was a smell of lilac that was coming in to us every time we opened a door or a window."'

'Don't talk to me about Stacy,' Kate said crossly. 'She has lilac on the brain, if you ask me. She never stops talking about it. What did she ever do to try and improve our situation?'

'Ah now Kate, as you know, Stacy is very timid.'

'All the more reason Father would listen to her, if she'd speak to him. He may not let on to it, but he'd do anything for her.'

Ros nodded.

'All the same she'd never speak to him. Stacy would never have the heart to cross anyone.'

'She wouldn't need to say much. Didn't you hear him, today, saying he supposed it was the smell of the dung was giving her her headaches? You let that pass, but I wouldn't – only I know he won't take any more from me, although it's me has to listen to her moaning and groaning from the minute the first cart rattles into the yard. How is it that it's always on a Wednesday she has a headache? And it's been the same since the first Wednesday we came home from the convent.' With that last thrust Kate ran into the bedroom and came out with a raincoat. 'I'm going out for a walk,' she said, 'and I won't come back until the smell of that stuff has died down a bit. You can tell my father that, too, if he's looking for me.'

'Wait a minute, Kate. Was Stacy asleep?' Ros asked

'I don't know and I don't care. She was lying with her face pressed to the wall, like always.'

When Kate went out, Ros took down the tea-caddy from the dresser and put a few pinches of tea from it into an earthenware pot on the hob of the big open fire. Then, tilting the kettle that hung from a crane over the flames, she wet the tea, and pouring out a cup she carried it over to the window and set it to cool on the sill while she went on watching Phelim.

He was a hard man when you went against him, she thought, a man who'd never let himself be thwarted. He was always the same. That being so, there wasn't much sense in nagging him, she thought, but Kate would never be made see that. Kate was stubborn too.

The last of the carts had gone, and after shutting the gate Phelim had taken a yard-brush and was sweeping up the dung that had been spilled. When he'd made a heap of it, he got a shovel and gathered it up and flung it up on the dunghill. But whether he did it to tidy the yard or not to waste the dung, Ros didn't know. The loose bits of dung he'd flung up on the top of the trough had dried out, and the bits of straw that were stuck to it had dried out too. They gleamed bright and yellow in a ray of watery sunlight that had suddenly shone forth.

Now that Kate was gone, Ros began to feel less bitter against Phelim. Like herself, he was getting old. She was sorry they had upset him. And while she was looking at him, he laid the yard-brush against the wall of one of the sheds and put his hand to his back. He'd been doing that a lot lately. She didn't like to see him doing it. She went across to the door and opened it.

'There's hot tea in the pot on the hob, Phelim,' she called out. 'Come in and have a cup.' Then seeing he was coming, she went over and gently opened the bedroom door. 'Stacy, would you he able for a cup of tea?' she asked, leaning in over the big feather-bed.

Stacy sat up at once.

'What did he say? Is it going to be moved?' she asked eagerly.

'Ssh, Stacy,' Ros whispered, and then as Stacy heard her father's steps in the kitchen she looked startled.

'Did he hear me?' she asked anxiously.

'No,' said Ros, and she went over and drew the curtains to let in the daylight. 'How is your poor head, Stacy?'

Stacy leaned toward Ros so she could be heard when she whispered. 'Did you have a word with him, Mother?'

'Yes,' said Ros.

'Did he agree?' Stacy whispered.

'No.'

Stacy closed her eyes.

'I hope he wasn't upset?' she said.

Ros stroked her daughter's limp hair. 'Don't you worry anyway, Stacy,' she said. 'He'll get over it. He's been outside sweeping the yard and I think maybe he has forgotten we raised the matter at all. Anyway, Kate has gone for a walk and I called him in for a cup of tea. Are you sure you won't let me bring you in a nice hot cup to sip here in the bed?'

'I think I'd prefer to get up and have it outside, as long as you're really sure Father is not upset.'

Ros drew a strand of Stacy's hair back from her damp forehead. 'You're a good girl, Stacy, a good, kind creature,' she said. 'You may feel better when you're on your feet. I can promise you there will be no more arguing for the time being anyway. I'm sorry I crossed him at all.'

It was to Stacy Ros turned, a few weeks later, when Phelim was taken bad in the middle of the night with a sharp pain in the small of his back that the women weren't able to ease, and after the doctor came and stayed with him until the early hours of the morning, the doctor didn't seem able to do much either. Before Phelim could be got to hospital, he died.

'Oh Stacy, Stacy,' Ros cried, throwing herself into her younger daughter's arms. 'Why did I cross him over that old dunghill?'

'Don't fret, Mother,' Stacy begged. 'I never heard you cross him over anything else as long as I can remember. You were always good and kind to him, calling him in out of the yard every other minute for a cup of tea. Morning, noon and night I'd hear your voice, and the mornings the carts came with the dung you'd call him in oftener than ever. I used to hear you when I'd be lying inside with one of my headaches.'

Ros was not to be so easily consoled.

'What thanks is due to a woman for giving a man a cup of hot tea on a bitter cold day? He was the best man ever lived. Oh why did I cross him?'

'Ah Mother, it wasn't only on cold days you were good to him but on summer days too – on every and all kind of days. Isn't that so, Kate?' Stacy said, appealing to Kate.

'You did everything you could to please him, Mother,' Kate said, but seeing this made no impression on her mother she turned to Stacy. 'That's more than could be said about him,' she muttered.

But Ros heard her.

'Say no more, you,' she said. 'You were the one was always at me to torment him. Oh why did I listen to you? Why did I cross him?'

'Because you were in the right. That's why!' Kate said.

'Was I?' Ros said.

Phelim was laid out in the parlour, and all through the night Ros and her daughters sat up in the room with the corpse. The neighbours that came to the house stayed up all night too, but they sat in the kitchen, and kept the fire going and made tea from time to time. Kate and Stacy stared sadly at their dead father stretched out in his shroud, and they mourned him as the man they had known all their lives, a heavy man with a red face whom they had seldom seen out of his big rubber boots caked with muck.

Ros mourned that Phelim too. But she mourned many another Phelim besides. She mourned the Phelim who, up to a little while before, never put a coat on him going out in the raw, cold air, nor covered his head even in the rain. Of course his hair was as thick as thatch! But most of all, she mourned the Phelim whose hair had not yet grown coarse but was soft and smooth as silk, like it was the time he led her in off the road and up a little lane near the chapel one Sunday when he was walking her home from Mass. That was the time when he used to call her by the old name. When, she wondered, when did he stop calling her Rose? Or was it herself gave herself the new name? Perhaps it was someone else altogether, someone outside the family? Just a neighbour maybe? No matter! Ros was a good name anyway, wherever it came from. It was a good name and a suitable name for an old woman. It would have been only foolishness to go on calling her Rose after she faded and dried up like an old twig. Ros looked down at her bony hands and her tears fell on them. But they were tears for Phelim. 'Rose,' he said that day in the lane. 'Rose, I've been thinking about ways to make money. And do you know what I found out? There's a pile of money to be made out of dung.' Rose thought he was joking. 'It's true,' he said. 'The people in the town – especially women – would give any money for a bagful of it for their gardens. And only a few miles out from the town there are farmers going mad to get rid of it, with it piling up day after day and cluttering up their farmyards until they can hardly get in and out their own doors!

Now, I was thinking, if I got hold of a horse and cart and went out and brought back a few loads of that dung, and if my father would let me store it for a while in our yard, I could maybe sell it to the people in the town.'

'Like the doctor's wife,' Rose said, knowing the doctor's wife was mad about roses. The doctor's wife had been seen going out into the street with a shovel to bring back a shoveful of horse manure.

'That's right. People like her! And after a while the farmers might deliver the loads to me. I might even pay them a few shillings a load, if I was getting a good price for it. Then if I made as much money as I think I might, maybe soon I'd be able to get a place of my own where I'd have room to store enough to make it a worthwhile business.' To Rose it seemed an odd sort of way to make money, but Phelim was only eighteen then and probably he wanted to have a few pounds in his pocket while he was waiting for something better. 'I'm going to ask my father about the storage today,' he said, 'and in the afternoon I'm going to get hold of a cart and go out the country and see how I get on.'

'Is that so?' Rose said, for want of knowing what else to say.

'It is,' said Phelim. 'And do you know the place I have in mind to buy if I make enough money? I'd buy that place we often looked at, you and me when we were out walking, that place on the outskirts of the town, with a big yard and two big sheds that only need a bit of fixing, to be ideal for my purposes.

'I think so,' Rose said. 'Isn't there an old cottage there all smothered with ivy?'

'That's the very place. Do you remember we peeped in the windows one day last summer. There's no one living there.'

'No wonder,' Rose said.

'Listen to me, Rose. After I'd done up the sheds,' Phelim said. 'I could fix up the cottage too, and make a nice job of it. That's another thing I wanted to ask you, Rose. How would you like to live in that cottage – after I'd done it up, I mean – with me, I mean?' he added when he saw he'd startled her. 'Well Rose, what have you to say to that?'

She bent her head to hide her blushes, and looked down at her small thin-soled shoes that she only wore on a Sunday. Rose didn't know what to say.

'Well?' said Phelim.

'There's a very dirty smell off dung,' she said at last in a whisper.

'It only smells strong when it's fresh,' Phelim said, 'And maybe you could plant flowers to take away the smell?'

She kept looking down at her shoes.

'They'd have to be flowers with a strong scent out of them!' she said – but already she was thinking of how strongly sweet rocket and mignonette perfumed the air of an evening after rain.

'You could plant all the flowers you liked, you'd have nothing else to do the day long,' he said. How innocent he was, for all that he was thinking of making big money, and taking a wife. She looked up at him. His skin was as fair and smooth as her own. He was the best looking fellow for miles around. Girls far prettier than her would have been glad to be led up a lane by him, just for a bit of a lark, let alone a proposal – a proposal of marriage. 'Well, Rose?' he said, and now there were blushes coming and going in his cheeks too, blotching his face the way the wind blotches a lake when there's a storm coming. And she knew him well enough, even in those days, to be sure he wouldn't stand for anyone putting between him and what he was bent on doing. 'You must know, Rose Magarry, that there's a lot in the way people look at a thing. When I was a young lad, driving along the country roads in my father's trap, I used to love looking down at the gold rings of dung dried out by the sun, as they flashed past underneath the horses' hooves.'

Rose felt like laughing, but she knew he was deadly serious. He wasn't like anybody else in the world she'd ever known. Who else would say a thing like that? It was like poetry. The sun was spilling down on them and in the hedges little pink dog roses were swaying in a soft breeze.

'Alright, so,' she said. 'I will.'

'You will? Oh, Rose! Kiss me so!' he said.

'Not here Phelim!' she cried. People were still coming out of the chapel yard and some of them were looking up the lane.

'Rose Magarry, if you're going to marry me, you must face up to people and never be ashamed of anything I do,' he said, and when she still hung back he put out his hand and tilted up her chin. 'If you don't kiss me right here and now, Rose, I'll have no more to do with you.'

She kissed him then.

And now, at his wake, the candle flames were wavering around his coffin the way the dog roses wavered that day in the summer breeze.

Ros shed tears for those little dog roses. She shed tears for the roses in her own cheeks in those days. And she shed tears for the soft young kissing lips of Phelim. Her tears fell quietly, but it seemed to Kate and Stacy that, like rain in windless weather, they would never cease.

When the white light of morning came at last, the neighbours got up and went home to do a few chores of their own and be ready for the funeral. Kate and Stacy got ready too, and made Ros ready. Ros didn't look much different in black from what she always looked. Neither did Stacy. But Kate looked well in black. It toned down her high colour.

After the funeral Kate led her mother home. Stacy had already been taken home by neighbours, because she fainted when the coffin was being lowered into the ground. She was lying down when they came home. The women who brought Stacey home and one or two other women who had stayed behind after the coffin was carried out, to put the furniture back in place, gave a meal to the family, but these women made sure to leave as soon as possible to let the Mulloys get used to their loss. When the women had gone Stacy got up and came out to join Ros and Kate. A strong smell of guttered-out candles hung in the air and a faint scent of lilies lingered on too.

'Oh Kate! Smell!' Stacy cried, drawing in as deep a breath as her thin chest allowed.

'For Heaven's sake, don't talk about smells or you'll have our mother wailing again and going on about having crossed him over the dunghill,' Kate said in a sharp whisper.

But Ros didn't need any reminders to make her wail.

'Oh Phelim, Phelim, why did I cross you?' she wailed. 'Wasn't I the bad old woman to go against you over a heap of dung that, if I looked at things rightly, wasn't bad at all after it dried out a bit. It was mostly only yellow straw.'

'Take no heed of her,' Kate counselled Stacy. 'Go inside you with our new hats and coats, and hang them up in our room with a sheet draped over them. Black nap is a caution for collecting dust.' To Ros she spoke kindly, but firmly. 'You've got to give over this moaning, Mother,' she said. 'You're only tormenting yourself. Why wouldn't you let him see how we felt about the dung?'

Ros stopped moaning long enough to look sadly out the window.

'It was out of the dung he made his first few shillings,' she said.

'That may be! But how long ago was that? He made plenty of money other ways as time went on. There was no need in keeping on the dung and humiliating us. He only did it out of obstinacy.' As Stacy came back after hanging up their black clothes, Kate appealed to her. 'Isn't that so, Stacy?'

Stacy drew another thin breath.

'It doesn't smell too bad today, does it?' she said. 'I suppose the scent of the flowers drove it out.'

'Well, the house won't always be filled with lilies,' Kate said irritably. 'In any case, Stacy, it's not the smell concerns me. What concerns me is the way people look at us when they hear how our money is made.'

Ros stopped moaning again for another minute. 'It's no cause for shame. It's honest dealing, and that's more than can be said for the dealings of others in this town. You shouldn't heed people's talk, Kate.'

'Well, I like that!' she said. 'May I ask what you know, Mother, about how people talk. Certain kinds of people I mean. Good class people! It's easily seen you were never away at boarding school like Stacy and me, or else you'd know what it feels like to have to admit our money was made out of horse manure and cow dung!'

'I don't see what great call there was on you to tell them!' Ros said.

'Stacy! Stacy! Did you hear that?' Kate cried.

Stacy put her hand to her head. She was getting confused. There was some truth in what Kate had said, and she felt obliged to side with her, but first she ran over and threw herself down at her mother's knees.

'We didn't tell them at first, Mother,' she said, hoping to make Ros feel better. 'We told them our father dealt in fertiliser, but one of the girls looked up the word in a dictionary and found out it was only a fancy name for manure.'

It was astonishing to Kate and Stacy how Ros took that. She not only stopped wailing but she began to laugh.

'Your father would have been amused to hear that,' she said.

'Well, it wasn't funny for us,' Kate said.

Ros stopped laughing, but the trace of a small black smile remained on her face.

'It wasn't everyone had your father's sense of humour,' she said.

'It wasn't everyone had his obstinacy either!' Kate said.

'You're right there, Kate,' Ros said simply. 'Isn't that why I feel so bad? When we knew how stubborn he was, weren't we the stupid women to be always trying to best him? We only succeeded in making him miserable.'

Kate and Stacy looked at each other.

'How about another cup of tea, Mother? I'll bring it over here to you beside the fire,' Stacy said, and although her mother made no reply she made the tea and brought over a cup. Ros took the cup but handed back the saucer.

'Leave that back on the table,' she said, and holding the cup in her two hands she went over to the window, although the light was fading fast.

'It only smells bad on hot muggy days,' she said.

Kate gave a loud sniff. 'Don't forget summer is coming,' she said.

For a moment it seemed Ros had not heard, then she gave a sigh.

'It is and it isn't,' she said. 'I often think that in the January of the year it's as true to say we have put the summer behind us as it is to say it's ahead!' Then she glanced at a calendar on the wall. 'Is tomorrow Wednesday?' she asked, and an anxious expression overcame the sorrowful look on her face. Wednesday was the day the farmers delivered the dung.

'Mother! You don't think the farmers will be unmannerly enough to come banging on the gate tomorrow, and us after having a death in the family?' Kate said in a shocked voice.

'Death never interfered with business yet, as far as I know,' Ros said coldly. 'And the farmers are kind folk. I saw a lot of them at the funeral. They might think it all the more reason to come. Knowing my man is taken from me.'

'Mother!' This time Kate was more than shocked, she was outraged. 'You're not thinking, by any chance of keeping on dealing with them – of keeping on dealing in dung?'

Ros looked her daughter straight in the face.

'I'm thinking of one thing and one thing only,' she said. 'I'm thinking of your father and him young one day, and the next day, you might say, him stretched on the bed inside with the neighbours washing him for his burial.' Then she began to moan again.

'If you keep this up you'll be laid alongside him one of these days,' Kate said.

'Leave me be!' Ros said. 'I'm not doing any harm to myself by thinking about him. I like thinking about him.'

'He lived to a good age, Mother. Don't forget that,' Kate said.

'I suppose that's what you'll be saying about me one of these days,' Ros said, but she didn't seem as upset as she had been. She turned to Stacy. 'It seems only like yesterday, Stacy, that I was sitting up beside him on the cart, right behind the horse's tail, with my white blouse on me and my gold chain that he gave me bouncing about on my front, and us both watching the road flashing past under the horse's hooves, bright with gold rings of dung.'

Kate raised her eyebrows. But Stacy gave a sob. And that night, when she and Kate were in bed, just before she faced in to the wall, Stacy gave another sob.

'Oh Kate, it's not a good sign when people begin to go back over the past, is it?'

'Are you speaking about Mother?'

'I am. And did you see how bad she looked when you brought her home from the grave?'

'I did,' said Kate. 'It may be true what I said to her. If she isn't careful we may be laying her alongside poor Father before long.'

'Oh Kate. How could you say such a thing?' Stacy burst into tears. 'Oh Kate. Oh Kate, why did we make her cross Father about the dunghill? I know how she feels. I keep reproaching myself for all the hard things I used to think about him when I'd be lying here in bed with one of my headaches.'

'Well, you certainly never came out with them!' Kate said. 'You left it to me to say them for you! Not that I'm going to reproach myself about anything! There was no need in him keeping that dunghill. He only did it out of pig-headedness. And now, if you'll only let me, I'm going to sleep.'

Kate was just dropping off when Stacy leant up on her elbow.

'You don't really think they will come in the morning, do you Kate – the carts I mean – like our mother said?'

'Of course not,' Kate said.

'But if they do?'

'Oh go to sleep Stacy, for Heaven's sake. There's no need facing things until they happen. And stop fidgeting! You're twitching the blankets off me. Move over.'

Stacy faced back to the wall and lay still. She didn't think she'd be able to sleep, but when she did, it seemed as if she'd only been asleep one minute when she woke to find the night had ended. The hard, white light of day was pressings on her eyelids. It's a new day for them, she thought, but not for their poor father. Father laid away in the cold clay. Stacy shivered and drew up her feet that were touching the icy iron rail at the foot of the bed. It must have been the cold wakened her. Opening her eyes she saw, through a chink between the curtains, that the crinkled edges of the big corrugated sheds glittered with frost. If only – she thought – if only it was summer. She longed for the time when warm winds would go daffing through the trees, and when in the gardens to which they delivered fertiliser, the tight hard beads of lilac buds would soon loop out into soft pear-shaped bosoms of blossoms. And then, gentle as those thoughts, another thought came into Stacy's mind, and she wondered whether their father, sleeping under the close, green sods, might mind now if they got rid of the dunghill. Indeed it seemed the dunghill was as good as gone, now that Father himself was gone. Curling up in the warm blankets Stacy was preparing to sleep again, when there was a loud knocking on the yard-gates and the sound of a horse shaking its harness. She raised her head off the pillow, and as she did, she heard the gate in the yard slap back against the wall and there was a rattle of iron-shod wheels travelling in across the cobbles.

'Kate! Kate!' she screamed, shaking her. 'I thought Father was leading in a load of manure.'

'Oh shut up, Stacy. You're dreaming – or else raving,' Kate muttered from the depths of the blankets that she had pulled closer around her. But suddenly she sat up. And then, to Stacy's astonishment, she threw back the bedclothes altogether, right across the footrail of the bed, and ran across the floor and pressed her face to the window pane. 'I might have known this would happen!' she cried. 'For all her lamenting and wailing, she knows what she's doing. Come and look!' Out in the yard Ros was leading in the first of the carts, and calling out to the drivers of the other carts waiting their turn to come in. She was not wearing her black clothes, but her ordinary everyday coat, the colour of the earth and the earth's decaying refuse. In the raw cold air, the manure in the cart she was leading was still giving off, unevenly, the fog of its hot breath.

'Get dressed, Stacy. We'll go down together!' Kate ordered and grabbed her clothes and dressed.

When they were both dressed, with Kate leading, the sisters went into the kitchen. The yard door was open and a powerful stench was making its way inside. The last cart was by then unloaded, and Ros soon came back into the kitchen and began to warm her hands by the big fire already roaring up the chimney. She had left the door open but Kate went over and banged it shut.

'Well?' said Ros.

'Well?' Kate said after her, only louder.

Stacy sat down at once and began to cry. The other two women took no notice of her, as they faced each other across the kitchen.

'Say whatever it is you have to say, Kate,' Ros said.

'You know what I have to say,' said Kate.

'Don't say it so! Save your breath!' Ros said, and she went as if to go out into the yard again, but Stacy got up and ran and put her arms around her.

'Mother, you always agreed with us! You always said it would be nice if –'

Ros put up a hand and silenced her.

'Listen to me, both of you,' she said. 'I had no right agreeing with anyone but your father,' she said. 'It was to him I gave my word. It was him I had a right to stand behind. He always said there was no shame in making money any way it could be made, as long as it was made honestly. And another thing he said was that money was money, whether it was in gold coins or in dung. And that was true for him. Did you, either of you, hear what the priest said yesterday in the cemetery? 'God help all poor widows.' That's what he said. And he set me thinking. Did it never occur to you that it might not be easy for us, three women with no man about the place, to keep going, to put food on the table and keep a fire on the hearth, to say nothing at all about finery and fal-lals.'

'That last remark is meant for me I suppose,' Kate said, but the frown that came on her face seemed to come more from worry than anger. 'By the way, Mother,' she said. 'You never told us whether you had a word with the solicitor when he came with his condolences? Did you by any chance find out how Father's affairs stood?'

'I did,' Ros said. But that was all she said as she went out into the yard again and took up the yard-brush. She had left the door open but Stacy ran over and closed it gently.

'She's twice as stubborn as ever Father was,' Kate said. 'There's going to be no change around here as long as she's alive.'

Stacy's face clouded. 'All the same, Kate, she's sure to let us clear a small corner and put in a few shrubs and things,' she said timidly.

'Lilacs, I suppose!' Kate said, with an unmistakable sneer, which however Stacy did not see.

'Think of the scent of them coming in the window,' she said.

'Stacy, you are a fool!' Kate cried. 'At least I can see that our mother has more important things on her mind than lilac bushes. I wonder what information she got from Jasper Kane? I thought her very secretive. I would have thought he'd have had a word with me, as the eldest daughter.'

'Oh, Kate.' Stacy's eyes filled with tears again. 'I never thought about it before, but when poor Mother –' she hesitated, then after a gulp she went on – 'when poor Mother goes to join Father, you and I will be all alone in the world with no one to look after us.'

'Stop whimpering, Stacy,' Kate said sharply. 'We've got to start living our own lives, sooner or later.' Going over to a small ornamental mirror on the wall over the fireplace, she looked into it and patted her hair. Stacy stared at her in surprise, because unless you stood well back from it you could only see the tip of your nose in that little mirror. But Kate was not looking at herself. She was looking out into the yard, which was reflected in the mirror, in which she could see their mother going around sweeping up stray bits of straw and dirt to bring them over and throw them on top of the dunghill. Then Kate turned around. 'We don't need to worry too much about that woman. She'll hardly follow Father for many a long day! That woman is as strong as a tree.'

But Ros was not cut out to be a widow. If Phelim had been taken from her before the dog roses had faded in the hedges that first summer of their lives together, she could hardly have mourned him more bitterly than she did when an old woman, tossing and turning sleeplessly in their big brass bed.

Kate and Stacy did their best to ease her work in the house. But there was one thing Kate was determined they would not do, and that was give any help on the Wednesday mornings when the farm carts arrived with their load. Nor would they help her to bag it for the townspeople, although as Phelim had long ago foreseen, the townspeople were often glad enough to bag it for themselves, or wheel it away in barrowfuls. On Wednesday morning when the rapping came at the gates at dawn, Kate and Stacy stayed in bed and did not get up, but Stacy was wide awake and lay listening to the noises outside. And sometimes she scrambled out of bed across Kate and went to the window.

'Kate?' Stacy would say almost every day.

'What?'

'Perhaps I ought to step out to the kitchen and see the fire is kept up. She'll be very cold when she comes in.'

'You'll do nothing of the kind I hope! We must stick to our agreement. Get back into bed.'

'She has only her old coat on her and it's very thin, Kate.'

Before answering her, Kate might raise herself up on one elbow and hump the blankets up with her so that when she sank back they were pegged down.

'By all the noise she's making out there I'd say she'd keep up her circulation no matter if she was in nothing but her shift.'

'That work is too heavy for her, Kate. She shouldn't be doing it at all.'

'And who is to blame for that? Get back to bed, like I told you, and don't let her see you're looking out. She'd like nothing better than that.'

'But she's not looking this way Kate. She couldn't see me.'

'That's what you think! Let me tell you, that woman has eyes in the back of her head.'

Stacy giggled nervously at that. It was what their mother herself used to tell them when they were small.

Then suddenly she stopped giggling and ran back and threw herself across the foot of the bed and began to sob.

After moving her feet to one side, Kate listened for a few seconds to the sobbing. Then she humped up her other shoulder and pegged the blankets under her on the other side.

'What ails you now?' she asked then.

'Oh Kate, you made me think of when we were children, and she used to stand up so tall and straight and with her gold chain and locket bobbing about on her chest.' Stacy gave another sob. 'Now she's so thin and bent the chain is dangling down to her waist.'

Kate sat up with a start. 'She's not wearing that chain and locket now, out in the yard, is she? Gold is worth a lot more now than it was when Father bought her that.'

Stacy went over to the window and looked out again. 'No, she's not wearing it.'

'I should hope not!' Kate said. 'I saw it on her at the funeral but I forgot about it afterwards in the commotion.'

'She took it off when we came back,' Stacy said. 'She put it away in father's black box and locked the box.'

'Well, that's one good thing she did anyway,' Kate said. 'She oughtn't to wear it at all.'

'Oh Kate!' Stacy looked at her.

'What?' Kate asked, staring back.

Stacy didn't know what she wanted to say. She couldn't put it into words. She had always thought Kate and herself were alike, that they had the same way of looking at things, but lately she was not so sure of this. They were both getting older of course, and some people were not as even-tempered as others. Not that she thought herself a paragon, but being so prone to headaches she had to let a lot of things pass that she didn't agree with – like a thing Kate said recently about the time when they were away at school. Their mother had asked how many years ago it was, and while Stacy was trying to count up the years, Kate answered at once.

'Only a few years ago,' she said. That wasn't true but perhaps it only seemed like that to Kate.

Gradually, as time passed, Stacy too, like Kate, used to put the blankets over her head so as not to hear the knocking at the gate, and the rattle of the cart wheels, or at least to deaden the noise of it. She just lay thinking. Kate had once asked her what went through her head when she'd be lying saying nothing.

'This and that,' she'd said. She really didn't think about anything in particular. Sometimes she'd imagine what it would be like if they cleared a small space in the yard and planted things. She knew of course that if they put in a lilac bush it would be small for a long time and would not bear flowers for ages. It would be mostly leaves, and leaves only, for years, or so she'd read somewhere. Yet she always imagined it would be a fully grown lilac they'd have outside the window. Once she imagined something absolutely ridiculous. She was

lying half awake and half asleep, and she thought they had
transplanted a large full grown lilac, a lilac that had more flowers than
leaves, something you never see. And then, as she was half-dozing, the
tree got so big and strong its roots pushed under the wall and pushed
up through the floorboards – bending the nails and sending splinters of
wood flying in all directions. And its branches were so laden down
with blossom, so weighted down, that one big pointed bosom of
bloom almost touched her face. But suddenly the branch broke with a
crack and Stacy was wide awake again. Then the sound that woke her
came again, only now she knew what it was – a knocking on the gate
outside, only louder than usual, and after it came a voice calling out.
She gave Kate a shake.

'Do you hear that, Kate? Mother must have slept it out.'

'Let's hope she did,' Kate said. 'It might teach her a lesson – it might
make her see she's not as fit and able as she thinks.'

'But what about the farmers?'

'Who cares about them,' Kate said. '*I* don't! Do you?' When the
knocking came again a third time, and a fourth time, Stacy shook Kate
again.

'Kate! I wouldn't mind going down and opening the gate,' she said.

'You? In your nightdress?' Kate needed to say to say no more. Stacy
cowered down under the blankets in her shame. All of a sudden she sat
up again.

'There wouldn't be anything wrong with Mother, would there?' she
cried. This time, without heeding Kate, Stacy climbed out over her to
get to the floor. 'I won't go out to the yard, I promise, I'll just go and
wake Mother,' she cried. She ran out of the room.

'Come back and shut that door,' Kate called after her. Stacy mustn't
have heard. 'Stacy! Come back and shut this door,' Kate shouted.

Stacy still didn't come back.

'Stacy!' Kate yelled. 'Stacy?'

Then she sat up.

'Is there something wrong?' she asked. Getting no answer now
either, she got up herself.

Stacy was in their mother's room, lying in a heap on the floor. As
Kate said afterwards, she hardly needed to look to know their mother
was dead, because Stacy always flopped down in a faint the moment
she came up against something unpleasant. And the next day, in the
cemetery, when the prayers were over and the gravediggers took up

their shovels, Stacy passed out again and had to be brought home by two of the neighbours, leaving Kate to stand and listen to the stones and the clay rumbling down on the coffin.

'You're a nice one, Stacy! Leaving me to stand listening to that awful sound.'

'But I heard it, Kate,' Stacy protested. 'I did! Then my head began to reel, and I got confused. The next thing I knew I was on the ground looking up at the blue sky and thinking the noise was the sound of the horses going clipclap along the road.'

Kate stared at her.

'Are you mad? What horses?'

'Oh Kate, don't you remember? The horses Mother was always talking about. She was always telling us how, when she and Father were young, she used to sit beside him on a plank across the cart and watch the road flashing by under the horses' hooves, glittering with bright gold rings of dung?'

Kate, however, wasn't listening.

'That reminds me. Isn't tomorrow Wednesday?' she said. 'Which of us is going to get up and let in the farm carts?' When Stacy stared vacantly, Kate stamped her foot. 'Don't look so stupid, Stacy? They came the day after Father was buried, why wouldn't they come tomorrow? Mother herself said it was their way of showing – showing that as far as they were concerned the death wouldn't make any difference.

'Oh Kate. How do you think they'll take it when you tell them –'

'Tell them what? Really Stacy, you *are* a fool. Tomorrow is no day to tell them anything. We'll have to take it easy – wait and see how we stand, before we talk about making changes.'

Kate was so capable. Stacy was filled with admiration for her. She would not have minded in the least getting up to open the gate, but she never would be able to face a discussion of the future. Kate was able for everything, and realising this, Stacy permitted herself a small feeling of excitement at the thought of them making their own plans and standing on their own two feet.

'I'll get up and light the fire and bring you a cup of tea in bed before you have to get up, Kate,' she said.

Kate shrugged her shoulders. 'If I know you, Stacy, you'll have one of your headaches,' Kate said.

Stacy said nothing. She was resolved to get up, headache or no headache. On the quiet she set an old alarm clock she found in the kitchen. But the alarm bell was broken, and the first thing Stacy heard next morning was the rapping on the gate. When she went to scramble out, to her surprise Kate was already gone from the room. And when Stacy threw her clothes on and ran out to the kitchen, the fire was roaring up the chimney, and a cup with a trace of sugar and tea leaves in the bottom of it was on the windowsill. The teapot was on the hob but it had been made a long time and it was cold. She made herself another pot and took it over to sip it by the window, looking out.

Kate was in the yard, directing the carts and laughing and talking with the men. Kate certainly had a way with her and no mistake. When it would come to telling the farmers that they needn't deliver any more dung, they wouldn't be offended.

One big tall farmer, with red hair and whiskers, was the last to leave, and he and Kate stood talking at the gate so long Stacy wondered if, after all, Kate mightn't discussing their future dealings with him. She hoped she wouldn't catch cold. She put a few more sods of turf on the fire.

'Do you want to set the chimney on fire?' Kate asked when she came in. Stacy didn't let herself get upset though. Kate was carrying all the responsibility now, and it was bound to make her edgy.

'I saw you talking to one of the men,' said she. 'I was wondering if perhaps you were giving him a hint of our plans and sounding him out?'

'I was sounding him out alright,' Kate said, and she smiled. 'You see, Stacy. I've been thinking that we might come up with a new plan. You mightn't like it at first, but you may come round when I make you see it in the right light. Sit down and I'll tell you.' Stacy sat down. Kate stayed standing. 'I've been looking into the ledgers, and I would never have believed there was so much money coming in from the dung. So, I've been thinking that, instead of getting rid of it, we ought to try and take in more, twice or three times more, and make twice or three times as much money. No! No! Sit down again, Stacy. Hear me out. My plan would be that we'd move out of here, and use this cottage for storage – the sheds are not big enough. We could move into a more suitable house, larger and with a garden maybe –'

When Stacy said nothing Kate looked sharply at her. It wouldn't have surprised her if Stacy had flopped off in another faint, but she was only sitting dumbly looking into the fire. 'It's only a suggestion,' Kate said, feeling her way more carefully. 'You never heed anything, Stacy, but when I go out for my walks I take note of things I see – and there's a plot of ground for sale out a bit the road, but not too far from here all the same, and it's for sale – I've made enquiries. Now if we were to try and buy that it wouldn't cost much to build a bungalow. I've made enquiries about the cost of that too, and it seems –'

But Stacy had found her tongue. 'I don't want to move out of here, Kate,' she cried. 'This is where we were born, where my mother and father –' She began to cry. 'Oh Kate! I never want to leave here. Never! Never!'

Kate could hardly speak with fury.

'Stay here so!' she said. 'But don't expect me to stay with you. I'm getting out of here at the first chance I get to go. And let me tell you something else. That dunghill isn't stirring out of where it is until I've a decent dowry out of it. Cry away now to your heart's content for all I care.' Going over to their bedroom Kate went in and banged the door behind her.

Stacy stopped crying and stared at the closed door. Her head had begun to throb and she would have liked to lie down, but after the early hour Kate had risen she had probably gone back to bed. No. Kate was up and moving about the room. There was great activity going on. Stacy felt so much better. She knew Kate. Kate had never been one to say she was sorry for anything she said or did, but that need not mean she didn't feel sorry. She was giving their room a good turn-out? Perhaps this was her way of working off her annoyance and at the same time show she was sorry for losing her temper. Stacy sat back, thinking her thoughts, and waited for Kate to come out. She didn't have long to wait. In about five minutes the knob of the bedroom door rattled. 'Open this door for me, Stacy! My arms are full. I can't turn the handle,' Kate called and Stacy was glad to see she sounded in excellent form, and as if all was forgotten. For the second time in twenty-four hours Stacy felt a small surge of excitement, as Kate came out her arms piled skyhigh with dresses and hats and a couple of cardboard boxes, covered with wallpaper, in which they kept their gloves and handkerchiefs. It was to be a real spring cleaning! They hadn't done one in years. She hadn't noticed it before but the

wallpaper on the boxes was yellowed with age and the flowery pattern
faded. They might paste on new wallpaper? And seeing that Kate,
naturally, had only her own things she went to run and get hers, but
first she ran back to clear a space on the table so Kate could put her
things down.

But Kate was heading across the kitchen to their mother's room.

'There's no sense in having a room idle, is there?' she said,
disappearing into it. 'I'm moving in here.'

There was no further mention of the dunghill that day, nor indeed
that week. Stacy felt a bit lonely at first in the room they had shared
since childhood. But it had its advantages. It had been a bit stuffy
sleeping on the inside. And she didn't have so many headaches, but
that could possibly be attributed to Kate's suggestion that she ignore
them.

Every Wednesday Kate was up at the crack of dawn to let the carts
unload. As their father had also foreseen, they were now paying the
farmers for the manure, but only a small sum, because they were still
glad to get rid of it. And the townspeople on the other hand were
paying five times more. Kate had made no bones about raising her
prices. The only time there was a reference to the future was when
Kate announced that she didn't like keeping cash in the house, and that
she was going to start banking some of their takings. The rest could be
put as usual in the black box, which was almost the only thing that had
never been taken our of their mother's room. A lot of other things were
thrown out.

Kate and Stacy got on as well as ever, it seemed to Stacy, but there
were often long stretches of silence in the house because Kate was
never as talkative as their mother. After nightfall they often sat by a
dying fire, only waiting for it to go out, before getting up and going to
bed. All things considered, Kate was right to have moved into the
other room, and Stacy began to enjoy having a room of her own. She
had salvaged a few of her mother's things that Kate had thrown out
and she liked looking at them. If Kate knew she never said anything.
Kate never came into their room anymore.

Then one evening when Con O'Toole – the big whiskery farmer with
whom Kate had been talking the first day she took over the running of
things – when Con started dropping in to see how they were getting
on, Stacy was particularly glad to have a room of her own. She liked

Con. She really did. But the smell of his pipe brought on her headaches again. The smell of his tobacco never quite left the house, and it even pursued her in through the keyhole after she had left him and Kate together, because of course it was Kate Con came to see.

'Can you stand the smell of his pipe?' she asked Kate one morning. 'It's worse than the smell of the dung!' She only said it by way of a joke, but Kate, who had taken out the black box and was going through the papers in it, a thing she did regularly now, shut the lid of the box and frowned.

'I thought we agreed on saying fertiliser instead of that word you just used.'

'Oh but that was long ago, when we were in boarding school,' Stacy stammered.

'I beg your pardon! It was agreed we'd be more particular about how we referred to our business when we were in the company of other people – or at least that was my understanding! Take Con O'Toole for instance. He may deliver dung here but he never gives it that name – at least not in front of me. The house he lives in may be thatched and have a mud wall, but that's because his old mother is alive and he can't get her to agree to knocking it down and building a new house, which of course they can afford – I was astonished at the amount of land he owns. Come Stacy, you must understand that I am not urging him to make any changes. So please don't mention this conversation to him. I'll tell him myself when I judge the time to be right. Then I'll make him see the need for building a new house. He needn't knock the old one either. He can leave the old woman in it for what time is left her. But as I say, I'll bide my time. I might even wait until after we are married.'

That was the first Stacy heard of Kate's intended marriage, but after that first reference there was talk of nothing else, right up to the fine blowy morning when Kate was hoisted up into Con O'Toole's new motor-car, in a peacock blue outfit, with their mother's gold chain bumping up and down on her bosom.

Stacy was almost squeezed to death in the doorway as the guests all stood there to wave goodbye to the happy couple. There had been far more guests than either she or Kate had bargained on because the O'Tooles had so many relations, and they all brought their children, and – to boot – Kate's old mother-in-law brought along a few of her own cronies as well. But there was enough food, and plenty of port wine.

It was a fine wedding. And Stacy didn't mind the mess that was made of the house. Such a mess! Crumbs scattered over the carpet in the parlour and driven into it by people's feet! Bottle tops all over the kitchen floor! Port wine and lemonade stains soaked into the tablecloth! It was going to take time to get the place to rights again. Stacy was almost looking forward to getting it to rights again because she had decided to make a few changes in the arrangement of the furniture – small changes, only involving chairs and ornaments. But she intended attacking it that evening after the guests left. However, when the bridal couple drove off with a hiss of steam rising out of the radiator of the car, the guests flocked back into the house and didn't go until there wasn't a morsel left to eat, or a single drop left to refill the decanters. One thing did upset Stacy and that was when she saw the way the beautiful wedding cake on which the icing had been as hard and white as plaster had been attacked by someone who didn't know how to cut a cake. The cake had been laid waste, and the children that hadn't already fallen asleep on the sofas were stuffing themselves with the last crumbs. Stacy herself hadn't as much as a taste of that cake, and she'd intended keeping at least one tier aside for some future time. Ah well. It was nice to think everyone had had a good time, she thought, as she closed the door on the last of the O'Tooles, who had greatly outnumbered their own friends. Jasper Kane, their father's solicitor, had been their principal guest. He had not in fact left yet, but he was getting ready to leave.

'It will be very lonely for you now, Miss Stacy,' he said. 'You ought to get some person in to keep you company – at least for the nights.'

It was very kind of him to be so concerned. Stacy expressed her gratitude freely, and reassured him that she was quite looking forward to being, as it were, her own mistress. She felt obliged to add, hastily, that she'd miss Kate, although to be strictly truthful, she didn't think she'd miss her as much as she would have thought before Con O'Toole had put in his appearance.

'Well, well. I'm glad to hear you say that, Miss Stacy,' Jasper Kane said, as he prepared to leave. 'I expect you'll drop in to my office at your convenience. I understand your sister took care of the business, but I'm sure you'll be just as competent when you get the hang of things.' Then for a staid man like him, he got almost playful. 'I'll be very curious to see what changes you'll make,' he said, and she saw his eye fall on a red plush sofa that Kate had bought after Con started calling, and which Stacy thought was hideous. She gave him a conspiratorial smile. But she didn't want him to think she wasn't serious.

'I intend to make changes outside as well, Mr Kane,' she said, gravely. And the very first thing I'm going to do is plant a few lilac trees.'

Jasper Kane looked surprised.

'Oh? Where?' he asked and although it was dark outside, he went to the window and tried to see out.

'Where else but where the dunghill has always been,' Stacy said, and just to hear herself speaking with such authority made her almost lightheaded.

Jasper Kane remained staring out into the darkness. Then he turned around and asked a simple question.

'But what will you live on, Miss Stacy?'

The Green Grave and the Black Grave

It was a body all right. It was hard to see in the dark, and the scale-back sea was heaving up between them and the place where they saw the thing floating. But it was a body all right.

'I knew it was a shout I heard,' said the taller of the two men in the black boat that was out fishing for mackerel. He was Tadg Mor and he was the father of the less tall man, that was blacker in the hair than him and broader in the chest than him, but was called Tadg Og because he was son to him. Mor means 'big' and Og means 'son'. But Mor can be taken to mean greater and Og can be taken to mean lesser than the greater.

'I knew it was a shout I heard,' said Tadg Mor.

'I knew it was a boat I saw and I dragging in the second net,' said Tadg Og.

'I said the sound I heard was a kittiwake, crying in the dark.'

'And I said the boat I saw was a black wave blown up on the wind.'

'It was a shout all right.'

'It was a boat all right.'

'It was a body all right.'

'But where is the black boat?' Tadg Og asked.

'It must be that the black boat capsized,' said Tadg Mor, 'and went down into the green sea.'

'Whose boat was it, would you venture for to say?' Tadg Og asked, pulling stroke for stroke at the sea.

'I'd venture for to say it was the boat of Eamon Buidhe,' said Tadg Mor, pulling with his oar against the sharp uppointing waves of the scaly, scurvy sea. The tall men rowed hard toward the clumsy thing that tossed on the tips of the deft green waves.

'Eamon Buidhe Murnane!' said Tadg Mor, lifting his silver-dropping oar.

'Eamon Buidhe Murnane!' said Tadg Og, lifting his clear, dripless, yellow oar.

It was a hard drag, dragging the body of Eamon Buidhe Murnane over the arching sides of the boat. His clothes logged him down to the water and the jutting waves jostled him against the boat. His yellow hair slipped from their fingers like floss, and the loose fibres of his island-spun clothes broke free from their grip. But they got him up over the edge of the boat, at the end of a black hour that was only lit by the whiteness of the breaking wave. They laid him down on the bottom boards of the boat on top of their haul of glittering mackerel, and they spread the nets over him. But the scales of the fish glittered up through the net and so, too, the eyes of Eamon Buidhe glittered up at them. And the live glitter of the dead eyes put a strain on Tadg Mor and he turned the body over on its face among the fish; and when they had looked a time at the black corpse with yellow hair, set in the silver and opal casket of fishes, they turned the oar blades out again into the scurvy seas, and pulled toward the land.

'How did you know it was Eamon Buidhe Murnane, and we forty pointed waves away from him at the time of your naming his name?' Tadg Og asked Tadg Mor.

'Whenever it is a thing that a man is pulled under by the sea,' said Tadg Mor, 'think around in your mind until you think out which man of all the men it might be that would be the man most missed, and that man, that you think out in your mind, will be the man cast up on the shingle.'

'This is a man that will be missed mightily,' said Tadg Og.

'He is a man that will be mightily bemoaned,' said Tadg Mor.

'He is a man that will never be replaced.'

'He is a man that will be prayed for bitterly and mightily.'

'Many a night, forgetful, his wife will set out food for him,' said Tadg Og.

'The Brightest and the Bravest!' said Tadg Mor. 'Those are the words that will be read over him – the Brightest and the Bravest.'

The boat rose up on the points of the waves and cleft down again between the points, and the oars of Tadg Mor and the oars of Tadg Og split the points of many waves.

'How is it the green sea always greeds after the Brightest and the Bravest?' Tadg Og asked Tadg Mor.

'And for the only sons?' Tadg Mor said.

'And the widows' sons?'

'And the men with one-year wives? The one-year wife that's getting this corpse' – Tadg Mor pointed down with his eyes – 'will have a black sorrow this night.'

'And every night after this night,' said Tadg Og, because he was a young man and knew about such things.

'It's a great thing that he was not dragged down to the green grave, and that is a thing will lighten the nights of the one-year wife,' said Tadg Mor.

'It isn't many are saved out of the green grave,' said Tadg Og.

'Mairtin Mor wasn't got,' said Tadg Mor.

'And Muiris Fada wasn't got.'

'Lorcan Og wasn't got.'

'Ruairi Dubh wasn't got.'

'It was three weeks and the best part of a night before the Frenchman with the leather coat was got, and five boats out looking for him.'

'It was seven weeks before Maolshaughlin O'Dalaigh was got, and his eye sockets emptied by the gulls and the gannies.'

'And by the waves. The waves are great people to lick out your eyeballs!' said Tadg Mor.

'It was a good thing, this man to be got,' said Tadg Og, 'and his eyes bright in his head.'

'Like he was looking up at the sky!'

'Like he was thinking to smile next thing he'd do.'

'He was a great man to smile, this man,' said Tadg Mor. 'He was ever and always smiling.'

'He was a great man to laugh too,' said Tadg Og. 'He was ever and always laughing.'

'Times he was laughing and times he was not laughing,' said Tadg Mor.

'Times all men stop from laughing,' said Tadg Og.

'Times I saw this man and he not laughing. Times I saw him and he putting out in the black boat looking back at the inland woman where she'd be standing on the shore and her hair weaving the wind, and there wouldn't be any laugh on his face those times.

'An island man should take an island wife,' said Tadg Og.

'An inland woman should take an inland man.'

'The inland woman that took this man had a dreadful dread on her of the sea and of the boats that put out in it.'

'Times I saw this woman from the inlands standing on the shore from his putting out with the dry black boat to his coming back with the shivering silver-belly boat.'

'He got it hard to go from her every night.'

'He got it harder than iron to go from her if there was a streak of storm gold in the sky at time of putting out.'

'An island man should not be held down to a woman from the silent inlands.'

'It was love-talk and love-looks that held down this man,' said Tadg Mor.

'The island women give love-words and love-talk too,' said Tadg Og.

'But not the love-words and the love-looks of this woman,' said Tadg Mor. 'Times I saw her wetting her feet in the sea and wetting her fingers in it and you'd see she was a kind of lovering the waves so they'd bring him back to her. Times he told me himself she had a dreadful dread of the green grave. 'There dies as many men in the inlands as in the islands. Tell her that,' I said. 'I told her that,' he said. 'But they get the black grave burial,' she said. 'They get the black grave burial in clay that's blessed by the priest and they get the speeding of the green sods thrown down on them by their kinsmen.' 'Tell her there's no worms in the green grave,' I said to him. 'I did,' said he. 'What did she say to that?' said I. She said, 'The bone waits for the bone.' 'What does she mean by that?' said I. 'She gave another saying as her meaning to that saying.' She said, 'There's no sorrow in death when two go down together into the one grave. Clay binds close as love,' she said, 'but the green grave binds nothing. The green grave scatters.' 'The green grave is for sons,' she said, 'and for brothers,' she said, 'but the black grave is for lovers,' she said, 'and for husbands in the faithful clay under the jealous sods.'

'She must be a great woman to make sayings,' said Tadg Og.

'She made great sayings for that man every hour of the day,' said Tadg Mor, 'and she stitching the nets for him on the steps of the pier while he'd be salting fish or blading oars.

'She'll be glad us to have saved him from the salt green grave. It's a great wonder but he was dragged down before he was got.'

'She is the kind of woman that always has great wonders happening round her,' said Tadg Mor. 'If she is a woman from the inlands itself, she has a great power in herself. She has a great power over the sea. Times – and she on the cliff shore and her hair weaving the wind, I'd point my eyes through the wind across at where Eamon Buidhe would be in the boat back of me, and there wouldn't be as much as one tongue of spite rising out of the waves around his black boat, and my black boat would be splattered over with white sea-spittle.'

'I heard tell of women like that. She took the fury out of the sea and burned it out to white salt in her own heart.'

The talk about the inland woman who fought the seas in her heart was slow talk and heavy talk, and slow and heavy talk was fit talk as the scurvy waves crawled over one another, scale by scale, and brought the bitter boat back to the shore.

Sometimes a spiteful tongue of foam forked up in the dark by the side of the boat and reached for the netted corpse on the boards. When this happened Tadg Og picked up the loose end of the raggy net and lashed out with it at the sea.

'Get down, you scaly-belly serpent,' he said, 'and let the corpse dry out in his death-clothes.'

'Take heed to your words, Tadg Og,' Tadg Mor would say, 'We have the point to round yet. Take heed to your words!'

'Here's a man took heed to his words and that didn't save him,' said Tadg Og. 'Here was a man was always singing back song for song to the singing sea, and look at him now lying there.'

They looked at him lying on his face under the brown web of the nets in his silver and opal casket And as they looked another venomous tongue of the sea licked up the side of the boat and strained in towards the body. Tadg Og beat at it with the raggy net.

'Keep your strength for the loud knocking you'll have to give on the wooden door,' said Tadg Mor. And Tadg Og understood that he was the one would walk up the shingle and bring the death news to the one-year wife, who was so strange among the island women with her hair weaving the wind at evening and her white feet wetted in the sea by day.

'Is it not a thing that she'll be, likely, out on the shore?' he asked, in a bright hope, pointing his eyes to where the white edge of a sandy shore-wash shone by its own light in the dark.

'Is there a storm tonight?' said Tadg Mor. 'Is there a great wind tonight? Is there a rain spate? Are there any other signs from the sea?'

'No,' said Tadg Og, 'there are none of those things that you mention.'

'I will tell you the reason you asked that question,' said Tadg Mor. 'You asked that question because that question is the answer that you'd like to get to that question.'

'It's a hard thing to bring news to a one-year wife and she one that has a dreadful dread on her of the sea,' said Tadg Og.

'It's good news you're bringing to the one-year wife when you bring news that her man is got safe, to go down like any inlander into a black grave blessed by a priest and tramped down by the feet of his kinsmen on the sod.'

'It's a queer thing him to be caught by the sea on a fine night with no wind blowing,' said Tadg Og.

'On a fine night the women lie down to sleep, and if a woman has a power over the sea, with her white feet in the water and her black hair fighting the wind and a bright fire in her heart, the sea can only wait until that woman's spirit is out of her body – likely back home in the inlands – and then the sea-serpent gives a slow turnover on his scales, one that you wouldn't heed to yourself, maybe, and you standing up with no hold on the oars; and before there's time for more than the first shout out of you the boat is logging down to the depths of the water. And all the time the woman that would have saved you, with her willing and wishing for you, is in the deep bed of a dark sleep, having no knowledge of the thing that has happened until she hears the loud-handed knocking of the neighbour on the door outside.'

Tadg Og knocked with his knuckles on the sideboards of the boat.

'Louder than that,' Tadg Mor said.

Tadg Og knocked another, louder knock on the boat's side.

'Have you no more knowledge than that of how to knock at a door in the fastness of the night and the people inside the house buried in sleep and the corpse down on the shore getting covered with sand and the fish scales drying into him so tight that the finger-nails of the washing women will be broken and split peeling them off him? Have you no more knowledge than that of how to knock with your knuckle-bones?' Tadg Mor gave a loud knocking with his own hand on the wet seat of the boat. 'That is the knock of a man that you might say knows how to knock at a door, day-time or night-time,' he said, and then he knocked again, louder, if it could be that any knock could be louder than the first knock.

Tadg Og listened and then he spoke, not looking at Tadg Mor, but looking at the oar he was rolling in the water. 'Two people knocking would make a loud knocking entirely,' he said.

'One has to stay with the dead,' said Tadg Mor.

Tadg Og drew a long stroke on the oar and he drew a long breath out of his lungs, and he took a long look at the nearing shore.

'What will I say when she comes to my knocking?'

'When she comes to the knocking, step back a bit from the door, so's she'll see the wet shining on you and smell the salt water off you, and say in a loud voice that the sea is queer and rough this night.'

'She'll be down with her to the shore if that's what I say.

'Say then,' said Tadg Mor, pulling in the oar to slow the boat a bit, 'say there's news come in that a boat went down beyond the point.'

'If I say that, she'll be down with her faster than ever to the shore without waiting to hear more, and her hair flying and her white feet freezing on the shingle.'

'If that is so,' said Tadg Mor, 'then you'll have to stand back bold from the door and call out loudly in the night, "The Brightest and the Bravest!"'

'What will she say to that?'

'She'll say, "God bless them!"'

'And what will I say to that?'

'You'll say, "God rest them!"'

'And what will she say to that?'

'She'll say, "Is it in the black grave or the green grave?"'

'And what will I say to that?'

'You say, "God rest Eamon Buidhe, that will be put down in the black grave in the holy ground, blessed by the priest and sodded by the people."'

'And what will she say to that?'

'She'll say, likely, "Bring him in to me, Tadg Og!"'

'And what will I say to that?'

'Whatever you say after that, let it be loud and raising echoes under the rafters, so she won't hear the sound of the corpse being dragged up on the shingle. And when he's lifted up on to the scoured table, let whatever you say be loud then too, so's she won't be listening for the sound of the water drabbling down off his clothes on the floor!'

There was only the noise of the oars after that for a time, till a shoaly sound stole in between the oar strokes. It was the shoaly sound of the pebbles dragged back from the shore by the tide.

A few strokes more and they beached, and stepped out among the sprawling waves and dragged the boat after them till it cleft its depth in the damp shingle.

'See that you give a loud knocking, Tadg Og,' said Tadg Mor, and Tadg Og set his head against the darkness and his feet were heard grinding down the shifting shingle as he made for the house of the one-year wife. The house was set in a thrifty sea-field, and his steps did not sound down to the shore once he got to the dune-grass of the thrifty sea-field. But in another little while there was a sound of a fist knocking upon wood, stroke after stroke. A strong hand coming down on hard wood. Tadg Mor, waiting with the body in the boat, recalled to himself all the times he went knocking on the island doors bringing news to the women of the death of their men. But island wives were the daughters of island widows. They knew the sea gave life, but it gave death. Life or death, it was all one in the end. The sea never lost its scabs. The sea was there before the coming of man. Island women had that knowledge. But what knowledge of the sea and its place in the world since the beginning of time had a woman from the inlands? No knowledge at all. An inland woman had not knowledge to bear her up when the loud knocking came on her door in the night. Tadg Mor listened to the loud, hard knocking of his son Tadg Og on the door of the one-year wife of Eamon Buidhe that was lying in his casket of fishes on the floor of the boat, cleft fast in the shingle sand. The night was cold. And even though it was dark the fish scales glittered in the whiteness made by the breaking of the waves on the black shore. The sound of the sea was as sad if not sadder than the sight of the yellow-haired corpse, but still Tadg Mor was gladder to be down on the shore than up in the dune-grass knocking at the one-night widow's door.

The knocking sound of Tadg Og's knuckles on the wooden door was a human sound and it sounded good in the ears of Tadg Mor for a time; but, like all sounds that go on too long, it sounded soon to be as inhuman as the washing of the waves tiding in on the shingle. Tadg Mor put up his rounded palms to his mouth and shouted out to Tadg Og to come back to the boat. Tadg Og came back running over the shore, and the air was grained with sounds of sliding shingle.

'There's no one in the house where you were knocking,' said Tadg Mor.

'I knocked louder on the door than you knocked on the seat boards,' said Tadg Og.

'I heard how you knocked,' said Tadg Mor. 'You knocked well. But let you knock better when you go to the house of her neighbour to find out where the one-night widow is from her own house this night.'

'If I got no answer at one door is it likely I'll get answer at another door?' said Tadg Og. 'It was you yourself I heard say one time that the man that knows how a thing is to be done is the man should do that thing when that thing is to be done.'

'How is a man ever to get knowledge of how to do a thing if that man doesn't do that thing when that thing is to be done?' said Tadg Mor.

Tadg Og got into the boat again and they sat there in the dark. After four or maybe five waves had broken by their side, Tadg Og lifted the net and felt the clothes of Eamon Buidhe.

'The clothes are drying into him,' he said.

'If I was to go up with you to the house of Seana Bhride, who would there be to watch the dead?' said Tadg Mor, and then Tadg Og knew that Tadg Mor was going with him and he had no need to put great heed on the answer he gave to him.

'Let the sea watch him,' he said, and after a wave went back with a fistful of little complaining pebbles, he put a leg out over the side of the boat.

'We must take him out of the boat first,' said Tadg Mor. 'Take hold of him there by the feet,' he said as he rolled back the net, putting it over the oar with each roll so it would not ravel and knot.

They lifted Eamon Buidhe out of the boat and the mackerel slipped about their feet into the place where he had left his shape. They dragged him up a boat-length from the sprawling waves, and they faced his feet to the shore, but when they saw that that left his head lower than his feet, because the shingle shelved deeply at that point, they faced him about again toward the waves that were clashing their sharp, pointy scales together and sending up spires of white spray in the air. The dead man glittered with the silver and verdigris scales of the mackerel that were over his clothing, every part.

Tadg Mor went up the sliding shingle in front of Tadg Og, and Tadg Og put his feet in the shelves that were made in the shingle by Tadg Mor because the length of the step they took was the same length. The sea sounded in their ears as they went through the shingle, but by the time the first coarse dune-grass scratched at their clothing the only sound each could hear was the sound of the other's breathing.

The first cottage that rose up blacker than the night in their path was the cottage where Tadg Og made the empty knocking. Tadg Mor stopped in front of the door as if he might be thinking of trying his own hand at knocking, but he thought better of it and went on after Tadg Og to the house that was next to that house, and that was the house of Seana Bhride, a woman that would know anything that eye or ear could know about those that lived within three islands of her. Tadg Mor hit the door of Seana Bhride's house with a knock of his knuckles, and although it was a less loud knock than the echo of the knock that came down to the shore when Tadg Og struck the first knock on the door of the wife of Eamon Buidhe, there was a foot to the floor before he could raise his knuckle off the wood for another knock.

A candle lit up, a shadow fell across the windowpane and a face whitened the door gap.

'You came to the wrong house this night,' said Seana Bhride. 'The sea took all the men was ever in this house twelve years ago and two months and seventeen days.'

'It may be that we have no corpse for this house, but we came to the right house for all that,' said Tadg Mor. 'We came to this house for knowledge of the house across two sea-fields from this house, where we got no answer to our knocking with our knuckles.'

'And I knocked with a stone up out of the ground, as well,' said Tadg Og coming closer.

The woman with the candle-flame blowing drew back into the dark.

'Is it for the inland woman, the one-year wife, you're bringing the corpse you have below in the boat this night?' she said.

'It is, God help us,' said Tadg Mor.

'It is, God help us,' said Tadg Og.

'The Brightest and the Bravest,' said Tadg Mor.

'Is it a thing that you got no answer to your knocking,' said the old woman, bending out again with the blowing candle-flame.

'No answer,' said Tadg Og, 'and sturdy knocking.'

'Knocking to be heard above the sound of the sea,' said Tadg Mor.

'They sleep deep, the people from the inland?' said Tadg Og, asking a question.

'The people of the inland sleep deep in the cottage in the middle of the fields,' said Seana Bhride, 'but when they're rooted up and set down by the sea their spirit never passes out of hearing of the step on the shingle. It's a queer thing entirely that you got no answer to your knocking.'

'We got no answer to our knocking,' said Tadg Mor and Tadg Og, bringing their words together like two oars striking the same wave, one on this side of a boat and one on that.

'When the inland woman puts her face down on the feather pillow,' said Seana Bhride, 'that pillow is like the seashells children put against their ears; that pillow has in it the sad crying voices of the sea.'

'Is it that you think she is from home this night?' said Tadg Mor.

'It must be a thing that she is,' said the old woman.

'Is it back to her people in the inlands she'd be gone?' said Tadg Og, who had more than the curiosity of the one night in him.

'Step into the kitchen,' said the old woman, 'while I ask Brid Og if she saw the wife of Eamon Buidhe go from her house this night.'

While she went into the room that was back from the kitchen, Tadg Og put a foot inside the kitchen door but Tadg Mor stayed looking down to the shore.

'If it is a thing the inland woman is from home this night, where will we put Eamon Buidhe, that we have below on the shore, with his face and no sheet on it, and his eyes with the lids not down on them, and the fish scales sticking to him faster than they stuck to the mackerels when they swam beyond the nets, blue and silver and green?'

Tadg Og stepped a bit further into the kitchen of Seana Bhride. 'Listen to Brid Og,' he said softly.

'Brid Og,' said the old woman, 'is it a thing that the inland woman from two fields over, went from her house this night?'

'Yes. It is a thing that she went,' said Brid Og.

Tadg Og spoke to Tadg Mor. 'Brid Og's talk is soft in the day, but her talk is soft as the sea in summer when she talks in the night in the dark.'

'Listen to what she says,' said Tadg Mor, coming in a step after Tadg Og.

'Is it that she went to her people in the inlands?' Seana Bhride asked.

'The wife of Eamon Buidhe never stirred a foot to her people in the inlands since the first day she came to the islands, in her blue dress with the beads,' said the voice of Brid Og.

'Where did she go then,' said the old woman, 'if it is a thing that she didn't go to her people in the inlands?'

'Where else but where she said she'd go?' said the voice of Brid Og. 'Out in the boat with her one-year husband?' There was sound of rusty springs creaking in the room where Brid Og slept, back behind the kitchen, and then her voice was clearer and stronger like as if she was sitting up in the bed looking out at the black sea and the white points rising in it, lit by the light of their own brightness. 'She said the sea would never drag Eamon Buidhe down to the green grave and leave her to lie lonely in the black grave on the shore, in the black clay that held tight, under the weighty sods. She said a man and a woman should lie in the one grave. She said a night never passed without her heart being burnt out to a cold white salt. She said that this night, and every night after, she'd go out with Eamon in the black boat over the scabby back of the sea. She said if he got the green grave, she'd get the green grave too, and her arms would be stronger than the weeds of the sea, to bind them together for ever. She said the island women never fought the sea. She said the sea needed taming and besting. She said there was a curse on the black clay for women that lay alone in it while their men washed to and fro in the eaves of the sea. She said the black clay was all right for inland women. She said the black clay was all right for sisters and mothers. She said the black clay was all right for girls that died at seven years. But the green grave was the grave for wives, she said, and she went out in the black boat this night and she's going out every night after!' said Brid Og.

'Tell Brid Og there will be no night after!' said Tadg Mor.

'Time enough to tell her. Let her sleep till day,' said Tadg Og, and he strained his eyes past the fluttering flame of the candle as the old woman came out from Brid Og's room.

'You heard what she said?'

'It's a bad thing he was got,' said the old woman.

'That's a thing was never said on this island before this night,' said Tadg Mor.

'There was a fire on every point of the cliff shore to light home the men who were dragging for Mairtin Mor.'

'And he never was got,' said Tadg Mor.

'There was a shroud spun for Ruairi Dubh between the time of the putting-out of the boats to look for him and their coming back with the empty news in the green daylight,' said the old woman.

'Ruairi Dubh was never got.'

'Mairtin Mor was never got.'

'Lorcan Og was never got.'

'Muiris Fada was never got.'

'My four sons were never got,' said the old woman. 'The father of Brid Og was never got,' said Tadg Og, and he was looking at the shut door of the room where Brid Og was lying in the dark, the candle shadows running their hands over the door. 'The father of Brid Og was never got,' he said again, forgetting he had said the same words before. 'Of all the men that had yellow coffins standing up on their ends by the gable, and all the men that had brown shrouds hanging up on the wall with the iron nail eating through the yarn, it had to be the one man that should never have been got that was got.' Tadg Og opened the top-half of the door and let in the deep sound of the tide.

'That is the way,' said Tadg Mor.

'That is ever and always the way,' said the old woman.

'The sea is stronger than any man,' said Tadg Mor.

'The sea is stronger than any woman.'

'The sea is stronger than women from the inland fields,' said Tadg Mor, going to the door.

'The sea is stronger than talk of love,' said Tadg Og, going out after him into the dark. It was so dark, he could not see where the window of Brid Og's room was, but he was looking where it might be while he buttoned his jacket.

Tadg Mor and Tadg Og went back to the shore, keeping their feet well on the shelving shingle, as they went towards the sprawling waves. The waves were up to the sea-break at the graywacke wall.

The boat was floating free. It was gone from the cleft in the shingle. And the body of Eamon Buidhe, that had glittered with fish scales, opal, silver and verdigris, was gone too from the shore. It was gone from the black land that was scored criss-cross with grave-cuts by spade and shovel It was gone and would never be got. The men spoke together.

'Mairtin Mor wasn't got.'

'Muiris Fada wasn't got.'

'Lorcan Og wasn't got.'

'Ruairi Dubh wasn't got.'

'The four sons of Seana Bhride were never got.'

'The father of Brid Og wasn't got.'

The men of the island were held down in the bed of the sea by the tight weeds of the sea. They were held by tendrils of sea anemone, green sea-grasses and green sea-reeds, and by the winding stems of the green sea-daffodil. But Eamon Buidhe Murnane would be held fast in the white arms of his one-year wife, who came from the inlands, where women have no knowledge of the sea but only a knowledge of love.

Sarah

Sarah had a bit of a bad name. That was the worst her neighbours would say of her, although there was a certain fortuity about her choice of fathers for the three strapping sons she'd borne – all three outside wedlock.

Sarah was a great worker, strong and tireless, and a lot of women in the village got her in to scrub for them. Nobody was ever known to be unkind to her. And not one of her children was born in the County Home. It was always the most upright matron in the village who slapped life into every one of them.

'She's unfortunate, that's all,' this matron used to say. 'How could she know any better – living with two rough brothers? And don't forget she had no father herself.'

If Sarah had been one to lie in bed on a Sunday and miss Mass, her neighbours might have felt differently about her, there being greater understanding in their hearts for sins against God than for sins against his Holy Church. But Sarah found it easy to keep the Commandments of the church. She never missed Mass. She observed abstinence on all days abstinence was required. She frequently did the Stations of the Cross as well. And on Lady Day when an annual pilgrimage took place to a holy well in the neighbouring village Sarah was an example to all – with her shoes off walking over the sharp flinty stones, doing penance like a nun. If on that occasion some outsider showed disapproval of her, Sarah's neighbours were quicker than Sarah herself to take offence. All the same, charity was tempered with prudence and women with grown sons, and women not long married, took care not to hire her.

So when Oliver Kedrigan's wife, a newcomer to the locality, spoke of getting Sarah in to keep house for her while she was going up to Dublin for a few days, two of the older women in the district felt it their duty to step across to Kedrigan's and offer a word of advice.

'I know she has a bit of a bad name,' Kathleen conceded, 'but she's a great worker. I hear it's said she can bake bread that's nearly as good as my own.'

'That may be!' said one of the women, 'but if I was you, I'd think twice before I'd leave her to mind your house while you're away!'

'Who else is there I can get?' Kathleen said stubbornly.

'Why do you want anyone? You'll only be gone for three days, isn't that all?'

'Three days is a long time to leave a house in the care of a man.'

'I'd rather let the roof fall in on him than draw Sarah Murray about my place!' said the women. 'She has a queer way of looking at a man. I wouldn't like to have her give my man one of those looks.' Kathleen got their meaning at last.

'I can trust Oliver,' she said coldly.

'It's not right to trust any man too far,' the women said, shaking their heads.

'Oliver isn't that sort,' Kathleen said, and her pale papery face smiled back contempt for the other women.

Stung by that smile, the women stood up and prepared to take their leave.

'I suppose you know your own business,' said the first one who had raised the subject, 'but I wouldn't trust the greatest saint ever walked with Sarah Murray.'

'I'd trust Oliver with any woman in the world,' Kathleen said.

'Well he's your man, not ours,' said the two women, speaking together as they went out the door. Kathleen looked after them resentfully. She may not have been too happy herself about hiring Sarah but as she closed the door on the women she made up her mind for once and for all to do so, goaded on by pride in her legitimate power over her man. She'd let everyone see she could trust him.

As the two women went down the road they talked for a while about the Kedrigans but gradually they began to talk about other things, until they came to the lane leading up to the cottage where Sarah Murray lived with her brothers and the houseful of children. Looking up at the cottage their thoughts went back to the Kedrigans again and they came to a stand. 'What ever took possession of Oliver Kedrigan to marry that bleached out bloodless thing?' one of them said.

'I don't know,' said the other one. 'I wonder why she's going up to Dublin?'

'Why do you think!' said the first woman, contemptuous of her companion's ignorance. 'Not that she looks to me like a woman would ever have a child, no matter how many doctors she might go to – in Dublin or elsewhere.'

Sarah went over to Mrs Kedrigan's the morning Mrs Kedrigan was going away and she made her a nice cup of tea. Then she carried the suitcase down to the road and helped her on to the bus because it was a busy time for Oliver. He had forty lambing ewes and there was a predatory vixen in a nearby wood that was causing him alarm. He had had to go out at the break of day to put up a new fence.

But the bus was barely out of sight when Oliver's cart rattled back into the yard. He'd forgotten to take the wire-cutters with him. He drew up outside the kitchen door and called to Sarah to hand him out the clippers, so he wouldn't have to get down off the cart. But when he looked down at her, he gave a laugh. 'Did you rub sheepraddle into your cheeks?' he asked, and he laughed again – a loud happy laugh that could give no offence. And Sarah took none. But her cheeks went redder, and she angrily swiped a bare arm across her face as if to stem the flux of the healthy blood in her face. Oliver laughed for the third time. 'Stand back or you'll frighten the horse and he'll bolt,' he said, as he jerked the reins and the cart rattled off out of the yard again.

Sarah stared after him, keeping her eyes on him until the cart was like a toy cart in the distance, with a toy horse under it, and Oliver himself a toy farmer made out of painted wood.

When Kathleen came home the following Friday her house was

cleaner than it had ever been. The boards were scrubbed white as rope, the windows glinted and there was bread cooling on the sill. Kathleen paid Sarah and Sarah went home. Her brothers were glad to have her back to clean the house and make the beds and bake. She gave them her money. The children were glad to see her too because while she was away their uncles made them work all day footing turf and running after sheep like collie dogs.

Sarah worked hard as she had always done, for a few months. Then one night as she was handing round potato-cakes to her brothers and the children who were sitting around the kitchen table with their knives and forks at the ready in their hands, the elder brother Pat gave a sharp look at her. He poked Joseph, the younger brother, in the ribs with the handle of his knife. 'For God's sake,' he said, 'will you look at her!'

Sarah ignored Pat's remark, except for a toss of her head. She sat down and ate her supper greedily, swilling it down with several cups of boiling tea. When she'd finished she got up and went out into the wagon-blue night. Her brothers stared after her. 'Holy God,' Pat said, 'something will have to be done about her this time.'

'Ah what's the use of talking like that?' Joseph said, twitching his shoulders uneasily. 'If the country is full of blackguards, what can we do about it?'

Pat put down his knife and fork and thumped the table with his closed fist.

'I thought the talking-to she got from the priest the last time would knock sense into her. The priest said a Home was the only place for the like of her. I told him we'd have no part in putting her away – God Almighty what would we do without her? There must a woman in the house! – we can't stand for much more of this.'

'Her brats need her too,' Joseph said, pondering over the plight they'd be in without her, 'leastways until they can be sent out to service themselves.' He looked up. 'That won't be long now though; they're shaping into fine strong boys.'

But Pat stood up. 'All the same something will have to be done. When the priest hears about this he'll be at me again. And this time I'll have to give him a better answer than the other times.'

Joseph shrugged his shoulders. 'Ah tell him you can get no rights of her. And isn't it the truth?' He gave an easygoing chuckle. 'Tell him to tackle the job himself!'

Pat gave a sort of a laugh too but it was less easy. 'Do you remember what he said the last time? He said if she didn't tell the name of the father, he'd make the new born infant speak and name him!'

'How well he didn't do it! Talk is easy!' Joseph said.

'He didn't do it,' said Pat, 'because Sarah took care not to let him catch sight of the child till the whole thing was put to the back of his mind by something else – the Confirmation – or the rewiring of the chapel.'

'Well, can't she do the same with this one?' Joseph said. He stood up. 'There's one good thing about the whole business, and that is that Mrs Kedrigan didn't notice anything wrong with her, or she'd never have given her an hour's work!'

Pat twitched with annoyance. 'How could Mrs Kedrigan notice anything? Isn't it six months at least since she was working in Kedrigan's?'

'It is I suppose,' Joseph said.

The two brothers moved about the kitchen for a few minutes in silence. The day with its solidarity of work and eating was over and they were about to go their separate ways when Joseph spoke.

'Pat?'

'What?'

'Oh nothing,' said Joseph. 'Nothing at all.'

'Ah quit your hinting! What are you trying to say? Speak out man.'

'I was only wondering,' said Joseph. 'Have you any idea at all who could be the father of this one?'

'Holy God,' Pat cried in fury. 'Why would you think I'd know the father of this one any more than the others? But if you think I'm going to stay here all evening gossiping like a woman, you're making a big mistake. I'm going out. I'm going over to the quarry field to see that heifer is all right that was sick this morning.'

'Ah the heifer'll be all right,' Joseph said. But feeling his older brother's eyes were on him he shrugged his shoulders. 'You can give me a shout if she's in a bad way and you want me.' Then when he'd let Pat get as far as the door he spoke again. 'I won't say anything to her, I suppose, when she comes in?' he asked.

Pat swung around. 'And what would you say, I'd like to know? Won't it be all beyond saying anyway in a few weeks when everyone in the countryside will see for themselves what's going on?'

'That's right,' said Joseph.

Sarah went out at the end of the day's work, as she had always done. And her brothers kept silent tongues in their heads about the child she was carrying. She worked even better than before and she sang at her work. She carried the child deep in her body and she boldly faced an abashed congregation at Mass on Sundays, walking down the centre aisle and taking her usual place under the fourth station of the cross.

Meantime Mrs Kedrigan too was expecting her long delayed child, but she didn't go to Mass: the priest came to her. She was looking bad. By day she crept from chair to chair around the kitchen, and only went out at night for a bit of a walk up and down their own lane. She was self-conscious about her condition and her nerves were frayed. Oliver used to have to sit up half the night with her and hold her moist hands in his until she fell asleep, but all the same she woke often and was frightened and peevish and, in bursts of hysteria, she called him a cruel brute. One evening she was taking a drop of tea by the fire. Oliver had gone down to the Post Office to see if there was a letter from the Maternity Hospital in Dublin, where she had engaged a bed for the following month. When he came back Oliver had a letter in his hand. Before he gave it to her, he told her what was in it. It was an anonymous letter and it named him as the father of the child Sarah Murray was going to bring into the world in a few weeks. He told Kathleen it was an unjust accusation.

'For God's sake, say something, Katty,' he said. 'You don't believe the bloody letter, do you?' Kathleen didn't answer. 'You don't believe it, sure you don't.' He went over to the window and laid his burning face against the cold pane of glass. 'What will I do, Katty?'

'You'll do nothing,' Kathleen said, speaking for the first time. 'Nothing. Aren't you innocent? Take no notice of that letter.'

She stooped and with a wide and grotesque swoop she plucked up the letter. She put it under a plate on the dresser and began to get the tea ready with slow, tedious journeyings back and forth across the silent kitchen. Oliver stood looking out over the fields until the tea was ready and only once or twice looked at his wife. At last he turned away from the window and went over to the dresser. 'I'll tear up the letter,' he said.

'You'll do nothing of the kind,' Kathleen said, and with a lurch she reached the dresser before him. 'Here's where that letter belongs.'

There was a sound of crackling and a paper-ball went into the heart of the flames. Oliver watched it burn, and although he thought it odd that he didn't see the writing on it, he still believed that it was Sarah's letter that coiled into a black spiral in the grate.

The next evening Sarah was sitting by the fire as Kathleen Kedrigan had been sitting by hers. She too was drinking a cup of tea, and she didn't look up when her brothers came into the kitchen. No one spoke, but after a minute or two Sarah went to get up to prepare the supper. Her brother Pat pushed her down again on the chair. The cup shattered against the range and the tea slopped over the floor.

'Is this letter yours? Did you write it?' he shouted at her, holding out a letter addressed to Oliver Kedrigan – a letter that had gone through the post, and been delivered and opened. 'Do you hear me talking to you? Did you write this letter?'

'What business is it of yours?' Sarah said sullenly, and again she tried to get to her feet.

'Sit down, I tell you,' Pat shouted, and he pressed her back. 'Answer my question. Did you write this letter?'

Sarah stared dully at the letter in her brother's hand. The firelight flickered in her yellow eyes. 'Give it to me,' she snarled, and she snatched it from him. 'What business is it of yours, you thief?'

'Did you hear that, Pat? She called you a thief!' the younger brother shouted.

'Shut up, you,' Pat said. He turned back to his sister. 'Answer me. Is it true what it says in this letter?'

'How do I know what it says! And what if it is true? It's no business of yours.'

'I'll show you whose business it is!' Pat said. For a minute he stood as if not knowing what to do. Then he ran into the room off the kitchen where Sarah slept with the three children. He came out with an armful of clothes, a red dress, a coat, and a few bits of underwear. Sarah watched him. There was no one holding her down now but she didn't attempt to rise. Again her brother stood for a moment in the middle of the floor irresolute. Then he heard the outer door rattle in a gust of wind, and he ran towards it and dragging it open he threw out the armful of clothing and ran back into the room. This time he came out with a jumper and a red cap, an alarm clock and a few other odds and ends. He threw them out the door, too.

'Do you know it's raining, Pat?' the younger brother asked cautiously.

'What do I care if it's raining?' Pat said. He went into the other room a third time. He was a while in there rummaging and when he came out he had a picture-frame, a prayer book, a pair of high-heeled shoes, a box of powder and a little green velvet box stuck all over with pearly shells.

Sarah sprang to her feet. 'My green box. Oh! Give me my box!' She tried to snatch it from him.

But Joseph suddenly put out a foot and tripped her.

When Sarah got to her feet Pat was standing at the door throwing her things out one by one, but he kept the green box till last and when he threw it out he fired it with all his strength as far as it would go as if trying to reach the dunghill at the other end of the yard. At first Sarah made as if to run out to get the things back. Then she stopped and started to pull on her coat, but her brother caught her by the hair, at the same time pulling the coat off her. Then, by the hair he dragged her across the kitchen and pushed her out into the rain, where she slipped and fell again on the wet slab stone of the doorway. Quickly then he shut out the sight of her from his eyes by banging the door closed.

'That ought to teach her,' he said. 'Carrying on with a married man! No one is going to say I put up with that kind of thing. I didn't mind the other times when it was probably old Molloy or his like that would have been prepared to pay for his mistakes if the need arose, but I wasn't going to stand for a thing like this.'

'You're sure it was Kedrigan?'

'Ah! didn't you see the letter yourself! Wasn't it Sarah's writing? And didn't Mrs Kedrigan herself give it to me this morning?'

'Sarah denied it, Pat,' Joseph said. His spurt of courage had given out and his hands were shaking as he went to the window and pulled back a corner of the bleached and neatly-sewn square of a flour bag that served as a curtain.

'She did! And so did he, I suppose? Well, she can deny it somewhere else now.'

'Where do you suppose she'll go?'

'She can go where she bloody well likes. And shut your mouth, you. Keep away from that window! Can't you sit down? Sit down, I tell you.'

All this took place at nine o'clock on a Tuesday night. The next morning at seven o'clock, Oliver Kedrigan went to a fair in a neighbouring town where he bought a new ram. He had had his breakfast in the town and he wanted to get on with his work, but he went to the door of the kitchen to see his wife was all right and called in to her from the yard. 'Katty! Hand me the tin of raddle. It's on top of the dresser.'

Kathleen Kedrigan came to the door and she had the tin of raddle in her hand.

'You won't be troubled with any more letters,' she said. Oliver laughed self-consciously. 'That's a good thing, anyhow,' he said. 'Hurry, give me the raddle.'

His wife held the tin in her hand, but she didn't move. She leaned against the jamb of the door. 'I see you didn't hear the news?'

'What news?'

'Sarah Murray got what was coming to her last night. Her brothers turned her out of the house, and threw out all her things after her.'

Oliver's faced darkened.

'That was a cruel class of thing for brothers to do. Where did she go?'

'She went where she and her likes belong; into a ditch on the side of the road!'

Oliver said nothing. His wife watched him closely and she clenched her hands. 'You can spare your sympathy. She won't need it.'

Oliver looked up.

'Where did she go?'

'Nowhere,' Kathleen said slowly.

Oliver tried to think clearly. It had been a bad night, wet and windy. 'She wasn't out all night in the rain?' he asked, a fierce light coming into his eyes.

'She was,' Kathleen said, and she stared at him. 'At least that's where they found her in the morning, dead as a rat. And the child dead beside her!'

Her pale eyes held his, and he stared uncomprehendingly into them. Then he looked down at her hand that held the tin of red sheep-raddle.

'Give me the raddle!' he said, but before she had time to hand it to him he yelled at her again. 'Give me the raddle Give it to me. What are you waiting for? Give me the God-damn' stuff.'

Brother Boniface

Brother Boniface sat in the sun. The sun shone full on the monastery wall, and brightened the gold coins of its ancient lichen. Its light fell through the leaves of an elm tree and littered the grass with yellow petals. It splattered the green and white palings that shut off the kitchen garden from the blazing flower-beds on the lawn and it fell full on the rough stone seat where Brother Boniface sat smiling.

There was no one to be seen out under the hot midday sun but Brother Boniface and the monastery cats. There were five cats. There was a big marmalade tom with green eyes, stretching his long paws up the bark of an elm. There was an old white cat sitting solemn in the grass, with her eyes shut tight against the piercing rays of the sun. There were two fat cats abask on the stone seat, one each side of Brother Boniface. And there would have been great peace in that sunny place had it not been for the fifth cat. The fifth cat was young and slender and she ran among the grasses. Her fur was grey with markings of gold, and her eyes were amber. She could not stay still for a second. She ran at the falling leaves. She ran at the splatters of sunlight and tried to pin them against the palings with her paw. Brother Boniface watched her for a little while, but with the other cats all around him closing their eyes every other minute – blinking, narrowing, then closing them – his own eyelids soon grew heavy and he, too, took a little nap.

Brother Boniface was sleeping soundly, with his chin on his chest, when a cinnamon-coloured butterfly, with black and brown spots on its wings, flew unsteadily over the flower-bed. At once the young cat sprang after it, leaping lightly through the flowers, but all the same the stem of a flower snapped and broke under her weight. The fat cats opened their eyes. The old white cat sat up. Brother Boniface jerked his head up and looked from right to left. When he saw the broken stem of the flower he rose to his feet as quick as he could, clapping his hands together and shuffling the gravel with his sandalled feet he called out to the cat.

'Pussy! Pussy! Pussy! Come out of that at once.' He waved his arms in distress. 'Pussy! Pussy! Pussy! Come out of that at once!'

The young cat started up with a pretty fright. She laid her ears back against her sleek head and arched her back fantastically. She looked at Brother Boniface and forgot the cinnamon butterfly, which fluttered away, but after a minute her body slackened and she leaped out of the flower-bed again and ran away, capricious, giddy and full of grace.

Brother Boniface watched the young cat as she ran away into the shade of the trees where she began to scramble from shadow to shadow whenever a breeze lightly moved the branches overhead. In his brown worsted habit he himself was almost too hot to move. The heavy folds seemed to tug at him with an insufferable weight. When he was a young monk he used to think that the folds of his sleeves and the scoop of his cowl gave him an added speed as he strode along the corridors, the way the sails of a ship speed it on before the wind. But at eighty the weight of the wool wearied him, although, in places, it was worn so thin it was little more than a network of thread. Still he got to his feet and shuffled over to the flower-bed to examine the broken flower. There was more than one broken! Two? Three! In dismay Brother Boniface picked up three flower heads that had been severed from their stems, and laid them sadly on the grass. Three flowers less before the high altar on the feast of Corpus Christi. The old monk sighed. He was looking forward to the great feast day, when there would be hundreds of candles blazing before the Host and hundreds of flowers as well. He would have to keep a more constant eye on that young cat. He went back to the stone seat, moving slowly over pebbles that had been rounded and smoothed by the soles of thousands of sandalled feet, and raked every day, winter and summer, by Brother Gardener.

Brother Gardener had joined the order exactly ten years after Brother Boniface, and so Brother Boniface always looked upon him as a very young man, although Brother Gardener himself was then fifty years in the garb of God. The day Brother Gardener came up the driveway to the monastery with a red carpet-bag in his hand, Brother Boniface was clipping the ivy on the chapel wall and the air was scented with its sap. The young man had asked to see the Father Abbot, and Brother Boniface got down from the ladder and went with him to the door of the Abbot's office. While they stood waiting for the Father Abbot to come out, they began to talk.

'Ivy should not be cut at this time of year,' said the young man, who had been a gardener out in the world before he got the notion of entering a monastery. Brother Boniface was just going to ask his reason for this statement when the Father Abbot – Abbot Anselm, God be good to his soul – opened the door, and, hearing the last sentence, joined in the conversation as if he had known the young man all his life.

'Will it grow again?' he asked.

'You can't kill ivy,' said the young man. 'But it looks better if it's clipped before the new growth starts.'

'I'm glad to know that,' said the Abbot. 'Still, we can't leave it the way it is!' He looked at the barren grey patch on the wall where Brother Boniface in his youthful vigour had perhaps been a bit too drastic with his shears, and then he looked at the rest of the wall where the ivy was so thick it gave shelter to hundreds of bees – and even a few birds – who, darting out, made the young leaves flutter as if they too had wings. He turned back to the young man and, glancing at his red carpet-bag, he looked him straight in the eye before he spoke again. 'Leave your bag in the hall, young man,' he said, 'and finish clipping that ivy. But see that you cut it at the right time next year,' he paused, 'and the year after and every year,' he said. He took the shears out of Brother Boniface's hand. 'You can help Brother Sacristan to clean the brasses,' he said. That was the kind of man he was, Father Abbot, God be good to his soul. He liked a job to be done right. Brother Boniface was very fond of him.

The young monk was given the name of Juniper, but it wasn't long till he was known as Brother Gardener, in the same way that Brother Boas was called Brother Sacristan, and Brother Lambert was called Brother Vintner. But Brother Boniface was always called by his own name because he never did anything well enough to be left at it for long. He was always being changed from one task to another. He cleaned the brasses and snuffed the candles. He sharpened knives and he fed chickens. He peeled apples and he turned the churn. He waxed the oak pews in the chapel and he chopped logs for the kitchen fire. And every October he went out with a basket and picked elderberries. Later he took the scum off the wine vats. He had a thousand tasks to do, and he loved doing them all. He helped with everything, and one day Father Abbot said he should have been called Brother Jack, because he was jack of all trades.

But when the Father Abbot felt his end had come, it was for Brother Boniface he sent, and although all his monks clustered round him, he wouldn't let anyone minister to him but Boniface. It was Brother Boniface who wet his lips. It was he who wiped the sweat from his brow and held the crucifix up for him to kiss. It was he who kept the candle firm in the Abbot's hand when the old man's soul was finally loosed to God. And when that soul had fled its clay, the hands of the corpse and the hands of Brother Boniface were bound together by a rope of twisted wax that had knotted its way down the candle, drop by drop, to their clasped hands.

Every year when the ivy was cut, and its green sap freed upon the air, Brother Boniface prayed for the old Abbot, and as he prayed thoughts of the past came back to him. His memories were not many but they were vivid. Memories stay greener where memories are few. There had never been much time, of course, for remembering anything at all. The years had gone by so swiftly one after another it seemed they had been but as the flight of the swallows that darted out at dawn from under the eaves of the chapel, almost faster than the eye could follow.

The earliest thing Brother Boniface could remember was standing between his father's knees in a big wagonette, painted black and yellow, with slippery leather cushions, as it rolled along a dark road in the middle of the night under rustling poplar trees. He had never been out so late. His mother hadn't wanted him brought. She thought it would be bad for him to stay up so late, but his father insisted, saying he could sleep in the brake coming home.

The journey home in the brake had been the real enchantment for Barney. It was the part of the picnic he remembered best. The rest of the day was a broken memory of sun and trestle-tables and people laughing and swaying from side to side on benches. He remembered a tall man pouring out lemonade from a bottle that foamed at the mouth. And he remembered a lady with a green feather in her hat who kept telling him to run away and play like a normal child. But he remembered every single moment of the drive home, along the darkening roads, up hill and down, with everyone singing. The voices volleyed back from the hills they passed between, and the horses' hooves, when they hit the road, rang like bells. He remembered looking down over the sides of the brake at the road that was travelling too, but travelling backwards, and he remembered his mother pulling him by the sleeve.

'Look up, Barney Boy,' she said. 'It will make you sick to lean down over the sides like that.' So he looked up, and when he did, another wonder of the world appeared. As his head jerked up he saw a shower of brilliant sparks riding down through the skies – riding straight towards him it seemed – and he screamed with fear and excitement, and everyone in the party was startled.

'Oh, look! Look, Father,' he shouted, as the gilt stars rode downwards.

'Where? What?' said his father, looking up in fright. 'What do you see?'

'Look,' shouted Barney, and he pointed at the stars.

'Is it the stars you mean?' his father said, and he gave a laugh and winked at the lady with the green feather in her hat.

'Is that what you call them?' Barney said, his voice full of awe. 'Why are they up in the sky?'

'They're always there. You often saw them before,' his father said, laughing again but a bit unsteadily.

'Were they there last night?' Barney asked.

'I suppose they were.'

'Why didn't I see them?'

'You were in bed.'

'Were they there last Sunday night?'

'They were. Now that's enough about them!' said his father, who had got quite testy. But Barney was persistent.

'When will I see them again?' he asked.

'If I have my way it will be many a day!' his father said, and he nudged the lady with the feather and she began to laugh and soon everyone was laughing as the brake went rolling along under the rustling trees, and Barney himself, who was staring upwards, felt his head begin to reel.

After that every night Barney used to beg to be let stay up until the stars came out. But long before that he was in bed, and although he tried hard to stay awake he always fell asleep before they rode forth. And so, in time, he forgot about them. And when he went to school he learned, among other things, that it was silly to get excited about common things like stars and even rainbows. They were natural phenomena, the teacher said, and he spent two days teaching Barney how to spell the word phenomena, because Barney was backward at his books.

All during his school days, Barney was slow. It took him all his time to avoid being made the butt of the master's jokes. And except for one poor lad that was simple in the head he would have been at the foot of his class. Of course, if he had had more time to do his homework and look over his lessons in the evenings he might have made better progress, but his father did not believe any real work could be done sitting down, and so Barney was more often helping in the shop than reading his books. His father kept him on the move. At nine o'clock he had to open the shop, although no one ever came into it until after ten. But between the time of taking down the lice-eaten shutters and the appearance of the first customers there were a hundred and one jobs to be done. He had to sprinkle the floor with tea leaves to keep down the dust before he swept it, and after he'd swept the dirt out into the gutter, he had to sweep the pavement in front of the shop as well.

One morning when he was sweeping the pavement his father

came out and saw he had sprinkled tea leaves on it the way he sprinkled them on the shop floor and his father gave him a clout on the ear. 'Waste not, want not,' his father said, and after that Barney had to be more attentive.

Sometimes there were large packing cases to be splintered open with a chisel, and cups and saucers and statues and lamp globes taken out and counted, one by one, and the tissue paper that was stuck to them peeled off with his fingernails. Then the articles had to be arranged on the shelves, and after that the sawdust had to be gathered up, and bits of shavings picked out by hand from the cracks in the boards, and carried in to the kitchen fire without any of it let fall. There was something to be done every minute, and on a Fair Day there was so much to be done Barney had to stay home from school.

On the night before the Fair Day he was up until ten or eleven o'clock rolling empty beer barrels into the street and nailing boards across them to make barriers to protect the plate-glass windows of the shop-front from the horns of the big heavy cattle. All the same he still had to hop out of bed at four on the morning of the Fair, and go out in the street and stand with an ash plant in his hand, ready to beat off any beasts that made bold enough to butt at the barrels

One morning when Barney stood in the dawn with his stick in his hand, a great red heifer gave a puck to one of the barrels and before Barney got time to raise his stick she had butted against it with such force that the nails in the boards were lifted out and a board rose up and crashed through the glass.

That was the worst day in Barney's life. He stood on the cold pavement while his father warmed his ears with curses and the drovers all came over to gape at the hole in the window. The cattle themselves were terrified and butted one another backwards and forwards and some of them slipped and fell on the wet dung that covered the street. When a beast fell the drovers yelled at it and kicked its rump and hurled curses at it so loud that in the end Barney couldn't hear the half of his father's curses.

But later that morning when he was thinking about it, the thing that seemed worst of all to him was the way his father kept flinging questions at him to which he had no answer. Why weren't you looking at what you were doing? Why didn't you see the beast? Where were your eyes?

And he was frightened because he couldn't remember looking at anything else but the big red-chalked barrels, and the dusty boards, and the great steaming nostrils of the cattle. He was looking at them all the time, and if he looked away it could only have been for a second when in the grey dawn a wisp of scarlet cloud floated out between the chimney of the barrack and the spire of the church. But later in the morning when he was thinking things over it seemed to him that there might be something odd about him, and that ordinary successful people – people who were respected in the town, like his own father – would never be foolish enough to stand and stare at a cloud.

But if Barney was beginning to notice the difference between himself and the other young fellows of his age in the town, his father, too, was beginning to notice it. One night, late, when his father was coming back from the railway station where he had been loading crates of china, he came upon Barney, leaning against the yard gate staring up into the sky. His father looked up too, but there was nothing in the sky only the everyday stars and the common, ordinary moon. The father flew into a rage. 'Are you soft in the head, I wonder?' he said as he pushed past Barney and went into the house, and Barney could hear him, telling his mother on him. 'That son of yours is abroad in the yard,' his father said, 'leaning up against the gate-piers, with his hands in his pockets, staring up into the sky like a half-wit. Can he never find anything to do without being driven to do it?'

'Leave him alone,' his mother said. 'You drive him too much as it is. You're always yelling at him, and sending him here and sending him there. He never gets a moment to rest his poor feet.'

'It's not his feet he's resting out there in the yard, gaping up at the sky,' his father said. Then Barney heard his step on the stairs, and he knew he was gone to bed leaving his mother alone in the kitchen. He was going to slip in then, when, happening to look around, he saw that every window of every house in the town was shuttered and curtained. And he shivered, partly because of the cold night air, partly because of the fear that he felt in his heart in case he was different from other men. He dreaded going into the lighted kitchen where his warm-hearted mother sat waiting for him, because he even felt different from her. All the same he opened the door and went in.

'Are you cold, son? Sit over here by the fire,' his mother said, kindly, pulling a chair across the tiles with a clatter. 'What were you doing out there in the dark by yourself?' she asked.

'Nothing,' Barney said, and he felt her gentle glance upon him although he was staring into the flames.

'People will think you're daft if you stand about like that gawking up at the sky,' she said, but he felt she was asking for an explanation rather than giving him advice. He knew that the simplest explanation would have made her his champion, but the need that drove him out into silent places, away from the company of his fellows, was a need too vague to be expressed even in thought, much less in words. He remained silent.

His mother felt rebuffed. 'It must be true for your father,' she said. 'You must be soft in the head. I don't know what kind of a person you are at all. But I know one thing! The devil makes work for idle hands! That's an old saying and it's a true one.' She picked up a candle and went out into the hall with her lips pursed together in annoyance. But half-way up the stairs she stopped and leaned down over the banisters and watched him as he sat without a word by the fire. Barney knew she was watching him, and his own perplexity deepened. He wanted to please his parents, but every day that passed made him feel more certain that their way of life was small and mean and he felt sure that there must be another way – one that would leave some time for taking in the glory of the earth and the heavens above it.

The week that his father found him in the yard gazing into vacancy, Barney was given more work to do than ever. Even in the evenings, when other boys went off to the ball-alley to play handball, or went off with their girls for a walk around the old town ramparts, Barney was often sent out on his bicycle into the country to deliver some parcel that could easily have been left for delivery next day. His father and mother were determined to prevent him from idling. They were determined to keep him on the go. But although for a long time there may seem to be something vague and indecisive about a man's destiny, after a certain point has been reached it often becomes clear, not only that there was a continuity in the events of his life but that the very events, which seemed to impede, had in fact accelerated his progress. So, cycling along the country roads on messages intended to stop him from dreaming, Barney's eyes were being opened more and more to the beauties of nature and he began to wonder more and more how it was that all the men he knew spent their leisure hours as drearily as their working hours, and only exchanged the stuffiness of the storehouse for the stuffiness of the card-room or the pool-room.

At first when he cycled out into the country Barney was little better than a city man, seeing only the blatant beauty paraded in the hedgerows, the wild rose, the hawthorn and the rambling honeysuckle. But after a time he learned to probe for subtler pleasures. Then he used to get off his bike and leave it on the side of the road and climb over the fences to penetrate into the green deeps of the fields where small flowers, nameless to him, gave up their secret fragrance only when he knelt and parted the grasses and found them where they hid close to the earth. And it was in a field one evening, with the curious cattle standing idle around him, that he resolved at last to evade the way of life that his father and mother had destined for him.

At first Barney's vow was pale and simple and merely freed him from the dread of spending his life behind the counter of a shop. But as time went on he realised that he must choose some other way of earning his bread. He set himself at once then to choose a way that would allow him some time to stand about and stare. But it was not an easy thing to find. For the first time in his life he was seen to take an interest in his fellow townsmen. He was seen to walk around the town, in such apparent search for something that people came out into the streets after he'd gone back home and furtively shuffled a foot in the gutter in the hope of some anonymous gain. But Barney was only looking for an idea. He stood at the great dark doorway of the smithy and watched the golden sparks threading up the flue. He stood at the door of the livery stable and watched the stable boy groom big horses with trembling withers, strange dappled roans, strawberry and grey, and bays and chestnuts dappled with their own sweat. He watched at the doors of shops bigger than his father's, and the only difference he could see between them and his own was that the big shops were noisier and had more spits on the floor. Then one evening when he was out in the country on message for the shop, just as the last of the light was ebbing from the sky, he saw a man sowing seeds in a few final furrows of his field. The picture the man made against the darkening sky was startling and it made Barney think for a moment that he himself had found the right life at last. But when he went nearer he saw that although the man made a picture of great grandeur standing out against the horizon with his raised arm flinging the unseen seed, the man himself was unaware of his grandeur, and never lifted his eyes higher than the hand that groped in the sack for the seed, to toss it on the ground. Realising this, Barney stepped down from the bank where he had been standing almost in a trance, and went home.

And as he cycled home his sadness deepened, for it seemed to him that whether you cobbled or whether you hammered, whether you weighed up rice on a scales or led a young colt round and round in a ring, or whether you stood at evening in a field opening or closing your hand to let fall a shower of seeds, you had to keep your eyes upon what you were doing, and soon you forgot that there was a sky overhead and earth underfoot, and that flowers blew and even that birds sang.

So at last he settled down to follow the life his father had planned for him. He let his mother buy him a yellow dust-coat to keep his trousers clean when he would be weighing out whiting or weedkiller. And everyone said that he was shaping out much better than had been expected. The canvas coat kept the dust from his trousers, but there was dust getting into his soul, and soon he would have been weighing the whiting and the weedkiller in the bag in order to make up weight and using newspaper to wrap up his customers' purchases in order to spare bags. And in no time at all he would be taking down the shutters from the shop windows five minutes before nine, instead of nine, in the hope of making an extra penny. But before he had quite

relinquished the last shreds of his dream, a message came down
to the shop one day from the Abbot of a monastery that was a few
miles outside the town. The Abbot wanted to know if the
monastery could be supplied with a gallon of colza oil three
times a week, and if it could be delivered?

'There's no need for you to go with it, Barney. I'll send one of
the shop boys,' his father said, because his father was anxious not
to impose too much on him just when he was beginning to show
some interest in moneymaking.

'I think I should go myself,' Barney said. 'I might arrange to
supply them with candles as well as colza.'

'Good man,' his father said proudly and he took the dust-coat
out of Barney's hands. 'I'll hang that up for you, my boy,' he said.
'And take your tea before you go. It's a long push on a bicycle out
to that monastery, and, if I remember, there's a rise in the road
most of the way.'

There was many a rise in the road, and Barney was so tired by
the time he reached the monastery gate he left his bicycle at the
gate-lodge and walked up the avenue. The night was coming
down between dark yews and cypresses, and there was a scent of
flowers in the air. But Barney's mind was occupied with thoughts
of what he would say to the monk who would open the door.

It was an old monk who came to the door, and he seemed to be
deaf. He took the can of colza oil from Barney and looked past
him at the open door. 'Shut that door,' he said, and then he told
Barney to wait for the can, while he himself doddered off down
a corridor. Barney was left alone in the bare hallway where the
yellow floorboards were so slippy with wax he was afraid to move
a foot. All of a sudden Barney felt very young. He looked around
him, and through the high, arched windows he saw the sharp-
pointed stars, because the windows had no curtains. And
suddenly it seemed to him that of all the silly things in the world
the silliest was to hang a curtain across a window and blot out the
glory of the sky and its welter of stars.

When the old monk came back with the empty can, and
handed it to him, Barney took it silently and went out into the
dark. There was no sound but the closing of the monastery door,
and he thought of all the foolish words another man would have
wasted upon the simple transaction. The monk was a wise old

man, he thought, and he was thinking about him as he walked down the driveway.

Half-way down the avenue there was a great elm tree, and Barney had nearly passed it when, by the light of the moon, he saw that underneath the tree a young monk was standing. There was such a strange stillness in the standing figure that Barney stopped and stared. The young monk's face was turned upwards to the stars, and his hands were lifted in adoration of the Creator. Barney raised his head. And it was all he could do to keep himself from falling to his knees and joining his own hands in adoration too.

All that night and all the next day Barney thought about the young monk whose face was lifted to the stars, and at the end of the second night he knew that his own eyes had been blinded for ever to the gross glare of coins. But the only difference his father and mother saw in him was that his yellow dust-coat was getting short in the sleeves.

So, one night soon afterwards his father was wakened in the early hours by what he thought was a rat down below in the shop and he went down in his nightshirt, with a spluttering candle stuck in a bottleneck, to see what was afoot. He got a shock. All the counters were piled with carefully weighed-out bags of tea, sugar, whiting, grass-seed, tacks, lime and a lot of other commodities. There was enough of everything weighed out to last all winter, and when he asked Barney why he had weighed out so much he was almost relieved at the answer he got, because when he first saw the laden counters he thought his son's tardily developed interest in business had driven him completely out of his mind.

Next evening Barney took an old fibre suitcase belonging to his mother, put a few of his things in it, and tied it to the back of the bicycle.

'I'll send one of the boys up to bring back the bicycle,' his father said.

'He can take back the case too,' Barney said. 'I won't need it after today.'

His mother wiped her eyes on the corner of his dust-coat which she held in her hand.

'Are you sure you'll be contented, Barney, inside those high walls?' she said.

'Remember,' his father said, 'there's only seven acres, all told, timber and pasture, inside those walls. It's a small place to spend the whole of your days.'

But Barney was thinking of the uncurtained windows up at the monastery and the great expanse of sky over it, and it seemed that the monastery was as wide and spacious as the whole world. And there, men had time to meditate and dwell on all the beauty the Lord had laid out before their eyes.

That evening, in fact, after he'd been shown to his cell, Barney found that the monastery was so big it was like a city and it took five or ten minutes to go from one end of it to the other. You'd need a scooter for the job. Three lengths of one corridor were equal to half a mile, He was shown over the whole place by a young and active lay brother, and when they came back to the place from which they had started out, the arches of Barney's insteps were aching and he could hardly believe that it was only nine o'clock, and time to go to bed. Nine o'clock seemed a ridiculous hour to retire to his pallet, but Barney was so tired he was glad to lie down. He meant to get up later and look out the narrow window of his cell at the garden below, but he fell asleep.

In the middle of the night Barney was wakened by a loud knock on the door of the cell and he sprang to the floor in fright because through a great windy crack in the door he had seen a flickering tongue of flame. Flinging open the door he was about to rush out, when a dash of holy water, cold as ice, cooled his face. The flame was only the flame of a candle in the lay brother's hand.

Dominus vobiscum.

Young Brother Boniface hastily donned his habit and joined the thronging feet that were descending a great flight of stone steps to the chapel. Once there, the knocking of wooden rosary beads, the sliding of sandals, the swishing of the monks' habits, the praying, the singing, but above all the blaze of candles on the altar, made him forget it was night and gave an impression of broad and busy day-time.

When the real day-time came at last and the birds began to

chirp and fly out from under the eaves, Brother Boniface was set the task that always fell to the last member to join the order, and that was peeling potatoes. It took a lot of potatoes to feed seventy-two monks, specially when they didn't eat meat. But it didn't take long to eat them. Brother Boniface was used to eating quickly and he would have been finished as soon as anyone, only he was so interested in the gospel story that the Brother Lector was reading during the meal that he had to hurry at the end and leave his meal half finished in order not to be left behind.

After the meal there was community prayer. Then there was private prayer. And after that there would have been recreation, but on that day some important person was coming to visit the monastery, and the Father Abbot wanted all the community present in the hall to receive her. The visitor, however, didn't arrive at the time arranged. She was so late coming that the monks had only seventeen minutes for supper; and it was a great rush clearing away the meal and laying the table for breakfast, before the great bell rang out to announce the hour of evening prayer. Next day an old monk died, an old monk who had clung to life longer than anyone could have imagined possible, and still at the end his soul lingered among the souls of the living while even the candle-flames around his pallet strove to part from the wick and fly heavenward. Boniface had never seen anyone dying before and death made a great impression on him. At dawn, when at last he went to his cell he stood for a while at his slit of window and said innumerable *pater* and *ave* for the dead man, but his thoughts were centred on the deathbed scene he had just witnessed, and then his mind flew forward to thoughts of his own last end. Afterwards, when he tried to remember whether the stars had gone in or not, and whether the moon had waned or not, he could not remember.

Next day Brother Boniface had to help dig a grave for the dead monk and the ground, under its rich covering of grass, was remarkably hard and strong and had to be attacked with a pick-axe. This took most of the day because the work had to be interrupted for prayers and meals and also for all the daily chores that would have had to be done by the living even if it were the Father Abbot himself who had died.

After that week there was a very wet week, and in wet weather there were always a great many things to be done in the monastery. Corridors were waxed, brasses shined and benches and pews were up-ended and examined to see that they were free from wood-lice. But on the evening of the seventh day when the rain ceased at last Brother Boniface went out into the grounds for a few minutes. Through the leafy branches of the trees he saw that the sky was pricked with stars and he walked a little way down the avenue towards the elm tree under which he had seen the young monk standing in adoration the first night he himself had come up to the monastery on a message. He was there again! As Brother Boniface had not made this monk's acquaintance, he stepped into the grass and was about to go across to him, when he saw that the young monk's eyes were closed and that his lips were moving. He was saying his office, and not looking at the stars at all. And Brother Boniface remembered that he himself had not yet said his office. So raising his eyes to heaven he began to say it there and then where he stood, in the damp evening grasses, under the starry heavens. But he soon found that he could not pray with his eyes open. The stars distracted him. He had to close his eyes, and when he came to the end of his office and opened his eyes again the sky was overcast.

That first year went flashing by so fast that at the end of it Boniface did not feel he was a week in the monastery. And in spring and summer when his father and mother came up to see him, if he was working in the fields he was so often busy working he did not see them and when his father called out to him by name – 'Barney! Barney!' – the other monks had to pluck him by the sleeve, because Brother Boniface had almost forgotten that he had once answered to the name of Barney. Time went flashing past fast as the wind, and life was blown with it as the wind blew the leaves from the trees. And Brother Boniface had stepped into his sandals some twenty thousand mornings before he realised one fine morning that he was eighty years old.

On the morning Brother Boniface was eighty he was coming out of the bakehouse with a trough of dough that he had kneaded for Brother Breadmaker, when he met the monastery doctor in the middle of the courtyard.

'Good morning, Brother Boniface. You get sprightlier every day,' the young doctor said, but he looked closely at him and watched after him when he went on his way. Then the doctor turned and went back to the Abbot's room.

'I met Boniface in the yard,' he said to the young monk who was Abbot at that time and who was a personal friend of the doctor's. 'I didn't like the way the veins on his forehead were swollen,' he said. 'He was carrying a heavy tray of dough. He does too much for a man of his age.'

'But he loves work,' the young Abbot said.

'That's the kind of person who needs rest most. He must be made to take life easier.'

'I will see that he is released from some of his duties,' the Abbot said.

'That's not enough,' the doctor said. 'He must be freed from all duties. He must sit out there in the sun, and remain as quiet as possible.'

'Poor Boniface,' the young Abbot sighed, as he and the doctor stood at the window in the Abbot's office and looked out at Brother Boniface, who had left the dough in the bakehouse and was now going across the grass with a saucer of milk, followed by five cats. As he went along, some of the cats ran in front of him with their tails up stiff as sticks, and others circled around him and lifted themselves up on their hind legs to caress him with the backs of their necks.

'You can't call that hard work?' the Abbot said.

'Any work that never ceases is hard work,' the doctor said.

'I suppose you're right,' said the Abbot. 'Very well, I'll send him out tomorrow morning to sit in the sun and I won't let him inside the door till night-time, except for meals and of course for prayers.'

Brother Boniface took to the sun like the monastery cats. He sat on a stone seat, and he had nothing to do but follow the ballet of the butterflies, or gaze – like the cats – who sometimes slit open their lazy eyes to gaze at a glossy black insect, perhaps as it ran up a green blade and bent it down.

And as he sat there Brother Boniface thanked the Lord that he had been led through the hustle and bustle of life to the peace and quiet of age. And he wondered what he had done to merit such happy contentment and rest. He tried to remember what it was that had first turned his thoughts to the cloister. He remembered the shop where he used to scatter tea leaves to keep down the dust. He remembered he wore a shopcoat that got too short in the sleeves. He remembered going out into the country on his bicycle to do errands for his father. And he remembered once when he was a small boy he had gone on a picnic with his father and mother in a black and yellow brake, under rustling poplar trees, while singing voices volleyed in the hills and stars showered down through the sky. And when he remembered that starry sky he slapped his hand on his knee and he gave a laugh, at which all the cats sprang up and arched their backs. But seeing they had nothing to fear, they relaxed, except for the young cat, who walked away in disdain.

Brother Boniface continued to chuckle. He realised that he had entered the monastery in order to have more time to meditate upon the glories of the earth, but his life had circled round, from matins to lauds, from daylight to starlight, with greater speed than it could possibly have sped by in the world. It had gone by so fast that he could hardly tell the colour of the leaves on the trees, and whether the stars were blue or green. But he was filled with joy to think that now, at the end of his days, having diligently earned his leisure, he would at last be able to spend long hours in appreciation of God's handiwork. Just then, however, there was the sound of another stem snapping and Brother Boniface had to get himself on his feet again. The young grey cat was chasing another butterfly, and once more she had jumped into the flower-bed. When she saw Boniface stand up she sprang out, but a yellow dahlia lay broken on the grass. Brother Boniface clapped his hands and toddled over to the flower-bed, but at that moment there was a light step on the gravel and the agile young Abbot came down the path, his flowing sleeves and his ample cowl, that belled out in the breeze as he walked, giving him an impressive air, although he was the youngest Abbot that had ever been anointed.

'Good morning, Brother Boniface,' he said, and quicker than Boniface he stooped and lifted up the broken dahlia. 'What will

we do with those cats?' he said, shaking his head. 'The feast of
Corpus Christi is only a few days away and we need every flower
for the decoration of the altars I wish we could dispense with the
cats, but there are unfortunately too many mice for that – did
you hear them behind the wainscoting in the chapel this
morning?' As he spoke he was bending to examine the stem of
another dahlia that looked a bit lopsided. 'What will we do?' he
said, and then he snapped his fingers. 'I have an idea,' he said,
and he strode across the casement of the refectory, and brushing
aside the strands of ivy he tapped on the window.

'Brother Almoner!' he called out, in his clear young voice.
'Hand me out a paper bag.'

Old Brother Almoner could be heard shuffling around inside,
and pulling out drawers and opening cupboards. At last he came
to the window and handed out a tinfoil tea-bag, open at the
mouth. The Abbot came striding back across the grass, and when
he reached the gravel path where Boniface sat on the stone seat
he bent and gathered up a handful of pebbles from the square
of gravel under the seat and he threw them into the tinfoil tea-
bag. Then nimbly bending down again he got another handful,
and another. When the bag was filled to the top with pebbles, he
set it down on the seat beside Brother Boniface. 'Here is a small
job for you, Boniface,' he said. 'You can do it without standing
up – without moving an inch. Every time you see a cat going near
the flowers, all you have to do is take up a little pebble and throw
it at him and frighten him away. In spite of the cats we'll have a
magnificent blaze of flowers yet for Corpus Christi.'

Brother Boniface took up the bag.

'I'll keep it in my lap,' he said.

'I'm delighted to have you out here, Boniface,' the Abbot said.
'Now I need not worry about the flowers. I know I can depend
on you.' Smiling, he went back to his own work.

Brother Boniface sat on in the sun. When the Abbot's footsteps
died away, there was no sound in Boniface's ears but the ringing
of the bells of silence. Beside him once a brilliant red insect
crawled up a blade of grass, and Boniface watched the blade
slowly bend until the insect was almost back on the ground. The
little creature put out a feeler and caught on to another blade

that was shorter and stabbed into the air more stiffly but when it started to crawl upward, this blade too began to bend. Boniface shook his head. Where were those little creatures heading, that they took such dangerous and devious paths?

But just then he heard another stem snap. The young cat was in among the dahlias once more. Stems were breaking to all sides and petals were scattering to the ground because this time there were two butterflies and the young cat sprang at each of them in turn.

'Pussy! Pussy! Pussy!' Brother Boniface shouted. 'Pussy! Pussy! Pussy! Come out of that at once!' He stamped his foot and groped for a pebble in his tinfoil bag. 'Pussy! Pussy! Pussy! Come out of that at once!'

And years and years afterwards, when Brother Boniface was long laid to rest in the close and secretive clay, the young monks who entered the monastery were told about his industry. They were told he was never, never idle for a moment. They strove to follow his example. And when they themselves were old they in their turn told younger men about him. And the part of the story that the old monks liked best to tell, and the young monks liked best to hear, was about the last days in the life of Boniface, when he was so old he couldn't hear even the bells of silence. Because then he was busiest of all. Day in and day out his voice could be heard, as he guarded the flowers for the feast days of the Mother Church, throwing pebbles at the cats and calling out to them.

'Pussy! Pussy! Pussy! Come out of that at once!'

At Sallygap

The bus climbed up the hilly roads on its way through the Dublin Mountains to the town of Enniskerry. On either side the hedges were so high that the passengers had nothing more interesting to look at than each other. But after a short time the road became steeper and then the fields that had been hidden were bared to view, slanting smoothly downward to the edge of the distant city.

Dublin was all exposed. The passengers could see every inch of it. They could certainly see every steeple and tower, although the dark spires and steeples rising out of the blue pools of distance looked little better than thistles rising up defiant in a pale pasture.

The sea that half-circled this indistinct city seemed as grey and motionless as the air. Suddenly, however, it was seen that the five o'clock mail boat, looking no bigger than a child's toy boat, was pushing aside the plastery waves and curving around the pier at Dunlaoghaire on its way to the shores of England.

'There she goes!' Manny Ryan said to the young man in a grey flannel suit who shared the bus seat with him. 'The fastest little boat for her size in the whole of the British Isles.'

'What time does it take her to do the crossing?' the young man asked.

'Two hours and five minutes,' said Manny, and he took out a watch and stared at it. 'It's three thirty-nine now. She's out about four minutes, I'd say. That leaves her right to the dot. She'll dock at Holyhead at exactly five forty.'

'She's dipping a bit,' said the young man. 'I suppose she's taking back a big load after the Horse Show.'

'That's right. I saw by the paper this morning she took two thousand people across yesterday evening.'

'You take a great interest in things, I see.'

'I do. That's quite right for you! I take a great interest indeed, but I have my reasons. I have my reasons.'

Manny put his elbow up against the ledge of the window and turned on his side in the tight space of the seat so that he was almost facing his companion, who, having no window ledge to lean upon, was forced to remain with his profile to Manny while they were talking.

'You wouldn't think, would you,' said Manny, 'just by looking at me, that I had my choice to sail out of Dublin on that little boat one day, and I turned it down? You wouldn't think that now, would you?'

'I don't know,' said the young man uncomfortably. 'Many a man goes over to Holyhead, for one class of thing or another.' But it was clear by his voice that he found it hard to picture Manny, with his shiny black suit and his bowler hat in any other city than the one they had lately left. So strong was his impression that Manny was – as he'd put it – a Dubliner-coming-and-going, that he hastened to hide this impression by asking what business Manny had in Holyhead, if that wasn't an impertinence? He forgot apparently that Manny had never actually gone there, but Manny forgot that too in his haste to correct the young man on another score altogether.

'Is it Holyhead?' he asked in disgust. 'Who goes there but jobbers and journeymen?'

'London?' asked the young man, raising his eyebrows.

'Policemen and servant girls,' Manny said impatiently.

'Was it to the Continent, sir?' said the young man, and the 'sir' whistled through the wax in Manny's ears like the sweetest note of a harp, plucked by a clever finger.

'To the Continent is right,' he said. 'I was heading for Paris – 'gay Paree,' as they call it over there – and I often wish to God I hadn't turned my back on the idea.'

'Is it a thing you didn't go, sir?'

'Well, now, as to that question,' said Manny, 'I won't say yes and I won't say no, but I'll tell you this much: I had my chance of

going. That's something, isn't it? That's more than most can say!
Isn't it?'

'It is indeed. But if it's a thing that you didn't go, sir, might I
make so bold as to ask the reason?'

'I'll tell you,' said Manny, 'but first of all I'll have to tell you why
I was going in the first place.' Taking out a sepia-coloured
photograph from an old wallet, he passed it to the young man
who looked at it, holding it close to his face because it was faded
in places and in other places the glaze was cracked. But he made
out quite clearly all the same a group of young men sitting stiffly
on cane-backed chairs, their legs rigid in pinstripe trousers, their
hair plastered down with oil, and their hands folded self-
consciously over the awkward contours of trombones, fiddles and
brass cornets. In the centre of the group, turned up on its rim,
was a big drum wearing a banner across its face with the words
MARY STREET BAND printed on it in large block letters. 'That
was us,' said Manny, 'the Mary Street Band. We used to play for
all the dances in the city, and as well, we played for the half-hour
interval at the Mary Street Theatre.' He leaned over. 'That was
me,' he said, pointing to a young man with a fiddle on his knee,
a young man who resembled him as a son might resemble a
father.

'I'd recognise you all right,' said the stranger, looking up at
Manny's face and down again at the photograph. Both faces had
the same nervous thinness, the same pointed jaw, and the same
cleft of weakness in the chin. Only the eyes were different. The
eyes in the photograph were light in colour, either from bad
lighting on the part of the photographer or from youthful
shallowness in the sitter. The eyes of the older Manny were dark.
They had a depth that might have come from sadness, but
whatever it came from, it was out of keeping with the cockiness
of his striped, city suiting and his bowler hat. 'There was a party
of us – the few lads you see there at the back, and the one to the
left of the drum – and we were planning on getting out, going
across to Paris and trying the dance halls over there – palais, they
call them. We'd stuck together for three years, but these few lads
I'm after pointing out to you got sick of playing to the Dublin
jackeens. I got sick of them, too. They were always sucking

oranges, and spitting out the pips on the floor, and catcalling up at the artistes. We heard tell it was different altogether across the water. Tell me this, were you ever in Paris, young fellow? 'Gay Paree' I should be saying.'

'No, I can't say that I was,' said the young man.

'Man alive!' said Manny. 'Sure that's the place for a young fellow like you. Clear out and go. That's my advice to you. Take it or leave it: it's my advice to you, although I don't know from Adam who you are or what you are. That's what I'd say to you if you were my own son. Cut and run for it.' Manny gave a deep sigh that went down the neck of the lady in front and made her shiver and draw her collar closer. 'Paris!' he said again, and again he sighed. 'Paris, lit up all night as bright as the sun, with strings of lights pulling out of each other from one side of the street to the other, and fountains and bandstands every other yard along the way. The people go up and down linked, and singing, at all hours of the day or night, and the publicans – they have some other name on them over there, of course – keep coming to the door every minute with aprons round their middle, like women, and sweeping the pavement outside the door and finishing off maybe by swilling a bucket of wine over it to wash it down.'

'You seem to have a pretty good idea of it for a man who was never there!'

'I have a lot of postcards,' said Manny, 'and myself and the lads were never done talking about it before ever we decided on going at all. In the end we just packed up one night and said, off with us! There had been a bit of a row that night at the theatre, and somehow or other an old dead cat got flung up on the stage. Did you ever hear the like of that for ignorance? "Holy God," we said, "that's too much to take from any audience."'

'All I can say is, it's no wonder you packed your bags!' said the young man.

'Is it now?' said Manny. 'That's what I tell myself. My bag was all packed and strapped, and what was more, before very long it was up the gangplank and on the deck of that little boat you see pulling out there!'

They looked out the window of the bus, down over the falling fields of the mountainside, to the sea and the vanishing boat.

'Is that right?' said the young man.

'That's right. Me and my bag were on the deck and there was Annie below on the quay, with the tears in her eyes. That was the first time I gave a thought to her at all. Annie is my wife. At least she is now. She wasn't then. I gave one look at her standing there in the rain – it was raining at the time – with her handkerchief rolled up in her hand ready to wave as soon as the boat got going. The porters were pushing past her with their truckloads of trunks and hitting up against her. Did you ever notice how rough those fellows are? Well, with the rain and the porters and one thing and another, I got to pitying her, standing there. I got to thinking, do you know, of all the things we'd done together. Nothing bad, you know. Nothing to be ashamed of, if you understand, but still I didn't like to think of her standing there, watching me going off, maybe for good, and she thinking over the things I'd said to her at one time or another You know yourself, I suppose, the kind of thing a man's apt to say to a girl, off and on?'

'I do,' said the young man.

'You do? Well, in that case you'll understand how I felt seeing her standing there. I felt so bad I tried to go back down the gangplank for a few last words with her before the boat pulled out, but there were people coming up against me all the time and I was having to stand aside every other step I took and crush in against the rails to let them pass. And some of them were cranky devils, telling me to get the hell out of the way, to come if I was coming, and go if I was going, and – for God Almighty's sake – to take my bloody bag out of the way. It was jabbing them in the legs without my noticing it, and as sure as I pulled it to one side it jabbed into someone on the other side. There was terrible confusion. You'd think, wouldn't you, that the officials would be able to put a stop to it? But I declare to God they were worse than the people that were travelling There was one of them clicking tickets at the bottom of the gangway, and all he did was let a shout at me to say I was obstructing the passage. Obstructing!

"Come on up, Manny," shouted the lads from up above on the deck.

"Goodbye, Manny," Annie said in a little bit of a voice you'd hardly hear above the banging of cases and the screaming of the seagulls.'

'You didn't go down?'

'Down I went.'

'And the boys?'

'They were staring like as if they were transfixed. They couldn't believe their eyes. They kept calling down to me from the deck above, but the wind was going the other way and we couldn't hear one word they were saying. Then the whistles began to blow, and the sailors began spitting on their hands and pulling at the ropes to let the plank up into the boat. The train was getting ready to go back to Westland Row: it was going to pull out any minute.

"I knew you'd come to your senses," Annie said. "Have you got your bag?" I held it up. "Your fiddle?" she said. By God, if I hadn't left the fiddle above on the deck! Would you believe that? I started shouting up at the lads, and Timmy Coyne – that's the little fellow with the moustache sitting next to me in the photo – Timmy put his hands up to his mouth like he was playing a bugle – it was the piano he played in the band, by the way – and he shouts out "Wha-a-a-at?" like that, drawing it out so's we could hear it.

"The fiddle!" I shouted. But 'fiddle' isn't a word you can stretch out, you know. No matter how slow you say it, it's said and done in a minute. 'Fiddle.' Try it yourself. 'Fiddle.' It's a funny sort of word, isn't it, when you say it over a few times like that? It sort of loses its meaning. Anyway, Timmy didn't hear me. "Ca-a-an t hea-er-ear!" says he. A couple of people round about me began to shout up too. "Fiddle. Fiddle", they shouted. The boat was pushing off from the pier. Suddenly one real game fellow that was after putting a fine young girl on the boat, and after kissing her too in front of everyone, ups and pulls off his hat, and crooking it under his arm, like it was a fiddle, he starts pulling his right hand back and forth across it for all the world as if it was a bow and he was playing a real fiddle. Timmy takes one look at him and down he ducks and starts rooting around on the deck. The next minute he ups and rests the fiddle case on the rails.

"Catch!" he shouts, and over comes the fiddle across the space of water that was blinding white by this time with the foam from the moving boat.

"It's into the water!" someone shouts.

"Not on your life!" shouts your man on the wharf, and he leaps into the air to catch it. But you know how slippy them wooden boards on the wharf are – with that green slimy stuff on them? You do? Well, to make a long story short, your man's foot slips, and down comes the fiddle on one of the iron stumps they tie the boat to, and fiddle and case, and even the little bow, were smashed to smithereens under my eyes. You should have heard the crowd laughing. I always say it's easy enough to raise a laugh when you're not doing it for money!'

'What did Annie say?'

' "It's the hand of God," she said.'

'What did you say?'

'Sure, what could I say? There was no use making the poor fellow feel bad, so I had to let on to make a joke of it. I went over and gave a kick with my foot to the bits of wood, and put them floating out on the water, along with a bucketful of potato-peels and cabbage-stalks that were just after being flung out of a porthole.' Manny looked down at the grey feather of smoke on the horizon that was all that now remained of the mail boat. 'Whenever I see that little boat,' he said, 'I get to thinking of the sea and the way it was that day, with the swill lapping up and down on it and the bits of the fiddle looking like bits of an old box. Walking back to the train, we could see the bits of it floating along on the water under us, through the big cracks in the boards. I never can understand why it is they leave such big spaces between those boards anyway. And just as we were going out the gate to the platform, what did I see, down through the splits, but a bit of the bow. And here's a curious thing for you! You could tell what it was the minute you looked at it, broken and all as it was. Oh look! you'd say if you happened to be passing along the pier, going for a walk and not knowing anything about me or the boys. Look! you'd say to whoever was with you. Isn't that the bow of a fiddle?'

'Did you ever hear from the boys again?' the young man asked.

Manny shook his head.

'If they wrote we never got the letter,' he said. 'I heard they broke up after a bit. When Annie and me got married we opened a shop in South King Street and went to live over the shop. You know South King Street? Our shop is down past the Gaiety. The shop took up pretty near all our time on account of us knowing nothing about business. We never got a minute to ourselves. Nor now either. Look at today! I've been out since early morning trying to find someone that would deliver eggs to the door. That's what I'm doing now, going up to Sallygap to see a man I was told about by one of the dealers in Moore Street. The dealer gets his eggs from this man twice a week, and I didn't see why he couldn't bring us in a couple of dozen at the same time. If he does, we'll put up a card on the window saying, Fresh Eggs Daily. The Dublin people go mad for a fresh egg. Did you ever notice that?'

The conductor came down the aisle and leaned in to Manny.

'We're coming near to Sallygap now,' said the conductor.

'Is that right?' said Manny. 'Give a touch to the bell so, and get the driver to stop. Anywhere here will do nicely.' He turned to the young man confidentially. 'I have to look for the place, you see.'

'I hope you find it all right, sir.'

'I hope so. Well, good day to you now. Don't forget the advice I gave you.' Manny pointed with his thumb in the direction of the sea. Then he got off the bus and for the first time in years found himself on a country road alone.

The farmhouse Manny was looking for was easy enough to find. And the farmer obligingly promised to send him down the eggs twice a week, and three times if the orders got bigger. He wanted to know if Manny ever tried selling chickens or geese? Manny said his wife took care of the orders. The farmer asked if he would mention the matter to his wife. Manny agreed to do so. They said goodbye and Manny went back to the road.

By that time Manny wanted a drink. He wasn't a drinking man, but he wanted a glass of beer just to take the thirst off him. He remembered that they had passed a public house a while before he got off the bus. He started walking back toward it.

As he walked along he thought of the boys again. It was the

boat had put him in mind of them. And the young fellow that had been sitting beside him was just about the age he was himself in those days. A nice young fellow! Manny idly wondered who he was, and he wondered, just as idly, at what time he himself would get a bus going back to Dublin.

But it was nice, mind you, walking along the road. He didn't care if the bus was a bit slow in coming. It was not as if it was raining or cold. It was a nice evening. He'd often heard tell of young lads from Dublin coming up here on their bicycles of a fine evening, and leaving the bicycles inside a fence while they went walking in the heather. Just walking, mind you; just walking. He used to think it was a bit daft. Now that he was up here himself he could see how a quiet sort of chap might like that class of thing. Manny looked at the hedges that were tangled with wild vetches, and he looked at an old apple tree crocheted over with grey lichen. He looked at the gleaming grass in the wet ditch, and at the flowers and flowering reeds that grew there. They all have names, he supposed. Could you beat that!

Walking along, he soon came to a cottage with dirty brown thatch from which streaks of rain had run down the walls, leaving yellow stripes on the lime. As he got near, a woman came to the door with a black pot and swilled out a slop of green water into the road, leaving a stench of cabbage in the air when she went in. It was a queer time to be cooking her cabbage, Manny thought, and then he chuckled. 'For God's sake,' he said out loud, 'will you look at the old duck?'

A duck had flapped over from the other side of the road to see if the cabbage water made a pool big enough to swim in. 'Will you just look at him?' Manny said to himself, the road being empty. He was giving himself very superfluous advice though because he was staring at the duck as hard as he could. But as he stood there a geranium pot was taken down from inside one of the small windows of the cottage, and a face came close to the glass. They don't like you stopping and staring, I suppose, he thought, and he moved along.

His thoughts for some time were on the smallness and darkness of the cottage. He wondered how people put up with living in a little poke like that, and his own room behind the shop in South

King Street seemed better to him than it had for a long time. After all, he and Annie had a range. They had gaslight. And they had the use of the lavatory on the upper landing. He was pleased to think of the many advantages he had over those people who had been peeping out at him. He used to think sometimes that South King Street was a dungeon in which he was imprisoned for life, while other men went here and went there, and did this and did that, and some of them even went off to Paris. But at that moment he felt it was a fine thing after all to have a place of your own to keep things in, a place where you could lie down if you were sick or worn out. And it was within a stone's throw of the Pillar.

He didn't get out enough – that was the trouble. If he got out and about more he'd have the right attitude to the house, and maybe to the shop, too. No wonder he was sick of it, never leaving it except like this, to do a message. He should take an odd day off. Man! What was he talking about? He ought to take a week. He ought to run over to Paris and look up the boys. Then, as if aghast at the magnitude of his revolt, he gave himself an alternative. He should go over to Liverpool, anyway, for one of the weekend race meetings. With a bit of luck he might make his expenses, and that would shut Annie's mouth.

The public house came into view just then, and very opportunely, because Manny walked in with the confidence of one who is contemplating a sojourn in distant lands.

He ordered his drink. There were two or three locals leaning against the counter, and a large man, obviously a commercial traveller, stood cleaning his spectacles and asking questions about the locality. The locals were looking sheepishly at their empty glasses that were draped with scum. The traveller gave orders for the glasses to be filled up again. He looked down the counter at Manny as if he would like to include him in the order, but there was a repelling air of independence about Manny, due perhaps to his bowler hat, which sat self-consciously upon the bar counter.

Manny listened to the talk at the other end of the bar. Once or twice the locals mistook the traveller's meaning, but Manny felt a warmth in his heart towards them. Their dull-wittedness gave him a feeling of security. He felt a great dislike for the talkative traveller. He hoped that they would not be on the same bus going back to the city.

Just then the sound of a motor stole into the stillness outside. The bus was coming. Manny drank up, and put out his hand for his hat. Out of the corner of his eye he saw the traveller buttoning his overcoat. He heard his jocose farewells to the locals, who were already leaning back with greater ease against the counter.

Manny went towards the door. The traveller also went towards the door. In the doorway they met.

'I see you are taking this bus too?' said the traveller.

Manny had, of course, intended going back on that bus. He had no idea when there would be another one. But he took a great dislike to the idea of journeying back with the large, talkative man.

'I'm waiting for the next bus,' he said impulsively.

'Sorry!' said the traveller. 'I should have been glad of your company. Good evening.'

'Good evening,' said Manny, and he stood back from the dust of the bus as it started up again.

When the dust had blown into the hedges, Manny stepped into the middle of the road and doggedly faced the way the bus had gone. He would probably be walking for a long time before another bus caught up with him, but he did not care. A rare recklessness possessed him, and when shortly after night came down this feeling of recklessness strengthened. He walked along, looking from side to side, and in his heart the night's potent beauty was beginning to have effect. But he felt confused. The dark hills and the pale sky and the city pricking out its shape upon the sea with starry lights filled him with strangely mingled feelings of sadness and joy. And when the sky flowered into a thousand stars of forget-me-not blue he was strangled by the need to know what had come over him, and having no other way to stem the tide of desolating joy within him, he started to run the way he used to run on the roads as a young lad. And as he ran he laughed out loud to think that he, Manny Ryan, was running along a country road in the dark, not knowing but he'd run into a hedge or a ditch.

Yesterday, if anyone had come to him and suggested that he'd do such a thing, he would have split his sides laughing. And tomorrow, if he were to try and persuade Annie to take a walk out in the country, she'd look at him as if he was daft. The Dublin people couldn't tell you the difference between a bush and a tree. Manny stood to recover his breath. And he thought of his wife with her yellow elbows coming through the black unravelled sleeve of her cardigan, as she leaned across the counter in the dismal shop, giving off old shaffoge with any shawley who came the way and had an hour, or maybe two hours, to spare. He thought of the bars filled with his cronies talking about the state of the country for all they were fit, men that never saw more of it than you'd see from the top of a tram. He thought of the skitting young fellows and girls outside Whitefriar Street after late Mass on a Sunday, and he thought of the old men standing at the pub ends of the streets, ringing themselves round with spits. He thought of the old women leaning against the jambs of their doorways, with empty crockery milk jugs hanging out of their hands, forgotten in the squalor of their gossip. He thought of the children sitting among the trodden and rancid cabbage butts on the edge of the pavements, repeating the gossip they had heard when they crouched, unheeded, under some public-house counter. He thought of the young and the old, the men and the women, and the pale, frightened children, who were shuffling along the kneelers in churches all over the city, waiting their turn to snuffle out their sins in the dark wooden confessionals. And it seemed as if the cool green light of day scarcely ever reached those people, and the only breezes that blew into their lives came from under their draughty doors thickened with the warm odour of boiling potatoes. The loathing he'd felt for the city, years before, when he first came to Dublin, stole over him again as it had done on that night long ago in the little theatre in Mary Street. Dublin jackeens! he thought.

'Dublin jackeens!' he said then out loud, the gibe coming forth from a dim corner in his mind where the memory of a buttercup field and a cobbled yard pricked with grass gave him the right to feel different from them. Once more he longed to get away from Dublin. But this time there was a difference. He wanted to get away from Dublin – yes – but not from Ireland. He didn't want to go away from Ireland, he thought with anguish. Not away from her yellow fields. Not away from her emerald ditches. He wanted only to get away from the stuffy Dublin streets and the people that walked them. Even to get away occasionally for an hour like this would satisfy him.

Wasn't it well, after all, he hadn't gone to Paris? Things always turned out for the best in the end. If he had gone away he might never have come up here to Sallygap, and then he would never have found out that peace was not a matter of one city or another, but a matter of hedges and fields and waddling ducks and a handful of stars. Cities were all alike. Paris was no better or no worse than Dublin when you looked into the matter closely. Paris was a wicked place too, by all accounts, even if people did have a good time there at night, with the lights and the band-stands. Who ever heard of the boys from the Mary Street Band since they went? Where were they? God alone knew! They were playing, maybe, in some cellar done up with striped tablecloths and posters on the walls, like he'd seen in the pictures, with smoke cutting their guts, and women with big thighs and dresses torn open to the waist sitting on their knees and cracking the strings of their sinews with the weight.

A sweat broke out on Manny, and he had to stand still on the road to let the wind cool his burning face. He was damn glad he had stayed at home. What was the need in anybody going across seas when all a man had to do, if he got sick of himself, was to take a bus and come up to a place like this? As long as a fellow could come up to a place like this, what was the need of going farther?

I'll come up here again, he thought. Upon my soul I will. 'I'll come back again,' he said out loud this time. 'I'll come back again all right.' He turned and took a last look at the hills before he went round a bend in the road, where the houses and shops of Rathfarnham would hide them from view.

With the first shops and the first beginnings of the city and its dazzling tramlines, its noises, and its shoving crowds, Manny felt a tiredness he had not felt in all the miles of rough road he had walked. His feet burned, and his back was weighed down with a knapsack of weariness. So at Terenure he took a tram and sat on the edge of the only seat that was vacant, his light weight joggling with every motion, and the elbow and hipbone of a fat woman on the inside of the seat nudging him with the insistence of inadvertency. Smells of gas and oil sickened him. Broken lights strained his eyes. But most of all a dread of returning home came over him as he remembered that Annie had told him to hurry back. The sharp notes of her voice echoed sudden and loud in his ears, and it seemed impossible that he had forgotten what she said. He felt like a little boy who had blotted his copy, a little boy who had lost the change, a little boy creeping home under fear of the whip.

The fear of Annie's tongue hung over Manny all the time the tram rattled through the suburbs and when he got out to walk down King Street. When he reached home and saw the closed shutters of the shop, his hand was so stiff and cold that when he put it into the letterbox he could hardly find the string by which the latch of the door could be pulled back from outside. His hand clattered the letter-box for a time before he found it. Then he pulled the string and the door opened. He went in and felt for the knob of the kitchen door, not seeing that the door was wide open because the room was dark and the fire only a powdering of hot grey ash. Then a red spark fell into the ashpit and he realised the door was open after all and that Annie was sitting by the range. Next minute his eyes became used to the dark, and, the customary position of things supplementing his eye where it failed, enabled him to reach the fire and sit down opposite her. He said nothing but sat watching her and wondering when she would speak.

Annie did not speak. The truth was that she had been so excited by his unusual absence that she was unfit for any emotion at his eventual return.

Marriage had been an act of unselfishness on Manny's part. He married Annie because he thought that was what would make her happy, and he was content to give up his own freedom for that object. She, however, had not thought of marriage as anything but a means of breaking the monotony. And she had soon found it a greater monotony than the one she had fled

from, and, unlike the other, it was no ante-room of hope leading
to something better. Manny accepted her so complacently from
the first day that she was bored in a week with his unchanging
kindness. At first she exhibited an artificial irritation at trifles in
the hope of stirring up a little excitement, but Manny was kinder
and more gentle on those occasions than he was before, and
gradually her irritability and petulance became more daring
until these sins could scarcely be classed as venial. Finally, what
had been slyly deliberate became involuntary, and the sour
expression on her face hardened into a mask. She sought in the
throbbing pulse and rippling flux of anger the excitement she
had unconsciously hoped to find in her marriage bed. But her
angers, too, were sterile, breeding no response in Manny. He was
the same always. It seemed, however, that she could never believe
this, and she tried from time to time to break the strength of his
weakness, and she fought against his kindness as if it were her
enemy, as, in an obscure way, it was. What Annie really wanted
was the flaming face, the racing pulse, the temper that raised red
weals on the skin, the heat of bodies crushed together in rage.
And this need of her nature had never been satisfied except
vicariously, leaning over the shop counter listening to the
whispered stories of other women; stories of obscene blows given
in drunken lusts, stories of cunning and cupidity and flashes of
anger and hate that rent the darkness of the tenement hallways
in the vicinity, when she and Manny had been in bed for hours.

'Ah, woman dear,' these other women would say to her, 'sure
you know nothing at all about life.' And then, as if she was to be
pitied, they'd roll up their sleeves indulgently and show her
scalds and scabs. 'Take a look at that!' they'd say.

And sometimes, standing at the hall door in the dark at night
after the shop was shut, she might hear a scream in a room across
the street, or round the corner, followed maybe by children's
voices sounding as if they were frightened out of their wits. Or
perhaps a neighbour might come down the street loudly
sobbing, linked on either side by her children, sobbing louder
and telling her in high childish voices not to mind; not to mind.
Not to mind what? Annie wondered. Which of the inciting words
and gestures she had heard the neighbours tell about had

provoked this woman? She used to draw back a bit into the doorway while they were passing, her thin shoulder-blades pressed against the wall so they wouldn't see her spying on them and she might then catch a glimpse of Manny sitting in the kitchen with his stocking-feet upon the cooling range, while he read the paper. Her eyes would flicker with hatred and resentment, and she would have an impulse to be revenged on him by going in and poking the range, to send clouds of ashes over him till he'd have to get up and go to bed.

This evening, when he did not come back on time, she set her mind to planning some taunt for him when he'd come into the shop. If there were customers there, so much the better. One time she wouldn't have risked a row before the customers, but she'd found it helped trade more than it hindered it, particularly when Manny never answered back or made trouble. But as the evening wore out and there was still no sign of him, she began to think better of him. She began to think that maybe in his weak way he was defying her at last. Maybe he was getting his temper up with drink? He wasn't a drinking man, but there was always a first time for everything.

A wild elation welled up inside her, waiting for a torrential release in shouting and screaming. Perhaps she had battered in his patience at last? At last he was going to try to get even with her. Well! She was ready. She went into the kitchen, leaving the door into the shop half-open while she knotted her hair as tight as she could, the pricking pain on her neck giving her a foretaste of the fight she would have, and her eyes glittered. She let the customers go without giving them their usual bit of chitchat. She put the shutters up before the time. Where was he? It was getting very late now for a timid man like Manny. And he had had no dinner. She lifted the saucer that was covering his plate on the range. She ought to let him get a bite of food into him before she started the row. But where was he?

She was on her way out to the door to look up the street when she saw the silhouette of the poorhouse hearse passing the door. Supposing he was gone for good? The little skunk! It would be just like him to go over the river wall, like a rat in the dark, and never be heard of again. She would be cheated in this like everything else. Then the blackness lifted a little in her heart and she began to consider other possibilities. Maybe he'd skipped off to better himself somewhere and given her a miss? Again anger throbbed in her breast, but it eased when she remembered that he wouldn't have any money. Thanks be to the Almighty – and to her own good sense – she hadn't given him any money for the eggs. She wondered if he'd got them. Had he gone for them at all?

One after another, then, pictures of horror came into her mind. She saw a sodden corpse, white and hideously swollen, being carried in across the shop, dripping water from muddy clothes upon the thirsty floorboards. She saw herself at the wake, moaning and rocking from side to side, with everyone pitying her.

He wasn't a bad sort really, always wanting to take her to the Gaiety when the opera was on. He wasn't to blame for being so weak. His hands always went dead when he was cold. His face got a terrible blue colour in frosty weather. She thought about the peculiar habit he had of sleeping with his feet outside the bedclothes. And she began to feel uneasy about the past as well as about the future. She walked up and down the dark room, letting herself be mauled now by remorse.

Once in a while she went into the street and looked up and down. She did that in an effort to anticipate the terror that she felt was coming nearer every minute, rounding each corner more rapidly than the one before. But the evening winds were cooling the air and breathing their clear sweet peace even into the city streets. The lights were lighted, but their rays were not yet drawn out from them because the day had still some brightness of its own. They kept their gold carefully coiled up inside their glass globes, against the hour when their light would be needed, and it seemed as if they had no other function than to decorate the streets. The trams too were lit up, and they sailed like gilded galleons down the evanescent evening blue. The noises of trucks and drays sounded singly in the stillness as if to announce that they were going off as fast as they could, and that soon the city would be given over to cars and taxis travelling to gaudy cinemas and to theatres pearled with light.

The evening was so fair and so serene, so green and gilt, it threatened to rob her of all her dreads and to soothe her fears. It was better to sit by the whitening fire and imagine that the city outside was dark and vicious as she had often felt it to be, crossing it late on winter nights; a place of evil shadows, with police standing silently in the alleyways, and its shops shut down and barricaded with boards like coffin lids, and all the private houses fortified with battered ashcans lined up along the path, and, dreariest of all, the dark Green with its padlocked gates and its tree-high railings, through which you heard the agonies of a thousand cats wailing in the shrubberies.

She did not know which of her black forebodings she felt to be the more likely, but the ones that brought terror without robbing her entirely of the object of her terror were the ones that most appealed to her. And so she more or less expected a living Manny to be brought home to her, but one in whom some latent mutinous instinct had at last set up a twanging of chords that would echo throughout the rest of their lives and put reality into their relationship. She waited for his coming with more eagerness than when he was coming to court her.

But the instant she heard his footfall she knew he was the same old Manny. He was all right. And he was sober. Her fears faded out in widening ripples, leaving stillness and stagnation in her heart once more. When he put his head inside the door she knew by his apologetic cough that whatever it was had kept him out late it was no high-riding revolt, just a pale and weedy shoot from the anaemia of his character. It was certainly not a bursting into leaf of unsuspected manliness.

She sat by the fire without moving.

At last Manny was driven to break the silence himself.

'Did you keep my dinner, Annie?' he asked timidly, going over to the range, stooping his head as he went to avoid a slap of the wet sheets and towels that hung across the kitchen on a piece of string. He opened the door of the oven and bending down looked in. There was nothing there, and he shut the door quietly and stole a look at Annie. She was sitting scratching her head with a hairpin she had pulled out of the tight knot of hair on her neck. When she had finished scratching she stood up.

'Get out of my way,' she ordered tonelessly, and, taking down a
damp cloth off the line over his head, she took a hot plate from
the top of the stove and went over to a pile of rubbish in the
corner of the room. Pulling out a piece of brown paper she put
it under the plate before she set it on the table. 'Light the gas,'
she ordered.

The nauseous smell of gas roamed around the room in
streamers that soon ran together into one thick odour, and the
glare of the gaslight took away the only dignity the room had –
its darkness. Manny sat down to the meal set before him on the
brown paper. It was a plate of meat flanked on two sides by
tallow-yellow potatoes and a mound of soggy cabbage that still
held the shape of the fork with which it had been patted. Meat,
potato and cabbage were all stuck fast to the plate. And around
the rim of the plate, the gravy was crusted into a brown paper
doily.

'It looks good,' Manny said appeasingly, 'and it smells good.'

'It smelled better four hours ago,' Annie said, cleaning a knife
with her fingers and putting it down beside the plate.

Manny wondered if this reference to keeping the dinner hot
was intended as an opening for him to say where he had been,
and what had kept him, but when he looked at her he decided
on saying nothing.

He ate his dinner in silence, and tried as best he could to keep
the food in his mouth from making noises, but the sounds of
chewing seemed so loud in his own ears that after a few
mouthfuls he began to swallow down the coarse lumps of beef
unchewed. Soon the silence became so terrible he could eat no
more. He pushed aside his plate and sat staring at the ring of
grease it had left on the absorbent brown paper. He was
reminded waywardly of the brown paper he had used the night
before his wedding to get a grease stain off the sleeve of his best
suit. In those days he used to read in bed and he'd get his clothes
covered with candle grease, because he used to hump them
under the candlestick to raise it higher beside the bed. That was
a long time ago, but the past had been coming into his mind all
day. He used to hear his mother say that you re-lived all your life
in your mind before you died, but he hated those ignorant old

superstitions. They'd drive you mad. Yet this silence in the kitchen was enough to make a man mad too.

He turned around in the chair and deliberately drew down the lash of her rage. 'I went up to Sallygap to get the eggs, but I missed the bus and walked home.'

'From Sallygap?'

He had expected a tirade. He looked at her. She was picking her teeth with a bit of brown paper she'd leaned over and torn off the paper under the plate.

'Gets in your teeth, doesn't it?' he said, in a fainthearted hope that there was not going to be any row.

'Are you finished?' she asked.

He looked at his plate. 'Finished,' he said. 'All except my tea. I'll wet the tea myself if you like.'

'The tea is in the pot,' she said, and as he poured the spluttering water into the cold teapot she got up and went over to the dresser and took down a cup and saucer. She put them on the table.

The cup had not been washed since it had last been used. There was a sediment of moist sugar in the bottom of it, and the outside was streaked with yellow tea stains.

'This cup is a bit dirty,' he said, moving over to the sink.

'It's your own dirt, then,' she said to him. 'It was you who had it last.'

He stood irresolute, and then he said he'd like a clean cup.

'There's a quarter pound of sugar in the bottom of that cup,' Annie said, and then she snapped a question at him suddenly, with some apparent relevancy in her own mind. 'What did you do with the return ticket?'

He rooted in his pockets and took out the half-ticket. She snapped it up and looked at it closely, and then she stuck it down in a jug that was hanging by its handle on the nail of the dresser.

'Is he going to send the eggs?'

'Every Monday and Friday.'

'Give me that cup.' She went over to the sink where she ran the cold tap on it. She clattered it back on the saucer, wet. Cold drops splashed on his hot hands from her wet hands. She stood looking down at him. 'It's a queer thing when a man disgusts to himself,' she said.

Her eyes were greener than ever. They used to remind him of the sea at Howth, where they used to go walking when they were courting. They were the same colour still, hut now they reminded him suddenly of the green water under the wharf at Dunlaoghaire. And as the sticky sea that day had been flecked with splinters of his broken fiddle, Annie's eyes above him now were flecked with malevolence.

Ever since their first quarrel, he'd been afraid of her sharp tongue. But it had been the fear of a timid soul. Now, looking up into her eyes, his immature and childish fear fell from him, and instead of it there came into his heart a terrible adult fear; a fear that came from his instincts, from his blood. He thought of all the talk he had heard at different times in public houses, talk of morgues and murders, and he remembered what he had said to himself up at Sallygap about the people of Dublin: that they were ignorant, with clogged pools in their blood that clotted easily to unjust hate. They hugged their hate. He thought of Paris, with its flashing lights and its flashing hates, its quick flashing knives; but the dangers in Paris seemed vivid and vital compared with the dead anger in the sullen eyes that were watching him. Desperately he thought of the hills, but the thought of them gave him no refuge. The happy hills were fading from his mind already. He would never seek a sanctuary among them again.

For there was no sanctuary from hatred such as he saw in Annie's eyes, unless it came from behind some night, from a raised hatchet brought down with a crack on his skull, or from a queer taste in the mouth followed by a twisting in the guts. She had him imprisoned for ever in her hatred. His little fiddle had crashed on the pier the day he gave up all his dreams for her, and it had floated in splintered sticks on the dirty water. He thought of it for a moment, and then he thought of nothing at all for a while, but just sat watching her as she went about the room.

Then he remembered that she had said something to him when she clattered down the wet cup on the saucer in front of him a little while before. He tried to think what it was she had said. He couldn't remember.

But he did remember, distinctly, thinking at the time, that whatever it was, it was true.

Love Is For Lovers

At the non-committal age of forty-five, Mathew Simmins began to think about marriage. Somehow or other he had never thought about it before. It took up nearly all his time and energy to get the day's work done in the day, because only for him, Mahaffy's Stores would have gone to the wall long ago. Paid hands never really put their heart into their work the way he did. Mathew drew a salary, too, of course, but it was how he felt about the shop that made the difference between him and the shop boys. He was like one of the family. For instance, the shop boys stopped work on the dot of six – actually stopped on the first stroke of the hour, and although Mathew could not himself swear to whether it was the first or the last stroke which indicated *exactly* the termination of one hour and the commencement of another, common courtesy would seem to have demanded that they wait for the last stroke before rushing to grab their coats and get away. For years Mathew had had it in mind to consult a jeweller on this delicate point, but there was no jeweller in the town, and gradually he let the matter slide. All the same he never quite lost a mild irritation at six o'clock when assistants and apprentices alike raced to the storehouse door behind which they hung their coats and caps. They always seemed to manage things in such a way that they were down at that end of the shop tipping up to six. And those of them who were held up by a customer coming in at the last minute, gave the customer short shrift and raced to make up the lost time. Mathew had more than once seen an apprentice – one of the cheekier sort – who, having got into the clutches of an admittably inconsiderate customer, actually vaulted over a counter in his haste to get out of the place. As if to make it known that once six had gone he owed no deference to anyone!

At precisely five minutes past six the blinds were down, the counters at the grocery end were covered with dust sheets, and Mathew alone remained to turn down the wicks of the lamps, and lock up for the night before leaving for his lodgings. On one memorable occasion when the shop door had shut on the last of the assistants, a mouse popped out from a hole in the wainscot and ran across the floor. Mathew thought at first it was a toy mouse on a string, a silly prank played by one of the apprentices. But it was a real mouse, and it took advantage of his hesitancy to get up on the counter and go at the cheese right under his very eyes. That meant another delay, laying down traps, as well as coming in earlier next morning to get rid of the dead mouse and block up the hole. There was always something over and above the day's work to be done in a big shop like Mahaffy's, if you had a proper sense of responsibility. It was almost unbelievable the odd jobs Mathew had to do. Once or twice he had found the day-book open, with a list of a last customer's purchases – a credit customer of course – properly entered, and with a neat line under the figures – but whoever made the entry had not waited to tot up the total. And he frequently found the till open, where someone hadn't taken the time to push the drawer back after flinging in the last coin of the day. Naturally, on these occasions Mathew did what was to be done, and moreover he said nothing about it next morning. He was not the type to be eternally picking on people over trifles. The assistants were almost all young and people nowadays could never be got to do a tap more than they were paid to do. They gave satisfaction from nine to six and that was what counted. In his quiet way Mathew kept order during shop hours. He prided himself that he gave his apprentices as good a training as they'd get in any shop in the town. Perhaps better? And it gave him real gratification on Friday evenings when he stayed behind, purposely and of his own volition, to make up the pay packets and have them in the safe ready for handing out on Saturday evening. He would have been quite within his rights to make them up during shop hours, but it was these small scruples that gave him what he considered a justifiable pride and self-respect. As he'd put each boy's pay into the separate paper packets, specially ordered for this purpose, with the name of the Store on one side and an advertisement for tea on the other, Mathew often felt exactly the same as if he was a partner – the active partner! Old Mahaffy – God rest his soul – had been extremely active, but when he died, Young Mr Mahaffy, who took over, was more of a sleeping partner. This was a private joke, of course, which Mathew enjoyed with himself alone, chuckling over it silently many a time. On those Friday evenings he sometimes indulged in these silent chuckles all the way up the street to the Mahaffy residence. For it was a custom established after the death of old Mahaffy that Mathew would call around in person to receive his cheque direct from the hands of Young Mr Mahaffy. It gave a nice touch to his association with the firm, Mathew felt. Sometimes in the big gloomy dining room, seated opposite the young man, Mathew often felt that young Mr Mahaffy too regarded him in the light of a partner. There was never any open reference to a partnership. And Mathew was quite satisfied to leave things as they were. It was enough for him to know that he had the gratitude of the Mahaffys. Yes. Yes. The gratitude was there all right. On his side too, there was also considerable gratitude. Where would he be if it were not for the Stores? He never let himself forget that he had not had one penny to rub against another the day he first put on his brown shopcoat and took his place behind Mahaffy's counter. Well he remembered that day – he began in the haberdashery, but he had done his stint behind the grocery and hardware also, a fact to which he attributed his overall knowledge of shopkeeping and management. He had a nice little sum tucked away in the bank today, but where had he made the money? In Mahaffy's! Where else? Young Mr Mahaffy might not have his father's ability, and Mathew had to work hard to make up for some of the young man's deficiencies, but he liked Young Mahaffy. He thought him an exceedingly nice man, and knew him to be one of the best chess players in the county, although he never entered for any competitions or contests. Mathew made a point of being just as deferential to the son as he had been to the father, who had always demanded the deference of everyone in his employment, from the highest to the lowest. The old man had been the glum type, testy and demanding, even with those who had served him for the whole of their lives. Young Mr Mahaffy was a gracious man, a man of great simplicity. No other words could so aptly describe him. Every Friday evening – after exchanging a few words of a more or less similar kind each week – he always made the exact same remark when it came time for him to slide the glossy white vellum envelope, with Mathew's cheque inside it, across the broad mahogany tabletop.

'You are Mahaffy's Mathew and Mahaffy's is you,' he'd say. 'I am a good-for-nothing. I only rake in the profits.'

And Mathew felt it to be in keeping with their relationship that his reply too be the same as always.

'Don't forget you write the cheques as well, sir.'

Those words of Mathews usually gave Young Mahaffy his cue for standing up and shaking hands with him. There was a sort of ritual touch to their encounters that Mathew liked. He liked to know precisely when to come and when to go. He liked to know for certain where he stood with people. It made it easier to deal with them. That, no doubt was why it upset him so much when one of his best customers, a widow, a Mrs Rita Cooligan, became so forgetful she was forever leaving something behind on one of the counters, and coming back in a state to look for it. To make matters worse she insisted on calling for him.

'Mr Simmins! Where is he? I must see Mr Simmins,' she'd call out as she'd come running back into the shop, regardless of whether or not there were other customers present. And when she'd see him, she'd rush up to him, pushing her hat back from her forehead in a manner that made her look younger and more helpless than she had seemed to Mathew when she first brought her custom to Mahaffy's. Then, he thought of her as a mature woman, and certainly strong-minded, and well balanced. But here she was arousing such feelings of protectiveness in him that he let the shop be turned upside down in his efforts to pacify her. For one thing, he'd send the shop-boys scurrying hither and thither all over the place, although he knew well they'd make it an excuse for tricking and fooling around under the counters. The tops of the counters he took care of himself, lifting up every blessed thing and looking under it, in search of whatever it was she had lost, although once it was only a handkerchief. Sometimes, however, Mrs Cooligan mislaid something less easily replaced – like a key-ring with the key of her house on it. She really was a featherhead, as indeed she called herself, when almost always, and with a rich, warm laugh, she would suddenly produce the missing article from somewhere on her own person, or from an inside pocket of her handbag which Mathew could have sworn she had searched, not indeed once, but several times. She was in such a state, however, one had to excuse her. And to show her that he did, Mathew always permitted himself to smile. The shop boys of course would have gone on screeching with laughter for the rest of the day, if he hadn't sent them about their business. Not that a little simple fun did anyone any harm, but it couldn't be carried too far. Mrs Cooligan herself almost carried the thing too far. When she'd finally leave the shop she'd still be laughing, as she went up the street. Mathew shook his head. Featherhead! he said to himself again, but he meant it in a kindly way. How long, he wondered, was it since her husband died? It was sad to see a woman like that so full of life left to live out the best years of her life alone. Here, however, Mathew put a strong rein on himself. It didn't seem proper to think about the poor woman's private life, such thoughts bordered on coarseness, and that was something he had always guarded against.

Then one day in early spring when the sun, for the time of year, was so strong, Mathew had thought he had better take the butter out of the window. Mahaffy's was giving a special offer in butter and a nice little display had been arranged to attract attention to it. His landlady had kindly made up a number of butter pats and Mathew had arranged them on a glass butter-dish from stock. But it would be disastrous if the unseasonable heat of the sun melted the butter. He just put his head into the window to take out the glass dish when he saw Mrs Cooligan coming down the street. What a fine figure she had, though to be truthful he had never considered himself a judge of such matters. Indeed, some of the young things that came into the shop these days looked so thin, so downright peaky, he often felt like commenting on their condition when talking to their parents, because one could not know people from the pram up – even in business – without taking a friendly interest in them. But to his astonishment these were the very girls he'd hear the shop boys gassing about as they were going out into the street in the evening, or when in the morning they would arrive at the door and he would be inside struggling with the lock to open up and let them in. Well, as the saying went, it took all kinds to make a world. And watching Mrs Rita Cooligan come sailing down the street, Mathew felt even a blind man could see that she was a well built woman. At this point he took out his handkerchief and vehemently blew his nose.

Meanwhile his customer was advancing rapidly, considering how highly arched were her shoes. She was wearing the same coat as usual, and although yesterday he could not have told what colour it was – not if his life depended on it – today in the spring sunlight he saw it was a nice colour. A sort of plum? It was tight, or perhaps he should say neat-fitting, and he liked the way she had pulled the belt tight like a man would, only of course, unlike a man her top rose up from it in a way that put him in mind of a swan on a pond. There again of course, swans were white and cold and Mrs Rita Cooligan exuded nothing but richness and warmth, being dark, and her complexion being the sort he understood to be called olive complexion.

But Mrs Cooligan had now almost arrived at the door and was clearly coming into the shop, since it was the end shop in the street. Realising that having watched her, when she had not known she was being watched, might make it hard for him to appear natural, Mathew made a lightning decision to stay where he was with his back turned. In fact when he heard the shop door open, he poked his head still further into the aperture of the window and busied himself with making slight alterations on the window display, moving things around a bit and trying to fill the space made by the removal of the butter. But he couldn't keep up this charade for long. There was one thing he could do. The sun was really strong. Even though he had taken out the butter, it would be quite reasonable to lower the window blind. He reached out for the cord, but his mind unfortunately was not properly centred on what he was doing and after he had lowered the blind, he let the cord slip from his grasp and the blind shot up again with a sound so loud and shocking that it brought the blood to his head. He didn't dare to turn around and see what Mrs Cooligan had made of his clumsiness. To hide this new flux of embarrassment he had no other course open to him hut bury his head still deeper into the opening of the window and continue to fiddle about with various articles and wait until she left the premises.

At last Mrs Cooligan concluded her purchases. Mathew knew when she was leaving by the tap-tap of her heels, and by a breath of heavy perfume that travelled through the shop, like a ring of smoke puffed into the air. He was almost relieved to find that as it neared him this intoxicating wreath of scent had begun to dissolve. Preoccupied in this way, he was still not giving his full attention to what he was doing and so when Mrs Cooligan, having gained the street, happened to stop and look in the window, he was struck dumb when he found himself staring straight into her face – that is to say, as clearly as he could see it with a fly paper hanging down between them, encrusted with dead flies. And immediately he had the uneasy feeling that she had known all along that he had been trying to avoid her, and this was her way of punishing him. He was contrite beyond words. Mrs Cooligan was one of Mahaffy's best customers. He resolved at once to make amends for having offended her, next time she came into the shop – if she ever did come in again. He might perhaps open a tin of biscuits and invite her to sample a new variety? Nothing pleased customers more than flattery like that – and his innocent little ruse served a double purpose, because most customers bought a pound or so of the biscuits, and the over-independent types, who felt obliged to give it as their opinion that the new variety was a bit on the sweet side, or else a bit on the plain side, nevertheless bought some sort of biscuits, if only to prove their point. It was a good business move in either case. In either case Mathew knew he was showing respect for the customer as well as putting a few more shillings in the till. There was no duplicity involved. After all, one man's meat was another man's poison.

Reassuring himself that Mrs Cooligan had really gone, Mathew was about to return to his station behind the desk, when, of a sudden, the shop door was thrown open with such violent force that a pile of empty biscuit tins that had been left near the door, ready when the van would arrive to collect returns, came toppling to the floor, making an indescribable din.

'Oh what have I done?' Mrs Cooligan cried as Mathew rushed forward to assist her in stepping over the wretched tins. In his attempt to be of assistance Mathew had to lift one of his legs with both hands over the heap of tins. But at least he was in command of the situation.

'What is the matter?' he cried.

'Oh Mr Simmins,' Mrs Cooligan was almost in tears. 'This time it's my handbag I've lost! I left it behind in some shop or other, but it's not in the butchers because I called there first of all. And it's not in the drapers, I didn't leave it there either. And I could not possibly have dropped it in the street on my way down here, or else the new chemist would have seen me drop it, because he assured me he never took his eyes off me for one moment – not for one second, if you want his exact words.

'Please, please, Mrs Cooligan,' Mathew cried. 'Please don't get excited. Perhaps you didn't bring your bag out with you? Perhaps you left it at home?'

'No, no, no,' Mrs Cooligan cried with extraordinary firmness. 'You must understand that I took my bag with me expressly because it contained a sum of money that I intended to lodge to my account in the bank.'

'Ah,' Mathew said, steadying himself still more to cope with this new aspect of the situation. 'Perhaps you left it behind in the bank?'

'I haven't been to the bank yet,' Mrs Cooligan replied with singular simplicity.

Mathew saw the matter, this time, was really serious. 'I hope there wasn't a large amount of money in the bag?' he asked, as he sent the shop boys scurrying off to look for it, and he having begun his usual lifting of things and putting them down again, not even bothering to rub a dab of butter off his cuff as he took his hand from behind the butterslab although it was improbable that the handbag could have got there, his intention having been to reassure her, nothing more. But she really was a strange woman.

'I don't care a rap about the money, Mr Simmins,' she said. 'What grieves me is the loss of a souvenir that was in an inner pocket of the bag – a paper knife – a little paper knife with an ivory handle that I've treasured ever since it was given to me years ago by someone I dearly loved.'

Mathew was struck to the heart, when her eyes filled with tears, he was so bewildered he didn't know what to say to her: but it did occur to him that it must have been given to her by that other fellow, her husband, and unaccountably he felt less sorry for her. Why didn't she keep things like that at home, instead of hawking them around in her handbag? His sympathy towards her lessened so much he went over and attended in person to another customer, although he seldom attended any customer in person any more. But, as if she had read his mind, at that very instant he overheard her talking to one of the shop boys and explaining that the paper knife had been given to her by her best friend when they had both been schoolgirls together before her friend married and went to Australia and was never heard from again!

Mathew could have kicked himself for being so hasty in misjudging her.

'Don't despair!' he cried. 'I believe we'll find it yet. If necessary I will paste a notice on the window.' Indeed, there and then he grabbed one of the assistants by the sleeve. 'Get a pencil!' he ordered. 'Say we are offering a reward.' He turned back to Mrs Cooligan 'This is not meant to convey that I have given up hope of yet finding it on the premises.' Here he plucked another of the boys by the sleeve. 'Did you try the sugar bin?' he demanded. The boy seemed a bit nonplussed but Mathew had turned away and was addressing himself to Mrs Cooligan. 'We lost one of the weights belonging to the scales, a few months ago – I forget which weight it was, the half hundred weight or the eight ounce, but whichever it was we were put to great inconvenience without it. We searched everywhere to no avail, and I myself was on the point of giving up and sending away to replace it, when I happened to pass the sugar bin and, partly to take my mind off my annoyance, I stopped to ascertain if there was sufficient sugar to last the weekend without sending out for more to the storeroom – something I usually do by eye, but which incredibly, I did that day by diving in my hand and running it through the sugar. And what do you suppose! Guess! I felt my hand hit against something hard on the bottom of the bin. "Come here, Joe," I cried. "There's something here in this bin. Put in your hand and see what it is!" Never did I suspect it to be the missing weight, but when Joe delved in his hand that was the very thing he pulled up and showed me. Isn't that right Joe?' he asked, but Joe, instead of confirming the story, had already dived his hand into the bin and begun to sift the sugar between his fingers.

'Any luck Joe?' Mrs Cooligan cried, as she leaned over the counter in such a way that Mathew was overwhelmed by her resemblance to a swan, with her top part swelling up over the counter and the rest of her hidden below it.

In the end, however, it had to be acknowledged by all that the handbag had vanished. It was not to be seen high up or low down. And Mrs Cooligan was forced to depart without it, although at the door she paused and called back to Mathew.

'Somehow or other I cannot help feeling that it is here somewhere,' she said.

Mathew felt that the shop boys must have been proud of the way he rose to the occasion.

'Rest assured, Mrs Cooligan,' he said. 'If we find it, I will send Joe, here, down with it to your house. Immediately.'

'You're more than kind,' Mrs Cooligan said, and then instead of going out, she came back into the shop. 'I do hope you believe me, Mr Simmins, when I say it's not the loss of the money that matters to me, but the loss of my little paper knife. I never took it out of the house before. I don't know what possessed me to take it with me today. It's a sort of a talisman, a charm. I always keep it on my bedside table. For luck! And if I think I hear a noise in the middle of the night, I put out my hand and feel around for it, and always, always, it gives me courage.' Then she left, having given Mathew a smile, a brave smile.

'I still believe we will find it,' Mathew said very solemnly, because it was, as far as he could recollect, the first lie he had ever told. The last he thought to see of her that day was when she smiled in at him again through the shop window before going bravely up the street. She was a woman of great self control, he thought, as he set about tidying up the counters. He could not but admire her sentiments towards an old friend, although he did, quite frankly, find it hard to understand how sentiment could take precedence over the loss of good money.

All that afternoon Mathew kept his eyes open for the missing handbag, while he went around readying up the mess that had been made in their search for it by those giddy shop boys. It was hard to see why they had to empty out three boxes of shoe laces. And it was harder still to explain why they had considered it necessary to unravel several balls of twine. Indeed, by the time six o'clock struck Mathew was almost as much put out by the state of the shop as he was by Mrs Cooligan's loss. And when the shop boys had gone gallivanting off, and as he himself went down to the storehouse door to get his outdoor clothes, he was actually frowning.

Mathew kept his coat and hat in the same place as his assistants, for convenience, but on a separate nail from the nails on which they hung their coats. There had to be some distinctions made in the interests of authority! But this evening, as he reached up to take down his coat, his foot hit against something and sent it sliding across the floor-boards. As he said to himself in bed that night, he knew, or to be accurate, he partly guessed, before stooping to pick it up, that it was Rita Cooligan's handbag. And so it was.

Mathew was as pleased as Punch. To think of how the shop boys had monkeyed about for hours looking for it, with no success, whereas he had only to walk down to the end of the shop and there it was under his feet as if placed there by magic. He picked it up. And seeing, that the clasp was open, he carefully closed it, although mind you, it took him some minutes to master that catch. There was a little trick to it – a very clever little trick. But he got it.

'Very clever!' he said out loud when he had ascertained that the clasp was well and truly closed, and he went over to put the bag into the safe. Before closing the safe he took a last look at it, and he marvelled at how extraordinary it was for women to feel the need of a contraption like it, whereas a man's wallet was so uncomplicated. Really, women were strange creatures.

This, therefore, may have been the point at which for the first time Mathew thought about marriage, but of course it was in a very negative way, because although other differences between women and men kept popping into his head, he assumed that by and large they were differences that he, personally, would never explore. However, after he had let himself out into the street, checking the shop door several times, due to the unusual tension caused by the events of the day, it crossed his mind that it was odd he had never thought about marriage – or, rather, never thought of it as being for him, within his province. Otherwise he felt no differently from any other evening as he plodded his way towards his lodgings, a little stiff after a long day's work, a trifle chilly in spite of his having on his heavy top-coat.

It was only by the merest chance, as he passed the entrance to a small road – a cul-de-sac really – where Mrs Cooligan lived – that he happened to look down at the terrace of small houses and saw that although most of the front windows were dark, there was one window so brightly lit that in spite of the curtains being drawn, a soft glow came through into the small front garden. Mathew stood for a moment. He knew that colour. Plum! It crossed his mind immediately that the house must be her house, Mrs Cooligan's. It was a pity he had not found her bag before closing time, or certainly he would, as he had promised, have Joe or one of the boys down with it to her Or would he? On consideration, it would have been better perhaps – had he found it in time – to send word that he had put it in the safe until such time as it could be passed from his hand to hers. Not that the assistants were untrustworthy! They would not be employed in Mahaffy's were that so, but that was solely with regard to money. With things of purely sentimental value they might not be so scrupulous. Supposing the paper knife were to be let fall out of the bag, unnoticed, into the gutter, to be picked up by some other careless person who in turn might toss it into a rubbish can. Yes, it would have been preferable to simply send word that the article had been found, just to put her out of suspense. Too bad he had not found it earlier.

Mathew was about to continue on his way when it struck him like a bolt from the blue that there was nothing to stop him from calling to her door himself, right there and then, and put her mind at ease. But now, Mathew was disturbed by the realisation that he was not certain of the number of her house, a fact for which he felt specially culpable since he often sent special deliveries to her door, and needless to say, as was only fitting in a place like Mahaffy's, that all labels on parcels should be in his own hand which he had perfected until it was copperplate. How could he have forgotten her number? Then, with a little spurt of jauntiness, he decided to take a shot in the dark, even if it was a long shot, and so next moment found him striding down the road, making for the house with the plum-coloured curtains. As he stepped up to the hall door, Mathew thought again what a pity it was he had not brought the bag with him. What a triumph it would have been when she'd open the door to hold it up without a word, just a knowing look, a telling smile! As he raised his hand to lift the iron door-knocker, however, Mathew was disconcerted to see it was fashioned in the shape of a mailed fist and he was overcome by an understandable timidity , He would feel as if he was banging on her door with his own fist. Fortunately there was a bell. And, assuming the bell to be one of the common, ordinary sorts, where you pushed a button with your finger, he was about to ring when another complication arose. The mechanism of the bell was most unusual. It consisted of two metal wings, like the wings of an ornamental butterfly, which presumably you pressed together. There was something vaguely familiar about the mechanism of the bell, he thought, as he gingerly pressed on the two bits of metal. Next minute he nearly fell off the doorstep with the twitter of sound just inside the door. For a moment he thought the sound was inside his ear, and that an insect had got into the ear and was trapped there. Before he was fully recovered the door was flung open.

'Your handbag, I found it,' Mathew said, summoning up the whole stock of his presence of mind to bring out the words.

Mrs Cooligan was quite composed.

'Mr Simmins! What a surprise! Do come inside!' she said, holding open the door and standing back. 'How nice of you to call. Welcome!' He had decidedly done the right thing by calling.

She made it seem the most natural thing in the world. And now, no doubt to put him still more at ease, she was drawing his attention to something on the back of the door. 'How do you like my bell, Mr Simmins. It's my own invention. It's just a bicycle bell fastened to the inside, with a hole bored so the two lugs can be squeezed from outside. So economical! And quite ingenious, don't you think? Listen!' she commanded, and before she closed the door she filled the hallway with twitter after twitter. Then she threw open the door of the front room, the room with the plum curtains, which was certainly comfortable, and hot. Mathew had not intended to do more than stand on the doorstep, but he was a bit con-fused by Mrs Cooligan's chatter, and the twittering of the bell, but above all by the incessant barking of a large liver-and-white spotted dog sitting on a plum coloured sofa. In two ticks Mathew was sitting on the sofa too.

'It was *so* nice of you to come,' Mrs Cooligan said, with such cordiality, she made it seem like a social call. He wondered if perhaps she had not heard what he'd said at the door?

'Your bag! I found it,' he said, and he almost had to shout to be heard above the din the dog was making.

'Be quiet, Pete!' Mrs Cooligan said. 'Be quiet.' And when the dog didn't stop she picked it up and held it in her arms. 'Nice Petey!' she coaxed. 'Petey mustn't bark at this kind gentlemen. The kind gentlemen brought back my bag, Petey.'

Mathew was relieved to see she had in fact registered the reason for his call, and he was even more relieved when the old dog yielded to the warmth of her arms and stopped yapping. Seemingly it had taken in what she'd said, because it looked at Mathew now with rich brown eyes, moist and red-brimmed. A well-meaning poor dog, Mathew thought, and forgave it the noise it had made.

'Isn't he sweet?' Mrs Cooligan was asking. 'He understands every word I say to him. You'll be firm friends, the two of you, from now on. You'll see! Pat him, Mr Simmins! Pat him! Take his paw. Make him shake hands! He won't bite. He's full of love, once he gets to know people. Make him give the paw.'

It was touching to see her devotion to the dog and its devotion to her, but Mathew had not patted a dog since he was a boy, and he was a bit nervous. Nevertheless he put out his hand and stroked Pete whose coat was certainly soft and silky. A very well kept animal! Stroking Pete's coat was like stroking human hair. Not that Mathew had ever done that in all his life, and involuntarily he glanced at Mrs Cooligan's hair that, seen without a hat, seemed to ripple like waves of the sea, ripple after ripple after ripple. When Mathew looked back quickly at the dog, Mrs Cooligan took its paw and began to pull it gently, making the loose flesh wobble. A most peculiar sensation went through Mathew – quite as if she was touching him. He stopped stroking the dog, but he went on looking into its wet eyes.

Mrs Cooligan saw at once that he was uncomfortable about something, and with a tact for which Mathew was more grateful than he could say, she tried to make him feel at home by talking to him playfully through the dog.

'Well, Pete? What do you think of Mr Simmins? Isn't he a nice man, Pete?'

And Pete understood every word, or so it would seem from the way he put out his tongue and tried to lick Mathew's hand.

'A wonderfully intelligent little creature,' Mrs Cooligan said, 'and with a heart brimful of human kindness. When poor Arthur – my husband, now dead, as I think you know, Mr Simmins – when he knew that his days were numbered, he picked up Pete one day and looking into his eyes, he told him he was leaving me in his charge. "Pete will take care of you, Rita my darling," he said.'

From that moment Mathew found himself thinking of her not as Mrs Cooligan, but as Rita. It was upsetting. He stood up at once.

'About your bag,' he said, in as practical a manner as possible.

Mrs Cooligan did not stand up, but she dropped Pete on the floor and she too became practical.

'I will call for it tomorrow,' she said.

Immediately Mathew recalled how she felt about her little keepsake. She'd be without it all night. Ah well, he thought, it might not be right to proffer to go back to the shop, it could make him appear altogether too accommodating, make him look as if he wanted to put her under a compliment to him.

Nothing was further from his mind. Then she herself brought up the subject of the paper knife, if indirectly.

'You do realise, don't you, Mr Simmins, it was never the loss of the ten pounds that bothered me, it was only –'

Mathew, however, heard no more.

'Ten pounds!' He was thunderstruck. 'You don't mean to say there was an amount of that size in the bag? Why didn't you tell me. I found it on the floor! The clasp was open! The money could have fallen out. I didn't look inside.' So great was his consternation that he had to mop his forehead with his handkerchief.

'Oh, I didn't mean to upset you, Mr Simmins,' Mrs Cooligan said. On the contrary! Do please sit down again.'

What a strange woman! She didn't care about losing ten pounds, and yet for the sake of economy she had installed that diabolical, twittering doorbell. It was almost irresponsible. He put away his handkerchief and returned to the subject of the money.

'May I ask if this money was in a single note, or if it was in two five pound notes?' he asked.

Rita shrugged her firm, rounded shoulders, which Mathew only now noticed were bare, but then the room was very hot. He himself was perspiring, but that may have been due to worry over the money.

'I really don't remember whether it was singles or fivers,' she said. Then she concentrated hard 'Wait a minute. I think it was two fivers. I know that last week it was a tenner, but it could have been two fivers this time.'

Evidently a regular income, Mathew thought. A pension perhaps? An annuity?

'Mrs Cooligan,' he said. He nearly said Rita! 'You must understand that although *you* may not be concerned about the safety of this money, I cannot remain unconcerned. Once the bag passed into my hands I hold myself responsible for it and also for whatever it contained. I think I simply must go back to the shop and make sure the money is alright.'

Rita sprang to her feet at that.

'You will do no such thing,' she cried. 'Not on my account, you won't! How could you think I'd be so inconsiderate, as to let you go back all that way – without your supper – which I'm sure you'd find flat and tasteless when you'd finally get it.' She was right there, Mathew thought, but all the same he went resolutely towards the door. 'No, I won't allow it,' Rita cried, and pushing past him, she stood with her back against the door, and threw out her arms as if physically to prevent his leaving. She sounded in deadly earnest, but again Mathew thought he detected a playfulness about her. A strange woman!

He, however, remained grave and earnest.

'I'm afraid I must insist,' he said. 'You don't understand, the money may be lying about on the floor.'

Let it lie there,' she said. 'Aren't you always the first one into the shop in the morning? What could happen it during the night?'

She'd nearly got him there! But he had his wits about him.

'A mouse might chew it up,' he said.

'A mouse? A mouse!' She was so taken by surprise she lowered her arms, which must have been tired stretched out like that, and she began to laugh so much and so heartily that she had to cross her arms over her bosom to prevent herself shaking to bits. Then, quite suddenly she gave way. 'Very well,' she said quietly. 'I will permit you to go and fetch it, but I warn you I don't like to be disobeyed and when you come back with it you may find yourself faced with paying me a forfeit.'

Mathew hadn't the foggiest idea what she was talking about. He was on edge to get back to the shop.

'Don't be long!' she called from the doorway.

'I don't intend to dally,' he called back gaily. And in fact he was striding along like a twenty year old, so fast he wasn't in the least chilly, and he didn't feel as stiff in the joints as usual either. What he did feel was hungry – famished in fact. He could hear his stomach rumbling. And to make matters worse when he got back to Rita's with the bag – in which the money was safe and sound, tucked away and zipped into an inner pocket – a tantalising smell of food rushed out into the air when she threw open the door. He held out the bag, coughing loudly to cover up the rumbling in his gut and preparing to dash off.

'Oh no, you don't!' Rita cried. She caught his arm and literally pulled him into the hall. Taking the bag she tossed it on the hall table and threw open the door of the front room where a small table, drawn up to the fire, was laid with places for two. 'Now you must pay your forfeit! You must keep me company for supper. Give me your coat,' she cried, and gave him a push that sent him into the middle of the room. As she took his coat she was talking ten to the dozen and Pete was beating the floor with his stubby tail. 'I love having people for a meal, specially in the evening. I never eat properly when I'm alone. Pete here always gets the best part of the meal. On top of his own share!' She picked up the dog. 'Isn't that so, Pete?' Then she put the dog down. 'Most evenings it doesn't seem worth while cooking for one person alone. I keep thinking how much Arthur loved my steak and kidney pie. That's what we're having tonight. I hope it's one of your favourite dishes?' It was. Mathew sat down beside Pete, who had scrambled back up on the plush sofa.

She was full of surprises. He would never have thought her the domesticated type. Only this morning he'd been thinking of her as a swan! Cooking was something he associated with landladies and downtrodden wives.

That night, however, after he had been invited to come again and try another of her culinary specialities, he felt it would have been boorish to refuse. And when in the course of the following weeks he had sampled several dishes and they'd got around to steak and kidney for the second time, Mathew discovered plenty of other differences, that he had not thought about, between men and women, only now he was beginning to think it might not be too late for him to investigate some of them more closely.

For although he hadn't thought of marriage ever, or certainly not for years, this did not mean that Mathew was not romantic at the white-hot core. As a young man, when he first came to Mahaffy's, he used to spend a lot of time looking at the girls in the town as they strolled about the streets, and thought how much nicer they were than big fat country girls. He would not have objected to making the acquaintance of one of these girls, but they seemed so quick, so smart, he didn't dare to speak to them. And it wasn't as if he knew anyone who would introduce him! Besides that, he was soon so wrapped up in Mahaffy's he was too tired after shop hours to do much more than crawl back to the lodging house for his evening meal and read the evening newspaper. Later in the night he might perhaps take a short walk, but by then there were no girls in the streets, they'd all have gone off somewhere. To the cinema perhaps? Or to the dance hall, from which, when he'd pass it, the music came out in gusts like wind blowing at gale force, against which he knew he would never push his way. He began then to content himself with looking at girls on the posters that were pasted to hoardings and the gable end of disused buildings, advertising some commodity like scented soap, or a camera. In his more fanciful moments he used to try to imagine what it would be like if they were real flesh and blood girls who might at any moment step down out of the poster and take his arm. Together, then, he and that girl would go up the street linked and laughing into each other's eyes.

There was one particular poster on a hoarding opposite Mahaffy's, which advertised a well known make of bicycle, and the girl on that poster was the one who really took Mathew's fancy. She wore a blue tam – blue was a nice colour – and she had blue eyes as well, and as she pedalled towards him, she rode right into the cool summer breeze, not caring that her golden hair got blown about. Indeed one golden strand of it blew right across her face. After a time he confined himself to that girl and it was always her, and not the others, that he'd dream of as stepping down and suggesting that he buy a bicycle and go for a spin with her. He was not in love with her. Needless to say! A girl on a poster! If he hadn't been a steady chap he would never have got where he got in Mahaffy's. Not in a million years!

All this, of course, was long ago. Girls never wore tams now. They never let their hair blow about. They sprayed something on it to keep the ripples in place. And most girls nowadays looked coarse on a bicycle. Anyway he had, quite properly, been brought up to understand that you couldn't have everything in this life. He had a good job in Mahaffy's and a nice little nest egg in the bank. What more could he have asked of life, not ever having thought that some women could be lonely too – not until the day one, of her own accord, flew down on to the path in front of him, asking to be caught. For Mathew was not as backward as he might seem. He knew what Rita had in mind. He didn't blame her either, and he made full acknowledgement that, if left to himself, he would never have come forward the way she did. She had made the blessings of marriage seem much more easily obtainable than he would ever have believed possible.

In other words Mathew decided to let events take their course. And in due time he and Rita were both overtaken by summer.

In the full heat of summer, an exceptionally hot Saturday in the middle of July, when he and Rita were having a cup of tea, Rita suddenly had one of her brainwaves. Running out into the garden she looked up into the sun. Then running back into the house, she pushed a cushion into Mathew's hand, and gave Pete an old newspaper to carry out in his mouth – just to please the dog. 'We're going to have tea in the garden,' she said. It seemed a good idea, but as they drank their tea in the small garden, which was almost burnt-up with the heat of that summer sun, Mathew found himself wondering why she had never planted a few trees, as a neighbour down the road had done. Trees – even bushes – could cast a nice shade in summer. And in Rita's garden no cool shade fell. Mathew was soon uncomfortably hot, and he wondered if she might not have looked cooler in some colour other than that eternal plum colour? Blue? Green? They were nice colours. He liked them better than that plum.

Putting his hand over his cup, as she went to pour more tea for him, Mathew casually remarked that in America people, or so he heard, drank iced tea.

America?' Rita cried. 'That's a place I'd give anything to visit!'

'Who wouldn't!' Mathew said. 'The fare is over a hundred and fifty pounds.'

'Oh well,' Rita said with a pout. 'As far as I am concerned, I might as well spend the money Arthur left me one way as another. After all, he did tell me that I was to spend it any way I liked, and put a recommendation into his will that I was to have as good a time as was possible for a woman alone. I'd have no hesitation at all in going to America, and seeing Niagara Falls, and the Statue of Liberty and all that, only I'm not really sure that I'd enjoy it on my own. What do you think, Mathew?'

'I don't know,' Mathew said, mopping his brow.

'Well? Would you enjoy going there all alone?' Rita challenged.

'I don't know,' Mathew repeated. 'I have never considered taking such a step.'

'Well, consider it now!' Rita said. 'Wouldn't you be lonely going off to America all alone?'

'But who said I was going?' Mathew asked. He was frankly bewildered by this turn the conversation had taken. In courtesy towards Rita, he felt obliged to give the prospect some consideration.

'I don't know anybody in America,' he said at last.

'But if you went there with a friend, what then?' she asked, leaning forward towards him.

'Since there isn't any question of my going, I don't see the point of all this discussion.' Mathew was becoming unbearably hot.

'Do have another cup of tea, Mat?' Rita asked, as she reached for and took his cup. 'Will I pour away the dregs?'

'Don't bother,' Mathew said listlessly.

But Rita looked into the cup and gave a little screech.

'There's a fly in your cup,' she said, and she spilled the cold slop out on the grass. The fly was not quite dead though, and feeling the firm ground under its feet, it shook the tea leaves from its wings and, crawling up onto a blade of grass, rubbed its forefeet together exactly as if clapping at its release. Alas, the celebration was premature, for Pete had spotted the fly. And Pete made a snap at it. In a desperate effort to save the fly Mathew aimed a kick at Pete's rump, but fat and all as Pete was, he was quicker than Mathew and Mathew missed. The fly went down Pete's gullet.

'Why didn't you take it out on a spoon?' he demanded of Rita. 'You could have put it down somewhere safe, where that damned dog wouldn't have got it.'

'Who are you talking about?' Rita was genuinely bewildered.

'That fly,' Mathew said.

Rita stared at him.

'But flies are a nuisance, Mathew. They get into the jam and into the honey – they get into everything. And if they land on meat they lay eggs and –'

Mathew's stomach turned upside down.

'Please!' he cried. 'Please,' and to settle his stomach he stared up into the sky, that was so blue and cool and remote.

'Mathew, you weren't listening to me a minute ago when I was talking about America,' Rita said. 'Wouldn't it be fun if we were both there at the same time, or better still if we went on the same ship? You may not know it, but you are very good company. And so efficient! You'd see to everything. You'd make such a success of the trip. Not like poor little me! I am no use at all outside my own little nest. I'd get lost within two seconds of walking down the gangplank.'

'I'd say you'd make out alright anywhere you'd go,' Mathew said, so stoutly, and so sure of what he was saying, Rita took another tack.

'Did I ever tell you about a cousin of mine who went over there, once? I didn't? Well let me tell you, Mathew, she met her Fate on board the ship.'

'What do you mean by that?' Matthew asked, roused at last to a small degree of interest.

'Oh Mathew! You are so funny! Did you never hear that old expression? It means she met the man Destiny had laid out for her to marry. As a matter of fact, they were married as soon as the ship docked.' Then, seeing by his face that Mathew still didn't appear to get her meaning, Rita threw back her head and laughed so loudly the tea cups rattled in their saucers. 'You are so innocent, my pet,' she said. But she wagged her finger at him. 'At least you pretend to be innocent, you cunning old fox!

She meant to be flattering, and that is the way Mathew would have taken her remarks, if only Pete hadn't started to bark again for no good reason that Mathew could see. Rita grabbed him up again and hugged him tight.

'He thinks I'm upset about something. Poor Pete! He wants to show he's here to protect me. He's a marvellous watch dog. Put him to the test, Mathew, if you don't believe me. Pretend to hit me! Go on. Please do. Just pretend. You'll see the state he'll get himself into, poor fellow. He'll bark his head off. You'll die laughing. Go on! Hit me. It's only make-believe!'

But Mathew was too hot for playing games of any kind. Anyway, Pete must have been too hot in Rita's arms because he was struggling to free his head, and Mathew thought the dog only wanted to reach out and lick him – lick his face – with its big, fat tongue that was disgustingly like a greasy slice of ham. He rapidly returned his gaze to the blue sky over them all, and stared up into it as hard as he could stare.

'Don't you think it's too hot to hold that dog in your arms?' he asked at last, when Pete began to pant.

'Too hot to cuddle my Petey? Nonsense!' Rita put a plump white hand on the old dog's fat, white belly, and she began to roll its belly round and round like a ball. 'I told you what Arthur said to me in the last moments before he left me.' She leant forward. 'Oh, Mathew, I do wish you had known Arthur. You two would have taken to each other on sight. But now it's too late. Poor Arthur!'

A tear, only one tear, ran down her face, but Mathew hoped that would be all.

'Arthur is happy wherever he is, Rita,' he said hastily. 'He is at peace. There's no reason to feel too sorry for him.' Mathew was hot and tired, but he always endeavoured to be honest. He did feel that Arthur had gone to a Better Place. At worst he was under the sod, his eyeballs stopped with clay. But when at that moment Pete took a notion and awkwardly jumped from Rita's lap on to Mathew's knees, that were tightly pressed together, and made a really determined effort to lick his face, Mathew, who put out his hand to fend off the dog, could feel its internal organs working inside the dog's baggy belly, and he thought he'd throw up.

'Get down! Get down!' he cried, perhaps too roughly, because Pete looked deeply hurt.

'Why Mathew!' Rita exclaimed. 'I'm beginning to think you don't like poor old Pete.'

'I don't dislike him,' Mathew said.

'That's not the point,' Rita said, gathering the dog up into her arms again. Then she stood up and went over and sat on one of the stone steps leading into the house. 'Come over here, Mathew,' she said. 'It's much nicer sitting here than on those deck chairs.'

'No, thank you,' Mathew said. He never felt safe in a deck chair, but he certainly didn't feel like sitting on a hot stone. There was a short silence, after which Rita suggested clearing away the tea things. Could she never sit still for a second? 'Let's leave them until later,' he said.

'What if it rains?' she asked, and held her hand palm upwards to the cloudless heavens.

'It won't rain,' Mathew said, without needing to raise his eyes. No such luck, he thought. Cool, sweet rain was a long way from falling on them. 'It won't rain,' he said again, and then, rather than try to think of anything else to say, he had an insane desire to go on repeating himself like a gramophone record with a crack in it.

At that moment he only wanted one thing from life and that was to be left alone to sit still, with his eyes closed, and not have to say a another word until he felt good and like it! And it occurred to him that perhaps if they were married – Rita and him – they would not have to keep talking all the time. If they were married she surely wouldn't be hurt if he wanted to be silent now and then? Wasn't it only before marriage one had to be over-polite? Marriage would surely allow for an occasional slump, even in an uncomfortable deck-chair?

As he turned over these thoughts in his mind, Mathew noticed that Rita had put out her hand to tweak Pete's ear. Pete, with a frantic wriggle, got off her lap to lay himself out flat on the grass. And Mathew put himself another question. Could he be sure that Rita felt the same as him, about marriage? He would like to have asked her there and then, point blank, how she felt about it, but he warned himself that such enquiries might compromise him, so he just stole a look at her from under his burning eyelids. She had reached out again and tweaked Pete's ear.

'Isn't he an old dote?' she said. 'He sleeps on the foot of my bed. Did you know that, Mathew?'

He didn't, but he might have guessed, Mathew thought.

'Why don't you let the poor brute sleep now?' he said irritably.

'Why would he want to sleep in the middle of a lovely hot summer afternoon?' Rita asked, and she stood up as if to come over closer to Mathew himself.

'The butter is melting,' Mathew said. 'I think maybe you should take it into the house.'

'True for you,' Rita said. 'Let's clear the table while we're at it. Give me a hand, Mat,' she said, as she herself took up the butter to go inside. Pete got up too and waddled after her. But Mathew sat tight. It was getting hotter instead of cooler as the afternoon wore on. He looked at poor Pete's fat rump disappearing into the house. Pete was no pup. Mathew felt sorry for Pete. But when he looked at the step where Pete had sprawled a short time before he saw that the stone was still wet with the grease marks left by Pete's lolling tongue, and all of a sudden he knew he'd be sick if he didn't get away from the sight of them. The fit of nausea that had been coming on for some time was about to peak. He'd have to get away, alone somewhere, and fight off the attack. The sky was no longer blue. His eyes must have become affected by the heat. Now, not only the sky but the grass and even the trees in the garden farther down the street, were all the one colour, a horrible brownish hue like in an old fashioned sepia photograph, that would fade into nothingness if exposed any longer to this sun. His head began to spin. He didn't dare call out for help, although he could scarcely make his way to the door. If Rita thought he was sick, she would want him to take something, she'd want to rub his forehead; make him lie down. The thought of swallowing anything made his stomach do another somersault. The thought of lying down on that awful plush sofa appalled him. The dog was on it the first night he came to the house. It smelled of dog.

Mathew ran. He ran through the house, without Rita hearing him, because she was talking to Pete and when he got out into the road, he crossed to the shady side. Immediately he felt cool again. Immediately he could see better. The sky regained its blue. The trees got back their green. And the railings along which he ran his hand were wonderfully cold.

When he reached his lodgings, Mathew, who couldn't wait to forage in his pocket for his keys, never felt so grateful for anything as for the clear clarion of the bell that sent a single peal and no more through the blessedly silent house, creating no echo. He appreciated the distant manner of the landlady when she opened the door. He liked the chilliness of the house. And when he repaired to his room, he liked the cold white glaze on the counterpane and the cold feel of it as he turned it back and lay down. And just as he had not thought about marriage for many a day, he realised that he had never thought about death either. He thought of it now, though. And the coldness and darkness of the grave didn't seem as bad as it once had seemed. It had its own appeal, like the shade of a tree on a stifling day. Life itself at that moment seemed as hot and pulsing as marriage. Sweat broke out again on Mathew's face.

He hoped, naturally, that he had a certain way to go yet before death's green shadow reached out over him, but meanwhile he told himself that he had better steer clear of the Rita Cooligans of this life, who could expect incessant chat all day long – and God knows how long into the night as well! A husband wouldn't be enough for Rita. She'd want to keep that smelly dog as well – sleeping on the foot of their bed. Mathew wouldn't be any use to a woman like Rita. To begin with, his feet were always icy, and he never minded it. In fact, in summer he often slept with his feet sticking out from under the covers. No. Marriage was not for him.

Late that night, however, when he lay between the sheets, Mathew remembered the girl on the poster with the blue tam, and the slender legs and the golden hair blown across her face in the breeze. Perhaps if he had met a girl like that in real life, a girl made of flesh and blood, instead of paper pasted to a board, he might have found marriage sweet and fragrant. But she had cycled away and left him. He could never see her again. Perhaps there were marriages in which people asked love to be no warmer than it ought to be, but he had not been one of the lucky ones. Death was the next step, for him, and as he was dropping off to sleep, he thought of stepping through green cemetery grass, and across cold grave-slabs. In his last wakeful moment Mathew looked up at the moon that was in its first quarter. It could be called gold no doubt, but it was the strange greenish gold of a young, young moon.

Say Could That Lad Be I?

This is my father's story. It isn't mine at all. I wrote it down one night so soon after hearing him tell it, I remembered every word. My father is not a man to bother writing a thing down, unless a message to pin on the stable door for the cow-man or the boy that feeds the dogs. He's not exactly a talking man either, unless about horses. Most of his yarning goes on in his head while he's walking the Meath fields, or leaning over the gate of a paddock. When I think of him, I think of him as I so often saw him, walking green fields dusty with buttercups, stopping only to stare at his prize cattle cropping the rich grass, or to scotch a thistle with a blade he had fitted to the butt of his walking-stick. His eyes were always quick to see the weeds that seemed to spring up overnight, and which, if left uncut, self-sowed themselves and multiplied seven times seven. In Meath a man must restrain the land, or else it would strangle him. But in Roscommon, where he was born, the fields were thin and the grass wiry and sparse. There, poverty had the dignity of a lost cause well fought. When my father talked of his bare-footed boyhood in blue Roscommon, it seemed very far away to me, as if he was a different person from the boy he talked about.

I think he himself must have found it hard at times to believe that he was once that boy – as hard as that boy would have found it to believe that he would one day be this quiet man who would not choose to leap over a wall if there was a gate or a stile, and who, if he went out in the evening-time, would go out only, as the poet says, to stand and stare.

But if I found it hard to imagine the lad he remembered was him, this story is his all the same, and not mine. It is his, even in the way one word goes before another.

'Did I ever tell you about a dog I had?' he asked me one day, 'a dog by the name of White Prince? He was the wonderfullest dog in the world. He was a cross between a wire-haired terrier and a blood-hound, and he was pure white, with the hair bristling on him like a hedgehog when he smelled a fight. A dog was no good to a fellow in those days if it wasn't a fighting dog. That was all we kept dogs for: to set them on one another. Every fellow in the village had a dog. And the fellow that had a dog to beat all the other dogs was a fellow that was looked up to the length and breadth of Roscommon. I used to have great dogs. But White Prince was about the best I ever had. I was very proud of him and I took him with me everywhere. On Saturdays I used to be sent over to my grandmother's to do the shopping for her in her own village that was a lot bigger than our village. My grandmother lived seven miles away, but by going over the fields as I did that was nothing. Not in those days! And naturally I brought White Prince along with me. We set off, the two of us, the dog and me, with me whistling, and kicking at sods of dry grass that were thrown up by the hooves of an old mare that was always breaking loose and clattering over anyone and everyone's few acres, and the dog running along in front of me barking for joy. I was glad I had him along with me for company, although I knew my grandmother hated the sight of him. Yes – well I knew it.

We got to my grandmother's house about two o'clock in the afternoon. It was drawing in towards winter and the days were getting short, so although it was only two o'clock the night was beginning to show in the sky. My grandmother was sitting on the side of her old settle bed, and she said she was sitting there for two hours waiting for me. "Take care would you think of bringing that blaggard of a dog into the village with you," she said, knowing he'd fight every dog in the village and that he wouldn't come home till he did. Nor me neither. "And take care would you think of leaving him here," she added.

I didn't know what to do. I thought things over for maybe a minute, and I decided that perhaps it was just as well not to bring my brave fighter into a village that was strange to him. I called him into the house and waited till my grandmother got up and went over to the dresser to take down her knitting. Then I went out quickly, stopping the dog from coming after me by blocking the door with the butt of my boot. When I was outside and the door shut I drew down the hasp. There used to be a hasp on the outside of the doors of most houses in those parts then and when it was caught down no one who was inside could get out. It seems queer, now I come to think of it, but then it seemed the most natural thing in the world. When I put down the hasp my grandmother and the dog were locked inside, and my mind was at rest on one score anyway. My grandmother was a kind woman at heart, and even if that was not the case, she was feeble, and she wouldn't be fit to lift a hand to the dog. There was only one thing she would do to him if she could, and that was the one thing I made sure she couldn't do: let him out and stray him on me.

I went down the pebbly lane, jingling the coins in my trouser pocket, and feeling a very big fellow, when all was said and done. But I was only half-way down the lane, when I heard a shattering noise behind me, and I looked around in time to see my fighting dog come leaping into the air through a gaping hole he'd made for himself in my grandmother's window. He glittered all over with sparkles of broken glass, and behind him on the sill a pot of red geraniums was reeling around like a drunk. I didn't wait to see if the pot fell, but went running down the lane, with White Prince after me, and now he was barking and yelping and snapping at my heels with his pride and his joy and his devilment. The more the dog ran the more excited he got. But the more I ran the more frightened I got. It was only when I came in sight of the village I stopped running and sat down on a stile, and took out the silver shilling my grandmother had given me and the six heavy coppers. Fast and all as I had run I hadn't lost the money. I looked at it for a long time and I felt a bit better. I felt some of the importance creeping back into me that I'd felt when I set out from the door after putting down the hasp. I started to plan in my mind the way I'd ask for my messages in the shops, but when I tried to remember what I was to buy I couldn't for the life of me remember. And I was afraid to go back and ask my grandmother to tell me again.

I'd get her tea and sugar anyway, I decided, and a loaf of bread, and if there was any money left, I'd get her a piece of bacon.

She'd be so mad about the broken window she wouldn't open the parcel till I'd be gone home. But I was sorry I reminded myself of the broken window, because the thought of it gave me a queer feeling. I looked around at the dog, thinking to give him a kick by way of thanks for all the trouble he'd got me into, but he was sitting in the middle of the road looking up at me, with his head cocked to one side and one ear up and the other ear down and I hadn't the heart to touch him. I couldn't think to do anything more than give him a whistle to get up and come along with me. And after that the two of us made for the main street of the village, trotting along together as great pals as ever we were.

It was half-dark by that time and the lamps were being lit in the shop windows. In every shop I could see shop-boys kneeling into the window spaces to trim the wicks of the lamps and in some shops they'd already touched a match to the wick and were putting down the globe over the flame. The lamps in the shop windows were hanging-lamps, and after they were lit they swung back and forth for a few minutes, sending big unnatural shadows of the shop-boys out over the footpath, in a way that would make you scared to look at them. I looked into the shops instead, where the lamps were fastened to the walls and their yellow light was steady. The crinkly tin reflectors behind them reminded me of our kitchen at home.

I went into the biggest shop in the street, where they sold drapery on one side, and, on the other side, tea and sugar and bread, and bullseyes in jars – a thing I never saw anywhere else but there. The window on that side was filled with plates of raisins and plates of flour, and plates of rice and plates of prunes. The window on the drapery side was filled with ladies' bonnets and caps, and yards of lace and coloured tape and strings of bootlaces in black and brown. I liked doing messages in this shop. We hadn't any as big as it in our village. I liked looking into the glass cases, and I liked looking at the big lamps as long as they were still and their shadows not flying about. Most of all I liked looking at the big ball of twine inside a tin canister with a hole in it, and listening to the whirl and spin of the twine every time a shop-boy gave it a tug and drew out enough to tie up a parcel. I liked the noise of the money, too, rattling about in a drawer under the counter, when the drawer was pulled out to give someone change.

I was so happy that evening looking around me and taking notice of everything, I didn't heed what my brave fighter was doing. The last I'd seen of him he was only smelling around, doing no harm to anyone and as long as no other dog came into the shop, I felt it safe enough to let him smell around as much as he liked. But, as I was leaning on the counter watching the boy totting up the price of my messages, I felt something brush past my leg, and what did I see but the white stump of the dog's tail disappearing under the counter. There was a space between two of the counters so the shop-boys could get in and out if they wanted, but there was a board across the opening, and they had to lift up that board going in or going out. The board was to keep out people that had no business behind the counter, but you'd never know there was a passage underneath, if you didn't happen to look close. White Prince wasn't one to miss much though, I can tell you, and he didn't miss that passage between the counters. He went inside, and I held my breath.

He was very quiet for a while. Then all of a sudden one of the boys bent down to pick up a penny he'd let drop, and he must have seen the white stump of a tail wagging away in the darkness under the shelves, because he let a yell out of him, and started ordering the poor dog out, stamping his feet at him and waving a sweeping brush that he'd grabbed up in a fit of rage. I don't know what the poor dog was doing, but whatever it was the shop-boy must have thought it was something he shouldn't be doing. And to make matters worse the shop-boy that was yelling at him to get out was standing up against the counter and blocking the way all the time he was yelling. So I suppose the poor dog got confused. I suppose he was sure and certain that fellow would kill him with the big sweeping brush if he didn't get out quick somehow. You never know what an animal is thinking, but they have very clever ideas. When White Prince saw there was no regular way out I suppose he started planning on getting out some irregular way. I suppose he said to himself if a trick was worth doing once it was worth doing twice. Anyway, however it was with the dog in his own mind, the next thing I saw was my flashing fighter rising up in the air and leaping into the window, knocking the bonnets to right and left and slapping up against the glass with a crash. Then there was a sound of splintering that was ten times worse than the one I'd heard in the lane back at my grandmother's, and down came a ten-times heavier shower of splinters as White Prince went flying into the street with his four paws stretched out still under him and streamers of lace and ribbon and tapes trailing after him into the street outside. I was struck cold with fright. I couldn't lift up a foot from the floor, much less get out of the shop. I thought as true as God I'd be put in prison for life. The shop was in an uproar, everyone running out and shouting and holding up their hands and whistling for the dog to come back, with one breath, and with another calling God to witness what they'd do to him if he did! Then everyone ran out into the street, shading their eyes with their hands and peering into the blackness to see which way the dog had gone, although it was easy to see the way he went, with the stream of muddy tapes and bonnet-strings he'd left behind him. Ribbons and tapes stretched half-way up the street, and maybe further, only it wasn't bright enough to see. Then the shop-boys started after him. The shopkeeper himself was fit to be tied. He divided his time between shaking his fist into the dark and running over to the window and pushing bonnets back through the hole in the glass.

There was a terrible lot of talk, I needn't tell you. Everyone was asking everyone else how much the cost of new glass would be. And the women were asking if the things that were muddy would be sold off cheap. I was alone in the shop but I could hear the talk outside in the street through the hole in the window. I'd have run off like the dog, if I had got my change, but I'd have thought it as bad to go back to my grandmother without that as I'd think it to go to prison with the dog. So I stood waiting in the shop, and cursed White Prince and planned what I'd do to him when I got him. But when I thought of the big bullies of shop-boys that were chasing after him at that minute, I got very sorry for him. And at the thought that if they caught him I might never see him again, I made up my mind that if only they'd come back and give me my change I'd go looking for him myself and that if I found him I wouldn't hurt a hair on his head.

I was standing in the shop for a long while, because the shopkeeper got a hammer and a fistful of nails and he was nailing boards over the broken window. Then when he came in at last he took up a piece of paper and a pen and began to write a notice. But he found the pen-work hard going and catching sight of me he said I looked as if I was at school long enough to be able to write. "Write down BUSINESS AS USUAL," he said. I am glad to say just then one of the shop-boys, that had gone after the dog, came back, and took the pen out of my hand and wrote it himself, although he was panting fit to burst his ribs. If only I'd had my chance that would have been the time for me to make off, when the fellow was winded, but I hadn't got it. I was glad to see though that he hadn't forgotten all about my change. "I'll have it for you in a tick," he said, and sure enough he gave it to me. When I counted it out and saw it was right I started for the street. But before I got to the door, the shop-keeper called me back. "Which road are you taking out of the town, young lad?" he asked. I went stiff with fright. I thought they'd found out the dog was my dog. But no! "Whichever way you're going," he said, "let you keep an eye out for that tinker of a dog. I'll give you sixpence if you come back with him."

"All right, sir," I said, and I was just going to go out of the door when he came after me again and insisted on escorting me into the street. "The cur was all white, but for an odd spot of black here and there on him," he said.

"He was pure white, sir," I said politely. "There was no black on him at all."

"Is that so?" said the man. "You've a good pair of eyes." He looked around at the crowd. "That information is worth something I suppose," he said, thinking maybe to encourage others to turn informer. "That information is worth at least a bag of sweets, I think," he said, and he went back inside the shop and I had to wait while he took down the jar of bullseyes and shook them into a big paper bag with a mitred mouth on it. He filled the bag so full it wouldn't close in the end. He had to swing it round and round, till it had two little paper ears sticking up on it. But the ears made me think of the way the dog cocked his ear when we stopped on our way into the village, and I wished I hadn't brought him with me at all. I took hold of the bag of sweets though, and I pelted off down the road towards my grandmother's, and I can tell you it was no snail's pace I went, at least until I was out of the village and back in the decent dark of the country road. I slowed down then because according as the road between me and the shop was growing longer the thought of the broken window of the shop was getting fainter, but according as it got shorter between me and my grandmother's house the thought of her broken window was getting stronger. But I was glad the dog had gone off with himself because it would have ruined everything if he'd come running up to me wagging his tail before I got out of the village. If he did there wouldn't be one in it that wouldn't know he was my dog, and there wouldn't be one in the place wouldn't be after me as well as after him I'd have had no chance at all against so many, and some of them maybe with bicycles. I hope he went home, I said to myself. I hope he didn't get himself lost.

I didn't need to worry. When I came out into the open country, what did I hear in the dark ahead of me but a growl and after that I heard a sort of scuffling on the gravelly road, and then more growling – and snarling. I wasn't long telling that the loudest snarl of all the snarls was the snarl of White Prince. Then I caught sight of him – shining bright against the black hedge. He was up on a rise of the bank, and there was a half-circle of dogs around him and he was snarling and baring his teeth at them. Not one of those other dogs would dare go an inch nearer to him, but not one of them would draw back an inch from him either. Then White Prince must have heard my footsteps, because he took courage, and giving a fiercer snarl than any before, he put his teeth into something that was lying on the grass beside him, and made off down the road, with all the other dogs after him barking fit to wake the dead. But I remember thinking, too, that as far as I was concerned they could wake every corpse that ever was planted, as long as they didn't draw down the living on me. I looked back in the direction of the village. There was nothing to be seen of it only a light here and a light there winking through the trees. So I ran after the dogs and I caught up with them in a bit. White Prince had stopped again on top of another bank and left down his precious load, whatever it was. But the half-circle of mangy curs was around him again in no time now and the poor dog gave me a look as much as to say, "What are you standing there for? Beat off these devils of dogs, will you, and come and look at what I have here!" I saw it was high time to put a stop to things as they were, and I took up a stick and began to beat off them dogs. It was no easy job, but I drove them off one by one until in the end there was only a lanky yellow cur left. But he was as hard to shake off as the whole pack. Forty times he slunk off and forty times he slunk back, till at last I threw the stick at him and gave him a crack on the skull. At that he let out a yell at the scudding clouds and off with him to wherever he came from.

"Come on now, you!" I said to White Prince, and I set off again for my grandmother's house, having forgotten he had been carrying something. But after a while I began to think it strange that he wasn't frisking along in front of me, and when I looked around there was the poor dog, staggering under the weight of whatever it was that he had hanging out of his jaws.

"What have you got, you blaggard?" I said, and at that he dropped the parcel down at my feet. What do you think it was? A leg of mutton! White Prince stared up at me. His little bright eyes were glinting, and his tail was wagging like a bush in the wind.

I was ready to kill him there and then for the robber and thief he was, when all of a sudden I remembered how mad my grandmother would be waiting for me, and I remembered, too, that she might still be hasped into the house, and that would make her ten times madder. I got an idea.

"Good dog!" I said, patting him on the head, and taking the parcel from him. "Come on!" I shouted, leaping over the hedge and into the fields with the groceries under one arm and the leg of mutton under the other.

May God forgive me, I washed that leg of mutton in a stream of clear spring water, and before my grandmother had time to know I was back at all I had the leg of mutton planted down on the kitchen table. Then I ran out again to where my white fighter was waiting for me, and half a hundred stars as well that had slipped out without my noticing them. We went back home, the two of us over the fields again, and the dog ran along in front of me, barking and wagging his tail again, as if nothing at all had happened. And if that dog was as happy as me, he had no conscience either.'

A Fable

She was the most beautiful woman they had ever seen and so they hated her. The women feared that she would dim their own glory, and the men disliked her because they felt she was inaccessible, even to the strongest and most fierce of them. The women need not have feared, for the orchid does not take from the beauty of the bluebell. The men need not have disliked her because they could not possess her body, for had they been wiser men than they were they would have realised that a woman of such incandescent beauty belonged to every eye that looked on her. So the beauty of Helen had belonged to every man in Greece, and Menelaus had not greater desire to drag her back from Troy across the coiling waters than had the least man among the men of Greece, hammering the curved boards, banging the singing rivets. But the men in the village where this beauty came to live were not wise men, nor were they generous, nor were they kind.

There is no need to try to describe her face, for faces such as hers cannot be described, except by some idea like the idea we have been given of the face of Helen by the man who said that it launched a thousand ships. You may say of her, if you wish, that she was like a bough of apricot blossom. She came to the village quietly one evening after dusk, to live in the house of her fathers that had been shut up for nearly a generation. She came without warning, and that in itself was a mark against her with the people of the countryside. The first they saw of her was on the top of a long and insecure ladder climbing up on to the roof of her house and poking at the lichen cushions on the tiles with a little cane. She was wearing trousers like a man and the lines of her lovely body were seen in silhouette against the blue breast of the sky. Her face was framed in the gold lace of her hair. She was beautiful every hour of the day, but in the early sunlight she was perhaps most beautiful, and the villagers got the full impact of her star-shining beauty upon their shrinking and unprepared eyes. They all saw her. The demesne was on a hilly ridge of the valley and so they all saw her. They felt a shock run through their bodies at the sight of her. They did their work badly all that day, as men and women do who work after the gusts of a great emotion have subsided and left an inexpressible lassitude of spirit and of body.

Next day they were themselves again, with energy to satisfy their curiosity about the newcomer. There was not much to be found out except that she intended to live in the old house permanently. She was reticent, but that was quickly translated into ungracious. She was going to have the house redecorated. That meant, to the minds of the people in the valley, that she was a spendthrift. They further decided that, as like as not, she would give big parties when the house was ready and that they would be attended by young and very gay people. That meant that she was fast. And so the legend grew that this exquisite creature was hateful in mind and heart. It was indeed a pity that she did not have one small flaw, even one. If one little ivory shell of her teeth were only turned or crooked they might have found her more human. If once in a while, even once, in the April of every year when the chemists in the valley put sarsaparilla in their windows, if, even then, she had one spot on her skin, they would not have been so grudging of praise whenever she passed them on the roads. But not one single flaw had she, and as she cantered over the fields the wind and rain could only blush and never redden her cheeks; they could cluster and tangle, but never untidy her hair.

Every day she rode along the roads, and if she sometimes shyly smiled at any of the people she met on the wayside they hurried home to tell their friends how she had sneered at them. Her own friends came from the city, and the windows in the big house on the hill were lit all night and patterned over with the passing and repassing of human figures. Presumably her friends were fond of her, although when their cars came careering into the market square, and they wanted to know the way to her house, they were not always careful, or just, in the description they gave of her in order to show who they meant and whose home they sought. Some of these friends were very pretty, too. The postmistress who lived just in the square, and who always rushed out into the dusty road to tell the drivers the way, before the wife of the haberdasher across the street could open her door to get out, gave it as her opinion that there was one very handsome girl among her friends. This girl was dark-haired with soft peach-skin cheeks. She had a clear-cut profile, and she would have been perfect only for a small cast in her left eye. The whole village was interested in the beautiful girl with the cast in her eye. When the people saw her at the Meet of the Harriers they were delighted with her. 'The poor girl. It was such a pity about her eye, because she was so beautiful.' They stood around the Town Hall to watch the riders and the hounds pass by, into the copse behind the demesne. They noticed with satisfaction that there were more gentlemen talking to her than talked to any other woman, and that there was always one ready to slip from his mount and do her a service; light her cigarette, tighten her girthstrap, or pick up her fallen whip. There was one other girl who was very popular, and she also was a guest from the big house. The gentlemen from the surrounding county seemed to be very attentive to her also. And she was very pretty too. As the postmistress said, she would have been nicer than the dark girl if only her nose were not a little bit too long. And she had a lovely expression. On that they were all agreed. In fact it was doubtful whether those who were mounted or those who were watching their performances had the greater enjoyment that morning at the first Meet of the year. The enjoyment of the villagers, and perhaps that of an odd person here and there among the members of the Hunt, was increased by an added pleasure later in the day, when the beautiful owner of the big house on the hill was forced to dismount at one point of the road and open a gate for herself. There had seemed to be no one on the spot at the moment, or no one was looking her way. No one looking her way I think. When she was on the ground and pulling off her yellow string gloves to open the wire knot that served as a lock, one or two of the gentlemen rode up and were about to help her, but she had opened the gate and was already leading the mare through. It did not seem worth while to knot up the wire for her, anyway she was nearly finished doing it up for herself. What extraordinary hands she had, like the unbelievable unflawed plaster hands of the draper's dummies! And watching the swiftly moving hands the men thought of the hands of wives and sweethearts that they had kissed and caressed, and strangely enough those hands were either red or slightly chapped or indeed definitely stubby.

To tell the truth, the perfection of this fabulously beautiful girl was really beginning to get on the nerves of the whole neighbourhood. If only she had managed to look tired after those energetic rides across country the spell might have been broken earlier than it was, but when she looked tired her eyes were deeper than the pools of the bog, and the blue veins that faintly beat in her forehead made her skin more like porcelain than ever. The veins were like the blue mark of the potter's underglaze. She looked more lovely than ever, but of course by this time what had unconsciously irritated everyone was the one thing that they would not admit to exist. In short, before very long, no one for miles away from the big house was aware that a face such as only forms in flesh once every hundred years had come to gaze on, and be gazed upon by, them.

Then one day when the Hunt was once more meeting at the square and the beautiful girl came riding down the hilly lawn from her house, an accident occurred. It was very slight, but it had a deep effect on the hearts and minds of the people who witnessed it. She had ridden down the hill, and those who had seen her coming through the branching trees were preparing to stare at her insolently as she sailed over the ditch that divided her own demesne from the tree-shaded village street where the horses and riders, the hounds and the spectators, were gathered. She rose in the air and with sure feet the mare brought her forelegs clear of the thorny bank. It was, as usual, a clean and graceful jump, and no one was prepared for the unexpected way the high-hanging strand of bramble switched her face.

The branch of brier switched her face and its thorns tore into her flesh. With the force of the slashing twig she was thrown from her mount, and with the pain of its lashing sting she lay where she fell, silent, still, face-upwards in the grass-tangled ditch. Her eyes were closed like the eyes of an old-fashioned china doll, and her lashes lay flat on her cheeks in an adorably old-fashioned way. Her hair was spread around her seemingly sleeping face like a fine gold filigree fan, and some strands still clung upwards caught on the thorns of the undergrowth, taut wires of finely spun white gold.

Everyone in the street seemed to see the accident in its least details. And perhaps the momentousness of her beauty and the momentousness of it having come among them dawned on their slow and dull-eyed minds, for they acted with a dignity beyond the power of prophecy to foresee in their heavy faces one moment before this moment. They did not rush. They did not shout or scream. Slowly they came over towards the ditch where she lay, like figures in a play acting at the will of some artistic producer rather than at the catcall of their instinct to stare at blood.

For the blood that had crept into the scratches and weals on her face had come slowly too, but with more sinister advance from cut to cut, until on the pale white porcelain cheek there was a blood etching of the brier branch itself.

After the first moments of unnatural calm, the wonder in the eyes of the villagers gave place to a sudden pity in their hearts, and that gave way to the skill and strength of their limbs as they lifted her up on strong shoulders and, wordlessly, carried her back to her house on the hill.

All day the image of her face as they had last seen it stayed in the minds of those people, and the colours and contours of things habitually in their minds ran together all day long to make images of what they had seen in slightly different forms. So, when the postmistress pressed down the deckle-edged and bright red stamp upon a white vellum envelope, she shivered. For her mind had made a new image of the porcelain skin with the brier etching on the face of a girl so beautiful that the postmistress let her tears fall freely on an envelope that had cost more to the dozen than her own black blouse. And when the gardener at the convent was picking up a red lady-bug from the frail white petals of a winter cyclamen, he sighed and thought he had never seen a more beautiful thing in all this world and in all his life than this white cyclamen petal, and nothing more cruel or more frightening than this red-backed insect that he flung to the ground in disgust. For, although he did not know it himself, he was thinking of a face in a ditch. And the schoolmaster went to his bookcase that day and took down *Macbeth,* although he did not particularly like it, and could not say to save his soul why he wanted to read it again. But when he came to the description of Duncan's death, he surprised himself by exclaiming 'Ah . . . here it is!' as he drew a pencil mark along the famous lines that tell how Duncan's silver skin was laced with his golden blood. He left the book open at that page and took out a cambric handkerchief to wipe his glasses. And the draper's wife, who had wrung the neck of a pure white pullet and seen the jet of red spurt over the silken feathers, had said that life was very cruel. The whole village felt that life was very cruel, and so they lined themselves up as allies of its most pitiful victim.

For she was pitifully scarred. After staying in a shaded room for three weeks she had come out one day determined to ignore the markings on her skin. It happened – for life is full of unrelated coincidences – that she had long been threatening to go up on the roof and see, if she could, whether or not there was room for a skylight between the two chimneys on the east side of the library. And for the first time since her fall the people down in the streets saw her, and it might almost have been the first day that she came among them, for they paused to look up at her figure against the blue, and they said they had never seen anyone or anything more beautiful; and that she would be the most beautiful girl in the world if it were not for her scarred face. And the postmistress called a messenger boy and told him to go up to the big house and tell the mistress that the letter she had sent to be posted that morning, the letter to the doctor in Vienna, was not sufficiently stamped. It was none of her business of course, but she was sure that the young lady wouldn't want such an important letter to be understamped. It must be important. It was probably a letter about her face to some clever foreign doctor. As the boy went up the hill she watched the figure on the distant roof. She was curling around the chimney pots like a great cat; light, deft, lithe, sleek and lovely. Those were the words of the schoolmaster and not the postmistress, for he too was watching her. He wondered how she managed for books; his were old, of course, but at any rate he'd mention it to her house steward, would say to him that she was welcome to any of his, he could make out a list of them some night, or perhaps if she was passing the schoolhouse some day he could give the children transcription, or perhaps she'd come after school hours?. . . But no ... better when the children would be there, because it would not be right that the breath of shame should fan such a lovely creature. It was really too bad about her face, only for that . . .

Her face was worse than might be imagined from the nature of the accident, but there were two reasons for this: firstly, the force with which she rode against the lash of the thorn was so great that the skin was displaced and had to be sewn; secondly, fine porcelain cracks easier than delft, and shows the mark of its mending. But if the villagers had been unable to bear the beauty of her unscarred face they seemed to long for the sight of her now. If a farmer's lad delayed and dallied with his fork or harrow when he saw her coming to a closed gate it was not in order to humiliate her into opening it herself, but in order that she might be forced to alight and be nearer to him as he ran with well-timed speed to fumble the wire lock, and mumble his regrets at not being quicker. And if he did not get there in time he would have a little spray of violets or a soft showery branch of pussy willow in his hat, and he would pull it out and offer it to her as naturally as if she were his sweetheart and they had lain in the hay together. And that evening he would say to his mother that she was a very civil lady and that if it wasn't for that mark on her face she'd be the finest lady in the land. And his mother would ask how her cheek looked, and the boy would say there was no sign of blood on it now at all, but her skin was all puckered up. 'I know,' his mother would assure him, 'like the grooves in a carving dish.' 'See,' she would say, and take one down from the dresser and show him the way a branching rill was made in the china to let the gravy flow into one well. And he had nodded that it was exactly like that, but whether he meant the colour and smoothness of the skin or the scar on the skin he did not really indicate. And he would tell his mother how he had given her the flowers, and his mother would boast about it to the rest of the villagers, for they all loved her dearly and were glad to serve her. Were it not for the scar on her face, would she not be the most beautiful girl in all the land?

For two years she lived quietly in the valley, beloved by all those who dwelt in it with her. Then one day she got a letter from the doctor in Vienna (and, although it is not important, let it be recorded that it was insufficiently stamped) saying that he was of the opinion that by now an adequate length of time had been let lapse since the wounds had been made, and that the time had come when it would be safe and advisable to have new skin grafted over the scars. She told the people in the valley, and they were glad, and they lit candles for her safety in the chapel on the hill. They went to the station to see her off, and one little cripple boy threw white heather into the smoky little carriage of the train as it left the station, noisily and fussily. Her pale and serene face was pressed to the plateglass window to see the last of the kind but stupid folk, and they thought how beautiful she would be were it not for the unfortunate mark on her cheek.

All the time that she was away they kept candles lighted before the shrine of the Beautiful Virgin, who was indeed very beautiful and would be more so still were it not for the fact that the paint from her blue mantle had run a little and stained her face a rather dark colour. They prayed that the girl would not be hurt by the foreign nurses and the foreign doctor, and they prayed that she would not be scarred worse when she returned. But for her return to beauty and perfection they did not pray, because they did not believe that such a thing was possible, and furthermore they did not remember what she looked like when she was perfect, and still furthermore they had loved her as she was. So when, one day, and unexpected, she arrived at the little station and walked up the street, the people ran out of the shops and the children ran out of the schools, and her mare put her bay head over the wall of the demesne, and all with excited clamour welcomed her home. But, since as in all public demonstrations of this kind they spoke more to each other than to her, and looked almost exclusively at each other rather than at her, she had passed in her own gates and up to her own hall door, and had entered the house and been seen in silhouette against her bedroom blind by the crowd of kind and happy people, before anyone noticed whether or not she had been cured. They consulted each other; and none of them – not even the postmistress, not even the schoolmaster, not even the stationmaster and not even the harbourmaster (this was a purely honorary appointment in the inland valley) – had noticed whether or not the scars were healed and concealed. Somehow they thought that they were not, and they lulled themselves with this decision so that they were enabled to rest all through that summer night and rise refreshed the next morning. She was not on the roof that morning, but she rode courageously out over the ditch where she had fallen, and they were all so impressed by her spirit and bravery that, of course, they forgot to look at her face that day too. On the third day she sent a messenger down to the chandler for some candles for her dinner table, and the messenger returned to say there were no candles to be had in the village. That is absurd, she thought; but she could not remedy matters by saying so, and she merely sent the messenger to the church to borrow a few unblessed candles with the promise of returning a dozen for every one she borrowed. The clergy were disappointed to lose the opportunity of closing such a friendly, uncommercial, and profitable deal, but the fact was they had no candles. That really was absurd. She put on a very becoming hat and went down to the village. The first person she met was the postmistress, but the draper's wife came over with her daughter and the daughter's fiancé the chemist, before they had spoken two words. So there was quite a crowd there when she asked about the shortage of candles. They all agreed with her that it was a ridiculous state of affairs, but they could not suggest any reason for it. Suddenly the postmistress clapped her hands together, but they did not ask her what she had remembered, because they knew she would tell them. Before they had time to go away she was reminding them that there were no candles because there had been so many burned in the chapel for the last month. That explained the shortage of candles, but when the beautiful woman asked what they were burning all those candles for anyway, there was not one who could remember. They called over a farmer's boy, who was sneaking by at the moment behind a wagon of hay in order that they should not notice the big bunch of bluebells in his hat, and they asked him if he could remember why they had lit so many candles before the Virgin last month. And he said quite simply that they had lit them for the safety of the operation. The woman from the big house was grieved to hear that someone had been operated on in the village, but they assured her that no one in the village had been operated on at all. Then she suddenly remembered her own operation, and asked if it could possibly be that out of their kindness they had . . . But she didn't get time to finish, for, of course, they all remembered with a rush and began to tell her together. But they stopped as suddenly as they began, and stared into her face. She was cured. She was completely cured, and there was not the least trace of her scars. In fact her sufferings had made her an impossible bit more lovely. She was indeed the most beautiful woman they had ever looked upon. And they hurried away with brief excuses to tell their husbands and children, for it will be remembered that she had not been up on the roof this time, and they had not all seen her. And as they hurried along the streets they began to wonder if her manner was exactly the same . . . if her clothes were in as perfect a taste as they had been when she was going away. For the force of the unendurable quality of perfect beauty was working in their minds already. The farmer's boy got suddenly impatient with his sentimental bouquet and was about to throw it in the hedge when he pondered on all that had happened. As they went their various ways they all pondered on what had happened; and next minute they were coming back with their husbands and children to ask the beautiful woman to be their Harvest Queen in the autumn of the year. For just as the unendurable pain of her perfect beauty was entering the heart of these people there entered also the steel and iron of a faint suspicion, and it grew with every step they took towards her where she stood at the stone trough in the market square while her bay mare with the cream-coloured mane drank the sun-warm water. For these people who were stupid did not believe in beauty, and so they did not believe either that the operation was really successful. They believed that after a time the scars would show out through the new skin again. They believed this so firmly that they loved her more than ever before. And the girls with moles on their faces, and the men who had married women with double chins, were one in secretly pitying her as she stood there lovely as the water in which she was reflected. The gods were good to these stupid people, for some reason of their own, and permitted many of them before they died to have their vision without in any way spoiling the beauty of the beautiful woman.

For after many, many years had passed, and she had married and borne children and held her grandchildren in her arms, Time at last cracked the porcelain skin into the faint red lines of broken veins. And the gappy gums of men who were old when she was young who was now old muttered that they had lived to see the prophecies of their fathers come true, and that the brambly brier had shown out through the new skin after all.

But if they were stupid they had gained some grain of wisdom, and they said, before they put their arms into the outheld shrouds, that they didn't know why she had bothered to go away and have new skin grafted over the brambly briery patches on her cheeks; for, indeed, they said, she was more beautiful with than without them.

Miss Holland

The cat decided Miss Holland.

The minute she saw it, she decided to take the room. After all the house seemed comfortable, and the landlady looked clean and quite good natured, like a superior type of housekeeper.

Miss Holland was not accustomed to interviewing landladies. She was not adept at asking the kind of questions that would elicit facts necessary for finding out if a lodging-house would, or would not, suit her.

The landlady now confronting her on this doorstep had already shown her the room, told her the rent, the number of meals she could expect, and had further volunteered the extraordinary information that all the beds in her establishment had hair mattresses. These facts, however, had not greatly interested Miss Holland, who did not really mind what rent she paid as long as it was within her means, a matter she had not yet taken up with her solicitor since her father's estate was not yet out of probate, and who had never in her life had cause for curiosity as to what was put inside a mattress as long as the springs were good and it was well aired. She was not, of course, quite so foolish as to give voice to these thoughts, but she did wish she could think of something to say. She simply could not make up her mind about the room.

There were a lot of things which Miss Holland did not voice, except under her breath, or to herself. This was firstly because she was shy, but secondly because she never really fully formulated her thoughts at any time. The things that passed through her mind were for the most part vague wonderings and imaginings with little or no coherence. She would like to have

been the kind of person to whom things happened that gave
cause for the making of sound, quick decisions. But she was not
like that. She would like to be able to stay in this house because
the beds had mattresses filled with hair, or some other such
reason. But no, here she stood, on the doorstep, hesitating and
unsure because she wanted to feel something about the place, to
be vaguely attracted to it, without being pinned down as it were
to mere practicalities.

That was the way she used to feel about her old home – feel
vaguely that it was where she belonged. Often times, in the
evenings, if she'd taken a last stroll on the terrace, when she'd
come in again through the French door she used to draw a deep
breath of satisfaction at the sheer delight in the beauty
surrounding her. But on those evenings she always deliberately
avoided looking at the beautiful Alken prints or the terra cotta
vase she and her father had once brought home from Egypt,
because she never wanted to single out any one particular object
in that old house, in case she might find her attachment to it in-
terfering with the wonderful over-all feeling of love for the dear
old house itself, and its rambling old garden, and grounds. Even
when she'd pass through the hall on her way upstairs she often
took care to turn her head aside so as not to see the third
banister rail from the bottom on which as a child she had one
day surreptitiously carved her name, because it might interfere
with the vague feeling of familiarity and homeliness that was
nearly as important to her as the beauty of the place.

If I had married, she thought, I would never have wanted to
find out what I liked best about my husband, and in this way I'm
sure our love would always remain a wonderful mystery, binding
us together – we knew not why – forever! If, for instance, he was
a very dignified man, I would never admit to myself that I loved
him for that reason, because then I would never be able to bear
the sight of him eating an egg in the shell, in case a trickle of egg
yolk might run down his chin without his noticing. Even if he
were to wipe it off, with his serviette, his dignity would have been
impaired for an instant and a crack, only a little hair-crack, but
still a crack, might come in our love. And if he was very
handsome, the most handsome man in the world, I would never

admit that I loved him for his looks because of what might happen then to my love when he got old and maybe bald and maybe start to tell the same story twice when we'd have guests to dinner. It was much wiser to be vague about things.

Here however, the landlady broke in on Miss Holland's thoughts, believing perhaps that the rent was worrying her and that it was this she was considering with such a look of concentration on her face.

'Perhaps you'd like time to think the matter over, Miss Holland,' she said.

Miss Holland came down to earth and gave the woman a grateful smile. It was nice of her to have remembered her name. She herself had forgotten the landlady's name, having lost the bit of paper on which the agent had written it.

'Thank you. Yes, I'd like very much to think it over,' she said. 'And perhaps,' she added, 'talk it over with a friend,' hoping this was not a lie, because her friends lived in the country, except for a few who lived in another locality, not quite as far from the centre of the city. But although she'd said she'd go, Miss Holland did nor move. If only she had had the vaguest feeling about the place, a feeling of warmth for instance, she'd have taken the room there and then. The house was nice enough of its kind, and the locality was not too bad. She liked the colour of the door, which was yellow, but she was not going to let herself take one of the most important steps of her life because of a door.

So, she was about to shake hands with the landlady and say goodbye, when she saw the cat. It was a big marmalade tom, and he was coming towards her, running through the flower beds of the next door garden, pushing his way through the heavy pink and yellow antirrhinums. Then, leaping over a bar of railings that divided the two houses, he rubbed himself ingratiatingly against her leg. All at once she got an indescribable sensation of warmth and welcome, and her interview with Mrs Lewis – whose name at that instant came back to her – ceased to be an impersonal matter of shillings, pence and bedding. A new element pervaded the entire transaction. Even the yellow door reminded her vaguely of summer in Tuscany, as yellow often did, certainly if it inclined towards ochre, although this door was a lot brighter than ochre. Then too the pink antirrhinums in the garden next door seemed to make the whole day pink as a day in June ought to be by rights. This was a little game Miss Holland had about the months of the calendar. April for instance was decidedly blue and October was—

But here Mrs Lewis coughed and tapped with her foot on the ground, and Miss Holland realised her little reverie, though pleasurable to herself, would perhaps appear silly to others, and was certainly inappropriate at that moment, when Mrs Lewis was no doubt wishing she'd go if she was going to go, or stay if she was going to stay. She turned to shake hands and take her leave when, looking up again at the landlady, she was amazed at how familiar her face seemed. It was now a face she knew! And if she met Mrs Lewis in the street next day, or even next week, she'd recognise her at once and would nod to her as to an acquaintance and Mrs Lewis would nod back at her. They might stop and exchange a few words, Mrs Lewis asking her if she had got suited, and she in turn enquiring if Mrs Lewis had succeeded in letting the room. Deciding that she really couldn't face any more strange landladies, Miss Holland smiled at Mrs Lewis and said that, on second thoughts, she would not bother to consult a friend, she would make up her own mind and take the room. When could she send her luggage?

She could send her baggage any time she liked, Mrs Lewis said. She could come in that same evening if she wished.

It did suit Miss Holland to come that evening. She came by taxi and the taxi man carried in her three trunks, treating them with great care, perhaps because they were plastered all over with the labels of foreign spas and watering places and he could have thought people who travelled extensively abroad gave enormous tips. How wrong he was! Her dear father despised over-tipping. In all their travels he had never been too ill to attend to the bills himself and also take care of the tips. She had always stood aside while these awkward negotiations were going on. averting her head, but never failing, when they were concluded, to turn and smile at the porter or the waiter or the taxi driver, as the case might be, and thank the man, in English of course, hoping he understood the language.

Now on the steps of her new home, Miss Holland was slightly embarrassed as she asked the price of her taxi fare, in what sounded, even in her own ears, far too conversational a tone. When the man named his fare she gave him the nearest even sum to the uneven amount of the fare. Luckily the fare had worked out to an uneven figure. What would she have done had it not? Given him sixpence, she supposed? The difficult business was over however, and the taxi man was stomping off down the cement path to the gate and Mrs Lewis, who must have heard the taxi, opened the door before Miss Holland knocked.

'Why has the taxi driver gone off and left those trunks on the step?' the woman enquired and she looked angrily after the taxi that had swung around in a half-circle and sped away. 'We'll have to drag them into the hall somehow,' she said. And this they did, after which Miss Holland was shown up to her room. Going up the stairs Mrs Lewis put her *au fait* with the customs of the house. Supper would be at six-thirty. It would be cold meat this evening, but something hot the following night. Every second night, Mrs Lewis explained. Then she came back to the matter of the trunks. If Miss Holland wanted something out of one of her trunks that night, she'd better take it out now and lock the trunks, until Mrs Lewis could find someone to haul them up the stairs. It would want to be someone hefty. What she simply could not understand was why they had not been taken up by the taxi man. And when she mentioned the man, she looked angry again, which seemed stupid to Miss Holland, since he was gone. Mrs Lewis made it seem as if it were her fault!

Opening the door of Miss Holland's room, the landlady expressed the hope that everything was in order. She switched the light off and on, twice, to show the general efficiency of the boarding house, reminded Miss Holland she must put out the light when leaving the room, and then went out herself, deftly closing the door although the knob seemed to Miss Holland to be loose on its spindle.

Left alone, Miss Holland looked around the room. It was quite large, and not too dark. The wallpaper was inoffensive and the furniture was certainly well polished, and here and there the gloss of the polish gave back a reflection of the window and a splash of blue from the sky. Miss Holland laid her coat across the iron footrail of the bed. The white counterpane was spotless. Indeed, it had been laundered so many times, a fringe of tassels, that must once have been fat and bobbing, were now flattened almost to extinction! No, it could not be considered an ugly room. She went over to an armchair that was turned to face the fireplace although the grate was blocked with a sheet of tin, and she sank into the chair, resolving that later she'd turn it to face the window. Then suddenly her eye took in the mantelshelf over the fireplace. Oh but it was hideous! Hideous! It was cast-iron, all in one piece, but an attempt had been made to paint it white, and dust must have settled on it before the paint had fully dried, and a thick coat of dust and grime had stuck fast to it. It was rather revolting. Tired as she was, Miss Holland got to her feet again and turned the chair to face the window.

The view from the window was not bad. The back garden was not as big as the front garden and most of it was taken up with cabbages, but there were flowers in the other gardens that you could see into over the dividing walls. Below her window there was a small square of grass across which a clothes line was strung, but there were also deckchairs stacked against a shed. I may be given permission to sit out there on a hot day, she thought. Meanwhile it was nice to sit at the window and look out. Tomorrow, she thought, when her trunks were brought up, she would take out her treasures, the Alken print, (which she had kept out of the auction because the auctioneer said it was in bad condition, and might take from the price he'd get for the good ones) and her terra cotta vase, which she had refused to sell. Well, then the room would be more homely. She would look and see if she might not have some piece of silk to drape around the shade of the lamp and make its light less harsh. She might even have enough silk to make a drape for the mantelshelf, a kind of a runner that would conceal its ugliness. To estimate how much silk she'd need, she looked again at the fireplace. To her surprise, from a distance it didn't look so bad and the design was not unpleasing. It was a motif of roses, stylised, of course, but roses were her favourite flower. The only thing was that she felt sad to see those little roses, really not much more than buds, covered up with paint, paint which, moreover, was crusted with dust. She went over and traced the outline of one poor little rose in particular that looked smothered to death. Poor little prisoner! 'I wish I could let you out, little rosebud,' she whispered to it. And immediately she felt better about the fireplace. She would have turned the chair back to face it again, if the grate hadn't been blocked up. 'But now, little rosebud, it's almost time to go down to supper,' she said, and she went over to the dressingtable and began to take down her hair and put it up again neatly. Since she didn't have her trunks, she wouldn't be able to put on something fresh. But just then anyway she heard the hall door open and shut – several times in fact at very close intervals. And then she heard voices – presumably the voices of the other paying guests – in the room below her. There was also a rattle of crockery. Her room must be over the diningroom. With some surprise, but also with relief on account of not having her trunks, she realised that the others were evidently not changing either – not even freshing-up. If they had been working all day they were probably quite hungry. So was she! Giving a last pat to her hair, she went down, feeling, as she told herself, like a child on its first day at a new school, when the rest of the children, who were already acquainted with each other, always appeared to be leagued against a newcomer.

There were five people in the diningroom when Miss Holland entered, three girls and two men, and they were already seated. They had in fact started on their meal. They looked up when she came in, but they did not speak, and Miss Holland saw with surprise that Mrs Lewis was nowhere around to introduce her. A maid, who was not in uniform, and who had put a platter on the table, had flounced out the door as she herself was making her way in through it. After she closed the door behind her (that knob too seemed badly fitted), Miss Holland wondered if she had fancied it, or had the other guests been talking about her before she'd come down? They had the self-conscious look on their faces of people caught out having a joke at the expense of someone they hadn't expected to appear at that moment. They were probably speculating on what she'd look like, and how

they'd get on with her. Not that she minded! Not in the least. It
was a very understandable situation. She would have liked to tell
them so and put them at their ease, but they had begun to talk
to each other, talking all together too. A sure sign of embarrassment! She wondered if she might break in on the crisscross
of talk and ask if they didn't agree that it was like the first day at
school? Still standing at the door, she glanced around the table,
since none of them was taking any notice of her. And as she did,
second by second she felt it less and less like a first day at school.
In school, for one thing, they'd all be dressed alike – the girls she
meant, of course. Not the men. She nearly tittered, to think of
these men being dressed like the girls! They were such real men,
not like some of her cousins who would deceive anyone when
they played the female lead in Gilbert and Sullivan! And at
school they would all speak with more or less the same accent,
whereas here a girl they seemed to call Betty had such an odd
accent Miss Holland could scarcely understand a word she said,
even making allowances for the general noiseiness of the room.
They didn't even hold their knives and forks as she would.
Finally, and this was the really awful thing, if this had been a
school, some girl, a prefect usually, would – however imperiously
– have told her what to do and where to sit if she saw her still
standing. Just then however, the younger of the two men nodded
at a chair she had not noticed, which was vacant between him
and a girl called Cissie. She supposed it was intended for her, and
nodding her thanks to him she sat down. Then another of the
girls, whose name, if she caught it correctly, was Marge, shoved
over the platter towards her, although by now there was not
much left on it, Miss Holland tried to concentrate on her plate.
She had already taken a slice of bread, feeling awful as she
reached for it – though no one else seemed to mind reaching for
things – but when she tried to hold the slice of bread, it was so
thick she couldn't fold it, or break it either, and she had to take
up her knife and cut it like the others. As if it was meat or cheese!
   Meanwhile the meal progressed, and at last, when they had
demolished the food, the others put their elbows up on the table
and showed no sign of leaving. Miss Holland, who didn't think it
polite for her to leave either, took another stealthy look at them

all. The girl named Betty was prettier than the others, and the red jumper she was wearing became her with regard to colour, but Miss Holland wondered how a pretty girl could not see how much more tasteful handknit woollens were than machine-knit ones. And Marge's green dress was quite becoming to her, too, although it was so badly fitting it must have been an off the rack purchase. If she was, as it would seem, a working girl, Miss Holland found it hard to understand why she couldn't get the name of a good dressmaker – some dressmakers, if recommended by the right people, could work wonders with a figure like Marge's, which was far from perfect.

In spite of herself, and certainly in spite of their having taken so little notice of her, Miss Holland felt herself drawn to her table companions. She found herself making allowances for them. That red jumper was new at least, whereas her own jumper was not at all new, although she washed it frequently, and was always careful to dry it between two towels so it would not stretch. Then, almost irrelevantly it crossed her mind that she had seen only one towel on the towel-rail in her room, but she didn't worry about that, as she probably had some monogrammed towels in her trunk – the auctioneer having suggested their withdrawal from the sale. Yes. Newness, neatness, those were qualities that counted for something. The girl in the green readymade had sewn – no, pinned – a nice little collar to the neck of the dress. It was a pity it hadn't a bit more starch in it, but limp and all as it was, it gave an added touch to the dress. The third girl at the table wore glasses. She was called Cissie. Miss Holland had been trying to avert her eyes from the poor girl because of a fearful bulge at her wrist, just above her cuff. But at that moment, the girl gave a frightful sneeze, and just too late she whipped out a handkerchief from her sleeve and Miss Holland saw it had been a handkerchief that had caused the bulge. What an odd place to keep your handkerchief. She was glad, however, that the girl had it handy to cover her mouth when she gave another sneeze, more violent than the first, and more far-reaching.

'Excuse me,' Cissie said when she tucked her handkerchief up her sleeve again, and marvellously, marvellously, Miss Holland felt herself to be included among those who were being

asked to excuse her. She tried to make the smile with which she
acknowledged the apology as radiant as possible. But Cissie had
turned to the older man – was his name Moriarty?

Miss Holland felt that she had been slow in catching their
names. She couldn't help thinking that Mrs Lewis had been
remiss in not introducing her. Introductions were really
frightfully necessary. She could hardly call the girls by their
Christian names on such short acquaintance. On the other hand,
it was by their surnames the girls called the men. Most
extraordinary! She had always been given to understand this to
be a privilege reserved by men for men.

At last Miss Holland felt she could leave the table with
impunity. 'Please excuse me,' she murmured faintly as she rose,
but as far as she could make out no one heard her. They had got
themselves involved in a furious argument. But tomorrow, or the
next day, she hoped that she would be in the thick of those
arguments, because she had begun to realise that they only
argued for fun.

As she hurried to the door, feeling it was a million miles away,
Miss Holland thought she'd never reach it, and so, when she did,
she must have grasped the knob with undue force, because to
her dismay it came off in her hand and fell to the linoleum and
rolled off somewhere out of sight under one of the huge pieces
of furniture that filled the room to capacity. It did not make her
feel any better that the others roared laughing. But then a
marvellous thing happened. The younger of the two men –
Harvey? – who she had decided must be a medical student,
called out to her. Unmistakably to her!

'You'll have to watch out for that knob. All the knobs in the
house are a bit poorly,' he said. It completely made up for their
not helping her to look for it. Anyway she had found it. She gave
the young man a smile and went out.

Miss Holland did like a joke, at least a joke made in a friendly
way. Father hadn't gone in for jokes. As she went upstairs she felt
nearer to the pulse of real life than she had felt for many a year.
These people might, to put it bluntly, belong to a different class
from herself and father, but, no matter what her father might
have made of them, she herself felt stimulated by them. Deep

down, for some years past she had felt that father and herself would eventually have to make changes in their way of life. Father had not admitted it, but the writing had appeared on the wall. It was a mercy for him that he had been spared seeing the wall collapse. But she felt she herself was well able for what was to come. A new world. And brave new people in it. Shakespeare? Huxley? It didn't matter who had originally said it. It was a fact. It had come to pass.

What harm if these people cut their bread with a knife instead of breaking it! What harm if they stretched for things instead of waiting for it to be passed to them. These things were no longer of any importance. And those who thought otherwise were fuddy-duddies, behind the times.

Sitting upstairs in her own room, listening to the babble of voices below that continued long into the night, Miss Holland pondered over the attributes of the people into whose company she had come, and she was more impressed by them in retrospect than she had been when she was downstairs among them. Mr Moriarty, for instance, the more elderly gentleman, seemed, like herself, to have had very deep sentiments towards his father. He had told a very touching anecdote about a present – she hadn't quite caught what it was – that he had received from his father when he was a young man, which, although he seldom found much use for it, he had never been able to bring himself to sell – or even to pop. Pop? It had taken her a few seconds to know this was a slang word for a pawnshop. He was most likely joking in any case, if she could judge by the screeches of laughter that greeted the word! She herself was a minute too late to laugh, but now in her room she made up for the omission by a real fit of the giggles. Oh, they were a lively bunch! Never had she heard such torrents of talk, such tempestuous arguments, and never had she known people to be so earnest about their views that they didn't hesitate for a moment to interrupt anyone expounding a different view. The interesting thing about their interruptions was that, instead of hindering the other speakers, interruptions seemed to put new wind into their sails – if she might so express it. The conversation had never for a moment flagged. And at times the interruptions sent everyone off on an altogether new tack! She herself had found it hard to tell when they were finished discussing the falling birth-rate, and had gone on to the high cost of living, or even to the need for free dental services in rural areas, but of course she would be the first to acknowledge that she was under a disadvantage, not always being quick enough to adjust to new turns of phrase.

But tomorrow, she thought, tomorrow she would feel less out of things. Or would she? A sudden dejection came down over her. Supposing she was never able to follow what they said? And supposing, worse still, she was never able to make any contribution of her own to the happy babel of voices around that table? Miss Holland stood up and went over and peered deeply into her dressingtable mirror, although she had not been thinking at all about her appearance, but about her personality.

This, without doubt, was the moment when there began a gradual deterioration, a paralysis of her personality. For two more weeks when she went down, regularly and punctually, to join them around the supper table, Miss Holland still held high hopes of adjusting herself to fit into the company of her fellow guests. She had had to rule out breakfast as an opportunity for getting closer to them, because not one of them got up in time to do more than snatch a cup of tea or coffee, and race to catch a bus. But towards the end of her second week, she had to admit to not having made significant progress. She had succeeded in engaging her table companions in a certain amount of small talk, but nothing more. She had enquired if the girl called Cissie was getting over her cold, although it didn't seem so from the way she was seized with those sudden fits of sneezing. And, one evening, she had brought down and offered the girl some throat lozenges belonging to her father, that she hadn't known she'd kept, until she opened her trunks which had in the end to be lugged up the stairs by Mr Harvey and Mr Moriarty with the girls pushing from below. Still she didn't feel they really accepted her. Even after she'd found out that they laughed every time she referred to herself as a paying guest, and had forced herself – hoping Mrs Lewis would not overhear – to refer to herself as a boarder, or a lodger – even this effort didn't mend matters.

One of the troubles was – or so she decided – that the others were out of the house all day, and were therefore continually picking up new items of interest with which to regale the table at suppertime, whereas she seldom left her room. She spent most of her day sticking stamps into her album, playing patience, and occasionally going for a walk to a park that was said to be nearby, but which turned out to be quite a trek. On fine days she felt for health reasons that she had to trudge off to that park because Mrs Lewis had disabused her of her earlier notion that the deck chairs in the garden were for the use of the lodgers.

That was it! The others came home in the evening agog with all they'd seen and done, while she had seen and done nothing. She had made one abortive attempt to interest them in an anecdote drawn from her travels with her father, but they'd made it quite clear they weren't interested, although Betty did interrupt to ask if she could tell her how much it would cost to bring a bicycle to Guernsey. And when on another occasion she had endeavoured to recommend a book she had recently read, she saw that as far as they were concerned books were only books. It was real life – action – people – that interested them. Sadly Miss Holland began to feel that a lot of money had been wasted on her own education and that she was totally uninformed on all major issues.

I am forty-five, she thought, and I do not know what constitutes a living wage. I don't even know what is the right tip to give a taxi man. More and more despairingly, night after night she listened to the talk at supper time, and more and more she felt she'd never enter more fully into it than by giving vigorous nods of her head, often in dissent, but more often, due to nervousness, in assent. She hadn't, however, given up the struggle, unequal though it was. And one evening, after a furious verbal encounter between the girls on the one side and the two men on the other, as to whether the recent death of a prominent politician had been the result of a terminal ailment from which he had been suffering for months, or whether it was a case of suicide – since there had apparently been some suspicion that he had embezzled party funds – Miss Holland came to an important decision: she would take a daily newspaper and keep herself abreast of the times.

It took her several hours next day to go out and get the paper, and then come back and read it, paying special attention to the death of the politician in whom her friends had been so interested, to which the newspaper gave extensive coverage. She felt it was time well spent all the same, when, armed with a few telling comments gleaned from the editorial, she prepared to go down to supper that evening and give as good as she got when the topic was brought up. But the others were no longer interested in the case. Something had cropped up in the office where Cissie and Marge worked, and they believed they had inside information to give to any and all whom it concerned about a plan to appoint a welfare officer – and about time too they said – to look into the schooling of itinerant children. Hugging tight to the comment she wanted to make on the deceased politician, Miss Holland stayed on longer than usual at the table, but in the end she had to excuse herself and go up to her room without having unburdened herself of it.

Later, in bed with the light out, she went back over things and in a whisper to herself she inserted her comment quite easily into the conversation! And everyone was most impressed. There were no interruptions, except when an imaginary Betty Stone said, in an aside to an imaginary Marge Moran, that it took a mature mind to get to the root of anything, and that experience always imposed a proper perspective. The young women even went so far as to suggest that Agnes Holland join them next evening when they were going to a public meeting and meet their friends, who, they felt sure, would be interested in her views – on various topics. Miss Holland willingly agreed to join them, and told them so, with a smile – a smile that when she fell asleep was still on her face.

After a while, however, Miss Holland got totally discouraged. She stopped making up conversations, and she stopped taking the newspaper. Gradually she slid back into her old habit of letting her mind roam loose – to go where it liked and settle on whatever pleased it. On days she did not go out, there was not, of course, a great deal to be observed in Mrs Lewis' garden – except the cat. But he was a source of daily delight to Miss Holland. To anyone, surely? He was a magnificent sight sitting on the wall under her window, particularly in the early morning when the sun was on that side of the house. When the sun went around to the front of the house, he went too. She never saw him late in the day. He was selfish of course, but that was his nature, the nature of all cats, like their vanity. His vanity was immense. You see, although he made a great pretence to the contrary, he knew very well that she was watching him, when shortly after breakfast, after the day had warmed up a bit, he'd advance like a tiger along the garden wall to his favourite spot under her window, where he would sit and wash himself, or perhaps just sit. Now and then he might see something stirring in among the flowers in the garden next door and then he might take it into his head to spring down and leap about for a few minutes as playful as a kitten in spite of being so big and strong. Miss Holland was sure that he was not meant to be in among the flowers, although he was so lightfooted, so deft and agile, she had never seen him break a single stem All the same, in case he'd get into trouble she never let him get too frisky, knowing the performance was most likely put on for her benefit, and so she'd clap her hands and call out to him. Ah then! Then he'd give the show away on himself by how he would look straight up at her window, never for a moment in doubt of who had called, and from where the call had come. After he sprang back onto the wall he'd sit facing her way, but with his eyes closed in make-believe disdain of everything around him. Now and then he'd open his eyes for a moment and then they'd narrow into mere slits again, but when they were wide open it almost made her gasp to see how they could change colour – go from a strange sea green to a curious yellow, the exact yellow of the glass buttons in a teddy bear, she thought. He was at his most teasing of all, however, when his back was turned and he sat as still as if he were a ceramic cat, and then the early morning sun shining down on him put a sheen on his fur, so that his outline was traced around him like a silver frame. Miss Holland would hardly have been surprised if, when he ran away, that silver silhouette remained behind, etched on the air.

One day she wondered idly if the other lodgers knew him. They left the house so early, and they were always in such a hurry, she doubted if they did. Being out of the house all day they'd have

no other opportunity of seeing him. She'd love to ask about him.
To whom did he belong? To one of the neighbours presumably?
He must have a good home to which he took himself off when
the shades of evening fell – to sit – she did so hope – in front of
a big blazing fire, blinking his eyes every time a flock of sparks
would fly up into the black flue.

Thinking of the big beautiful cat after he'd gone, Miss Holland
on more than one occasion felt a revival of confidence in her
power to engage the interest of the other lodgers. If she could
make them see that cat through her eyes! They none of them
seemed the kind of people who read poetry, but everyone had a
streak of poetry in them somewhere. If she could find the right
words, to build up a word picture of that tom, she really did
believe they'd respond, and find it evocative, original.

One evening therefore as she sat at her dressing table, getting
ready for supper, Miss Holland decided to make a last assault on
the company below. She had already rehearsed what she would
say, but she kept making small alterations, changing the order of
her words, dropping a word, or maybe two words, here and
there, where they seemed exaggeratedly ornate. Indeed she was
in grave danger of being late for supper, she thought, when she
glanced at her watch, but this was an important moment for her.
Her only trouble was that she could not find a striking phrase
with which to start. Once started, everything would go
swimmingly.

For that was one thing she had noticed about the others, they
all had an uncanny knack of coming out with an exclamation or
an introductory word, so striking that, when they uttered it, the
table fell silent. For example; the previous evening Harvey had
been a few minutes late and there had been a really quite
interesting discussion in progress when he burst into the room.

'Blood makes you people retch – the thought of it, I mean.
Only for that I'd tell you a good yarn I heard today at the
hospital.'

Immediately everyone clamoured to hear the yarn, which,
when he told it, Miss Holland, privately of course, without
betraying herself, thought dull and tedious. Nevertheless it was
greeted by roars of laughter. But she knew the secret for its

success – that striking opening, that powerful beginning. She glanced at her watch again. Time was flying. How would she begin her recital? For, willy nilly she was determined to make her debut that very evening.

Then, happening to glance out of the window – it was almost like the work of Providence – she saw her old friend the tom-cat, and before her eyes he did the most *extraordinary* thing she had ever seen a cat do. It was spectacular. Oh, he was a real playboy! An actor. Indeed it was almost as if he had put on a performance on purpose for her – to give her the opening she needed in order to introduce him to her friends!

He was not on the wall under her window, but up on the roof of the shed, where although the sun had left the garden, he had spotted a last ray of its dying light. And now he was etched not in silver but in pure gold. And, as soon as she went to the window, he stretched himself superbly and jumped down on to the wall to walk away as if no one was looking, as if he was alone in the world and Lord of all creation.

'Oh you lovely, lovely, pussy,' she called out, but of course he didn't turn, or pretend he had heard. But next minute he sprang off the wall, and went plomp on all fours into the flowerbed. And she saw that this time he had broken a big pink antirrhinum – one of the last in bloom. Miss Holland changed her tune, but only in fun.

'Bad cat! Bad cat!' she called out. He could hardly believe his ears! He looked up with such disbelief she had to stifle her laughter and forgive him. 'No. No. No. You're not bad!' she cried.

And then he did it. He opened his mouth and deliberately – oh yes it was quite deliberate – he snapped the head off another antirrhinum – snapped it off exactly as if it had been the head of a mouse! And then, oh then, he surpassed himself altogether. With the flower in his mouth he sprang back on to the wall and danced away into the shadows. Danced!

'He danced away' Miss Holland said out loud. 'Like a flamenco dancer,' she added. And she knew she had her opening line. Glancing at her watch she decided to allow herself a moment for a last rehearsal.

'Did you know we have a flamenco dancer living in the house next door?' How would that be? But did he live next door? Perhaps, since she didn't know for sure where he belonged, it might be better to speak of him just as living in this terrace, or on the road? One way or another she would have them captive.

'A flamenco dancer?' they would exclaim. She could imagine their astonishment.

Slowly then, keeping them on the *qui vive* as long as possible, she would triumphantly reveal the identity of the dancer.

'The cat!' she'd say. 'You must know him, the big marmalade tom-cat who sits on the garden wall all morning.' How they'd laugh. And once she had taken them unawares, she'd tell them all about the cat. Surprised by poetry: that was how her strategy could be described.

They'd see her company was worth cultivating! And she would not fob poetry off on them all the time. Another night, when they'd be complaining at mashed turnip again for the second time in one week although no one ate it, she'd tell them the wicked plan she had hatched in her own mind. Never, without their help, would she attempt to execute it. Her plan was to get some small object – a burnt match, or better still, a dead fly – and bury it in the mound of turnip and then wait and see if, the next time turnip was served, they might not unearth it!

Miss Holland giggled to think of the fun they'd have. Oh she'd succeed in being one of them yet, or more correct to say she'd narrow the gap between them. She'd end by having them reading, not just novels but instructive books – perhaps poetry in time! And when, if another change came in her fortunes and she were to move again to another lodgings, or a small residential hotel, they would think back to her, with gratitude. She would have made their life richer and they would always acknowledge their debt to her. She could imagine she heard them. 'Only for Agnes Holland,' they'd say. 'Only for Agnes Holland.'

But now she really was late for supper. She had heard them come home a few moments before and now she heard the clatter of knives and forks and a babel of voices. Rubbing her cheeks with the palms of her hands to give herself a bit of colour, because she was pale from excitement, Miss Holland ran down the stairs. She felt like an actress on a first night, with the curtain about to rise. Only this wasn't play-acting. This was real life.

In the diningroom the others as usual were seated and had already started to eat. But now of course they all nodded to her, and Mr Harvey actually lifted the lid of the covered-dish, and put out his hand for her plate in order to serve her. Miss Holland got the warm feeling one gets when a pattern has been established; because Harvey always served out the food when it was something like a stew, and she knew it was because it gave him an opportunity to use his pet joke. 'Some swill for you, Miss Holland?' he'd say. And, as she guessed, he did say it. To please him she laughed as she gave him her plate. When, in a few minutes, one of the girls would ask her to pass, not the butter but the margarine, she'd laugh again, because this was a joke too. It wasn't really margarine at all, or at least she didn't think so.

They were always joking. Not only did her father dislike jokes, but at the table he deplored them. He considered it very bad form to joke at meals, but that was because of the servant, who stood behind a screen at the service hatch. Here the maid never stayed in the diningroom for longer than to plant the food on the table and make off to the kitchen.

Taking her plate of stew, (Harvey had given her too much, but she'd try and manage it if she had enough bread to go with it) Miss Holland reached for the bread. Reaching for things was really very sensible. And taking a lesson from Cissie, Miss Holland took two pieces at the one time because she wanted to be finished eating herself when she'd start to tell her story. Her moment was about to come – the moment Betty Stone would come to the end of her boring account of a hockey match she'd been at that afternoon.

'The crowd was unbelievable,' Betty said. 'Going through the turnstile I was nearly squeezed to death.'

'No need to go far from here, Betty, if it's a squeeze you want,' Harvey said, and although it was a bit vulgar, Miss Holland felt that perhaps she wasn't the only one who thought Betty boring. Certainly, after Harvey's remark, Betty did not pursue her story. She closed up like a clam. And Miss Holland saw that her chance had arrived. She almost rose from her chair.

'A funny thing happened today,' she said, because in her excitement she forgot the exact words she had prepared.

No matter! She was about to rush on, when to her astonishment her words had clashed in mid-air with words that were almost exactly the same, uttered by Moriarty.

'A funny thing happened last night,' Moriarty said.

Miss Holland sank back, and fell silent – not so much defeated as stupified. Moriarty was just discomfited. He made a gesture for her to proceed – not with very good grace however, and there was a sudden tension as everyone waited to see what would happen. They looked from one speaker to the other.

'You were going to say something?' Moriarty asked coldly.

'It can wait. Please continue,' Miss Holland said. Her story was so good she felt she could afford to be generous. And Moriarty went ahead.

'You'll all be darned glad to hear what I have to tell you,' he said, and Miss Holland was somewhat mollified by thinking this may have been meant as a sort of apology to her for preceding her. 'I meant to tell you at breakfast, but I forgot. Do you know what I did last night? Wait till you hear! I'll expect a round of applause. You know that damn tom-cat, that dirty orange creature that's always caterwailing on the tiles just when one is about to go to sleep? Well, he was at it again last night. But not for long. I jumped out of bed, and I got out that old shot-gun – the one I was telling you about last week, that my father gave me when I was a boy – and I threw up the window and took aim at him. It was dark and I missed him. But I put a stop to his concert for one night. And at least he knows what to expect tonight! If he's at it again tonight he'll get something he won't forget in a hurry – a pellet in the backside!'

Miss Holland put her hand over her mouth. She thought she was going to faint. All around her the others were roaring with laughter, louder than ever before, and their faces looked so contorted she felt she must be getting dizzy. She'd have to get away from the table and out of the room. She stood up. Then suddenly her head cleared and she sat down – I must take one good, hard look at them – she thought, so I'll never forget how awful they are, and so I can try to protect myself from people like them in the future.

Miss Holland looked at Harvey. His jacket had several stains and she knew there was another big stain on the inside leg of his trousers, although at the moment it was hidden by the tablecloth. Marge Moran's green dress had stains of perspiration under her armpits. The wool fabric was matted and instead of a brilliant green it was the sickly green of frog's spawn. Cissie, the one with the perpetual cold in her head, had a drop at the end of her nose and one day it could fall into the stew. Betty Stone had a wart on the palm of her hand and if you shook hands with her, you'd feel you were shaking hands with a wart. Moriarty was the only one left, but Miss Holland couldn't face looking at him. She stayed sitting in her chair just long enough to recall all the times he left his false teeth behind him in the bathroom on the rim of the handbasin. No matter how hard she tried not to look at them, she could feel them sitting there – grinning at her.

Then she got to her feet. And when she reached the door, as on her first day in the house, the door knob fell off and rolled across the floor. Miss Holland made no attempt to pick it up and neither did anyone else, because no one had noticed that she was taking her departure.

The Dead Soldier

When he was going away his mother and his sister Solly went up to Dublin to see him off. When they got off the train, the sun still shone in the spaces between the city buildings, but by the time they had found their way to the docks it was dark. They stood under a lamp-post so they would be sure to pick him out from the other men as he marched past. When they heard the band in the distance they stood very close together, and when a crowd of children came running along in the dark, the old woman began to tremble. The soldiers would not be far behind.

The soldiers were marching four abreast. They advanced steadily, rank after dark rank, like the waves of the sea. And under the lamp-post, where the women stood, the black ranks foamed into faces, for a moment, and then went onward again, rank after rank, into the darkness where the river sirens wailed.

The women knew instinctively when Matty's rank was coming near, and when his face shone in the light they took the full advantage of their eyes in staring at him. They smiled, and they put their hands to their lips. They waved at him. But they couldn't be sure if Matty saw them.

In the train going home again the old woman was desolate.

'If we ran as far as the next lamp-post we would have seen him again!'

'Now, Mother!' said Solly. 'You know yourself that Matty would not have wanted us to do that. He'd only be saying afterwards that we made a laughing stock of ourselves before the other men, two women running along the street thinking they were fit to keep up with the soldiers.'

'That's like what a daughter would say,' said the old woman. 'A son would never say the like of that. A son would never see anything to laugh at in his own mother, no matter what she did.'

'All the same, I'm glad we stayed where we were. We might have lost the way, and missed the train, if we went any farther from the station.' She looked out the carriage window at the pattern of the lighted city that was fading into the black sky, and she wondered what got into men that they wanted to go off to fight in a foreign country that meant nothing to them, one way or another. Matty was a real Irishman, if ever there was one, and yet he was one of the first in the country to give his name and go off to France, although the old woman screamed and threw herself down on the floor begging him not to leave her.

'Women don't understand,' was all Matty said.

'Leave the way!' he said to Solly, who had gone over to stand between him and the door.

'Stay where you are, Solly!' the old woman cried.

'I can't stop him, Mother, if he's set on going,' Solly said, and she had to stand aside and let him pass.

That was only four days ago, and now he was gone; and in a few hours the two of them would be back in the empty house, making up the fire that had never been let die out before, since the day the old woman came into the house as a young bride in a blue dress. Solly knew all about the blue dress. It had cerise bows down the front. The old woman was always talking about it. I suppose she'll never talk about it again, thought Solly. She'll talk about nothing but Matty now till the day he comes home again.

The talk about Matty began the minute they got into the house. As they made up the fire the old woman told Solly stories about the time he was a child. Even when Solly went out to the well she could hear the old woman talking to herself: laughing over some things and sobbing over other things. When she thought of the times she had been hurt and worried while Matty was growing up, she laughed, because those times were gone; but when she thought of the gay times, and the happy times, she sobbed, and wiped her eyes with her skirt, because those times were gone as well.

Both the chaff and the grain had gone on the wind, and the barren days had begun. In the house where seven men had sat down to be served by the two women, there was no one now to sit down but the servers. Matty was the last of the men to leave home, and what lured him away was beyond the comprehension of any woman.

Week after week there was no other talk in the cottage, but talk about Matty. And when the priest called, he had to stay for an hour listening to an account of the time that Matty played hurley for the county. But when he was going he called Solly out into the yard.

'Let her talk about him all she wants. Don't stop her,' he said. 'It will be an ease to her mind.'

So when they got the news that Matty was killed, Solly knew she'd have to let the old woman talk away, day and night. So she went around the house all day listening to her and encouraging her. And when there was another death in the parish, she took the opportunity to try and console her mother.

'Murty Glynn is dead, Mother. He had a hard death. He was dying for three days and three nights. They said it was agony to look at him. Isn't any death better than that? Isn't a blow of a bullet a grand death compared with that?'

'I don't know. It's a grand thing to die in your bed,' the old woman said.

'It's a great thing to die quick! You wouldn't want to think Matty was lying inside there in the room, twisting in agony, would you? Isn't it better to think of him maybe laughing one minute and maybe lying at peace the next?'

'I suppose you're right,' said the old woman. 'But it's a nice thing to be able to lay a body out, and see that he gets the best in candles and linen. It's nice to get a last look at it before it's put down into the grave.'

'It's not right to talk like that, Mother. It's flying in the face of God's goodness. I think it's nice to remember Matty like we last saw him, marching along to the sound of the band with a smile on his face. I'm glad I don't have to remember him as a corpse. All corpses look alike in my opinion.'

'You don't know what you're talking about, Solly,' the old woman said. 'Your own father was the handsomest corpse that was ever stretched. People that never knew him when he was alive came from miles just to see him laid out, he was such a handsome sight then. I can see him to this day, when I close my eyes, looking as fierce as when he was a living man. You'd think to look at his hands that he'd raise up one of them any minute, and brush away a fly that was flying around his face.'

'I'm glad I don't remember him,' Solly said, 'and I'm glad I didn't see Matty dead. I'm glad I remember him alive.' She took up a picture from the mantelpiece, a picture of two swans standing in a clump of bulrushes. The frame was engraved steel and there was no glass in it.

'I was thinking we could take out this picture, and put in one of Matty,' she said, and she took a prayer book from a shelf under the mantelpiece and pulling out a photograph, began to put it into the frame instead of the picture of the two swans.

'Be careful you don't tear that photograph while you're putting it in,' the mother said, leaning anxiously over Solly's shoulder and watching her every action. When she was satisfied that Solly was doing it carefully she picked up the picture of the swans in the bulrushes and put it into the prayer book, and put the prayer book back on the smoky shelf. 'Give me that frame, I'll shine it up a bit,' she said, wiping it in her skirt by rubbing it back and forth. Then looking at it, she wiped it back and forth again, until, apparently she saw some improvement in it and satisfied, put it back on the mantelpiece. She stared into the eyes of the photograph.

'I often saw him looking just like that,' she said. 'Didn't you?

Solly took the picture and looked hard at it. 'Isn't it funny the different looks a person can have on his face, from one time to another, and yet when you think of them you think of them with the one look only on them. I always think of Matty the way he looked when he was passing under the lamp-post the night he went away.'

'If you were his mother you'd remember every look he had on his face from the day he was born to the last day you saw him. Do you mean to say you don't remember the way he looked when he came running in with the blood pouring down his face the time he fell on the broken pie dish in the yard and cut his head open?'

'No,' said Solly, 'I don't remember that day.'

'Don't you?' The old woman was surprised. 'Well, surely you remember the day he came racing up the yard with the geese after him, and his face red as the jersey on his back?'

'No,' said Solly, 'but now I come to think of it I do remember the way he looked in his uniform the first day he put it on, when he was showing us the map and marking out where France was. He had his cap pushed back on his head, and the track of it was across his forehead in a red weal.'

'It's my opinion that cap was too small for him' said the mother. 'It was too tight across the forehead. It should have been a half-size larger.'

'He told you himself, Mother, that they don't look into half-sizes in the army.'

She smiled into the eyes of the photograph, thinking Matty would be pleased if he could hear her now consoling their mother. But the words had not penetrated far into the old woman's sorrow.

'No matter how many memories I have,' she said, 'it doesn't make up for not seeing him laid out in his own house. I don't like to think of them burying him in a hurry, along with a lot of other poor young fellows. I think to myself that, for all we know, it may have been night-time and raining at that, and the place too dark and wet for them to kneel down and say a prayer for him!'

'Now, Mother, stop crying. You may be sure they knelt down and said a prayer for him, no matter how wet or dark it was, when they didn't know which of themselves would be the next to be shot.'

'I suppose you're right' said the old woman. 'Anyway I thought by the letter the officer wrote that he wasn't the kind of man to throw down the spade out of his hands after burying a lad and not kneel and say a prayer.'

'You may be sure he said many a prayer,' said Solly, 'but of course, I don't suppose it was the officer himself who buried Matty!'

'He said in the letter that he did! "We buried him under a little ash tree," he said. "I know you will be very glad to hear that." I was very glad to hear it. I say a prayer for that officer every night after I've said prayers for Matty and for his father, and for my own poor mother and father – God be good to them. I always say a special prayer for that officer who buried my son.'

'I suppose he was there at the time,' Solly said, 'but it's likely he got someone else to do the digging for him!'

'I wouldn't give in to that,' said the mother. 'Matty was a nice lad. Everyone liked him. I never knew anyone yet that didn't take a liking to him, specially when he smiled. He had a lovely smile.'

Solly took up the frame and looked again at her brother's face. 'I couldn't get him to smile when I was taking this picture of him,' she said. 'He kept telling me to hurry up all the time. "Take the picture, can't you, if you're going to take it?" he said. "I'm not aiming to stand here all day with the sun in my eyes!"'

'I hope he wasn't lying in the sun when he was wounded,' the mother said suddenly. 'I heard Marg Mack and Maggie Cullen talking in the shop yesterday about a young lad who was wounded. Maggie's son wrote home to say that the young lad, whoever he was, was lying in the blazing sun for six hours before they found him, and they only got time to pull him over under a bit of a tree or a bush before the poor fellow died. "I'm glad I'm not going to die looking up at the bloody sun," was the last thing he said. They stopped talking when they saw I was listening. I suppose they thought I'd feel bad on account of my boy being killed in the war too. But I'd only love to hear them talking. You like to hear about other people's troubles when you have trouble of your own.'

'All the same, I wouldn't like to listen to those old gossips,' said Solly, 'they love to talk about people that are dead or dying, just to make themselves important.'

'You don't understand. You don't understand at all,' her old mother said. 'When I was walking home along the road, afterwards, I was thinking of what they said, and I was wondering what was the last thing our Matty said. The officer didn't think to tell us that.'

'I'm sure Matty was praying' said Solly, 'but maybe if the officer wasn't a Catholic himself he wouldn't think to put a thing like that in a letter.'

'That's right. I'm sure he was praying. He was a good boy. Still it's a great consolation for a mother if she has to lose a son, to see him slipping out of this world with his grip on a crucifix, and his lips moving at least, if he wasn't able to repeat the prayers of the priest.'

'Don't talk like that now, Mother,' said Solly. 'I've often heard tell that a soldier gets a special grace when he's dying. Many a one, they say, is saved at the last minute, just by thinking of the Judgment.'

'That's right. God is good,' said the old woman. 'I hope I won't have too long to wait now till I'm called myself to meet my dear ones.'

'And what about me?' said Solly. 'Have you no consideration for me, Mother, that you sit there talking about dying, and not remembering that I'd be all alone then, with no one at all to care what becomes of me, or whether I get a bit to eat for myself of not?'

The old woman was staring into the fire and she didn't hear Solly. It was getting late and the fire was dying down. Solly took out a candle from the drawer of the dresser. She paid no attention to the fact that the old woman didn't answer her. She didn't expect an answer. Her own remark was an old one, well worn, and brought into use every time the old woman began to talk about dying.

'I think sometimes when I'm half asleep, I see his face in the fire,' said the old woman, again, after a few minutes' silence.

'Take heed would you fall into the fire some night, staring into it like that, and you half asleep,' Solly said. 'Will I get your pillow, Mother, and put it by the fire, for a spell, to take the chill off it before you go to bed? It's getting late.'

The old woman looked up.

'I'm not going to bed yet,' she said. 'Do you not know what night it is?'

'I do,' Solly had hoped her mother had forgotten. It was All Souls' Night.

'My own poor mother, God be good to her,' said the old woman, 'used to say that the dead are sometimes allowed come back to their own fireside tonight, and sit down by the hob until the first light steals up through the trees.'

Solly went into the other room and came out with the pillow in her arms. 'Here's your pillow. Hold it to the fire for a bit, Mother, and then we'll go to bed. Don't be talking about ghosts. Listen to the wind under the door! I wish there was a man in the house to put a bit of cement on the floor, there by the hinge. That's where the wind is coming in.'

'My father used to laugh at my mother,' the old woman continued, as if she had not been interrupted. 'He used to tell her that if it was as easy as all that to come back from the grave, there wouldn't be such a dread on people at the thought of going into it.'

'That's what I say too,' Solly said.

'When I was a child, old people had strange notions.'

'Old people are always the same. I wouldn't wonder to hear that you were thinking of sitting up all night yourself to see if Matty would come back!' Solly said, and she gave an awkward laugh, and stood back out of the circle of the lamp so that she could look at the old woman. She had an idea her mother might have a notion of staying up and she wanted to laugh her out of it. The old woman threw a big sod of turf on the fire.

'Why are you putting on turf at this hour of the night, when we're going to our beds?' Solly asked.

'It's raking down the fire every night that has this house as damp as it is,' said the old woman. 'It's no harm to have a good blaze on the hearth during the night in damp weather. The wall over there, by the dresser, is dripping wet. The lime is washed off it. There'll be a hole in it after another winter.'

'A man would mix up a bit of plaster for that wall while you'd be looking around you,' said Solly. 'Is your pillow warmed?'

'It is,' said the old woman, 'but don't light the candle yet awhile.' All the same, Solly stuck a bit of paper in between the red sods of turf on the hearthstone, and when it lit with a pout of flame, she held the flame to a candle-butt that she took out of her pocket.

'Are you coming to bed, Mother?' she said, going into the next room and standing the candle in a cup on the table beside the tufty bed with its white counterpane.

The old woman hoisted herself out of the chair by leaning on the arms and drawing herself up with a jerk.

'Stop that candle from guttering and spluttering,' she said.

Solly squeezed the burnt end of the wick with her finger and thumb and the candle blazed freshly and cleanly along the new piece of wick.

'Do you know what it is?' she said. 'The moon is so bright tonight you'd hardly want a candle at all.'

Through the small window, the rim of a hill behind the house could be seen against the bright moonlit sky. The light of the candle, the lamp, and the fire, all burning at their brightest, was not strong enough to keep out the light of the moon. Even an odd star, that shone brighter than the other stars, could be seen as clearly from where they stood as if the cottage were in darkness.

'The moon is in full bloom,' said the old woman.

Solly stood looking out and listening. The wind had risen, and somewhere away behind the cottage it sounded in the trees.

'It's odd for the wind to be so high on a moon-bright night,' she said.

The old woman went into the inner room and Solly turned down the lamp in the kitchen. She kicked in a sod that had fallen out from the hearth and lit another butt of a candle for herself.

'If you feel cold, Mother, be sure to give a rap on the wall, and I'll come down and put another blanket over you,' she said as she went up the steps of the loft. 'Give a good loud rap,' she repeated when she got to the top step.

'I won't want any more over me than I have every night,' the old woman said. 'Put another blanket over yourself. Young people nowadays haven't as good blood in their veins as we had in our day.'

Solly closed the door of the loft. The old woman left her door open and she went on talking to herself. Solly listened to her for a few minutes, and then she took off her clothes, and lay down on a trestle bed with her face to the gable window where she could see the moon high in the bright sky. But she was asleep before a travelling cloud had crossed the bright face of the moon.

Down below the old woman was still talking to herself. 'I don't know why Solly is so cold,' she muttered. 'Every one of my children felt the cold worse than me, but Solly and Matty were the worst. Perhaps it's because they came last of the family.' She sat on the edge of the bed and it sank under her with a creak. 'Matty could never get socks thick enough to suit him.' She stood up again and the bed sprang up with a rusty whinge. She went over to the yellow chest of drawers in the corner and pulled out the top drawer. She took out a thick grey sock and another unfinished sock that dangled from four steel needles. 'There's no harm in finishing a thing once it's begun,' she said. And she went over to the open door that led into the kitchen and listened to Solly's breathing. 'Who knows?' she said. 'Matty might come back. There was lot of sense in the things my mother said. I don't believe that everyone that dies has the power to come back, but a poor harmless boy like Matty, that died so far away from his home, might be allowed to come as far as the door, and step inside for a minute just to please his old mother.' She put the finished sock back in the drawer, and then on second thoughts she took it out again. 'If he came back he might like to see I was still knitting for him, even after he was gone,' she said. 'But of course it's only nonsense thinking that he'll come back.' She put her hand under the bolster, and drew out a pair of worn rosary beads that were polished from a lifetime of handling. 'Poor Matty!' she said. 'Poor Matty! Your old mother would give her senses for one sight of your darling face!' Then she went back out into the kitchen, talking to herself. 'He won't come, I know that. But it's no harm to stay up awhile. I couldn't sleep anyway. My father was right when he said that people wouldn't get it so hard to leave this world if there was any chance of getting back to it. He had good sayings. He wore my poor mother out with his talk, but she cried herself into a fit the day he died. It is a strange thing the way you value a person when he's gone from you. But it's a strange thing too that I never had any hankering to see my father or mother again, once they went from me – nor any of the other children either, not the way I hanker to see Matty.' She left the lamp unlit, finding her way in by the light of the fire that darkened and brightened every other minute, and pausing to feel the edges of the furniture like a blind person, with gentleness and timidity – yet with a kind of loving gratitude in the touch of her fingers. 'If I had seen him laid out I might have been satisfied,' she said as she sat down by the fire.

For a long time, then, there was no sound, as the old woman's fingers went silently up and down the knitting needles, except when the tips of the needles came together, accidentally, with a little knocking sound. Then a sod fell with a thud, and the bitter smell of smoke threaded the air. She let the sod burn out where it lay, until the bitter fumes made her eyes sore. When she stirred in her chair, to lift it, the chair made a harsh sound as it grated on the rough flagstones, and she looked anxiously up at the loft to see if Solly had wakened. But Solly slept on.

The clock on the dresser seemed to get louder and louder as she listened, and she could barely make out its face because of the way the clouds were passing over the moon every minute, darkening the kitchen. She could imagine that she saw the clock, but she could not possibly have been looking at it, because she imagined it as it was, when she was first married. Then the paint was fresh and bright. It was red, with blue and yellow flowers stencilled up the sides, and a cuckoo that came out on the platform with his beak open and called out the hours. But of course there was no paint on it now. It was as smoky as a pot, and there'd been no cuckoo in it since the day Matty knocked him off with a catapult, when he was a little lad. She was very angry with him that day. She was going to raise her hand to him, but he pleaded with her like a little girl.

'I wouldn't have touched him if he was alive, Mother, but I knew he was only made of cardboard and feathers,' he said, and he picked up the cuckoo, and plucked out the feathers to show her the cardboard body.

She put out her hand and groped along the mantelshelf till she found the framed photograph, and she lifted it carefully and held it low down near the flames to see the features more clearly.

'If you come back, Matty, you'll find your old mother waiting for you,' she said. 'But God is an obstinate man. He has his own ideas, but it's very hard on the like of me.'

The wind dropped suddenly. Then it rose again in a gust. Soot loosened in the chimney and fell down into the fire. From under the door there came a thin, whistling sound and then the clouds broke and the moon slipped out like a nut from the kernel. All at once the room was as bright as if a light had been flashed in through the window again.

And then there was a step outside the door.

The old woman remained where she was, crouched low over the flames with the picture in its steel frame in her hands.

'Good Christ,' she said. 'Good Christ deliver us!'

She didn't move. Then the moon was covered again, and the steps came nearer. They paused outside the window. They went past the window. Then they came back again – came to stand outside the window.

'Christ and His Blessed Mother,' said the old woman. She raised her eyes without raising her head. I can't be seen from here, she thought. If I was sitting between the fire and the window it would be another thing; but I can't be seen from here.

The wind dropped again. Now there was no sound.

Maybe I only thought I heard a step, the old woman thought.

Then the steps sounded again – this time outside the door.

The door is bolted she thought, staring at it, and as she stared her upper lip raised so that her yellow teeth, and her gapped gums, were to be seen. Her face looked like a mask with a hole for breathing cut out of the lower part.

Then a hand pressed down the latch.

'Good Christ deliver me! Matty, go back where you belong! Go back where you belong for the love of God and His Holy Mother, and leave me in peace to live out the bit of life that is left to me. Good Christ deliver me. Holy Mother ward off from us all wicked spirits who wander through the night!' She longed to scream out for Solly, but she couldn't raise her voice beyond a whisper. Then the steps went away from the door. But they paused again at the window and she could make out a dark form. 'Good Christ keep the clouds travelling,' she implored, and she raised her eyes again as high as she could, without moving her head, till she felt the veins swelling and throbbing at the back of her eye sockets. She saw a great rent coming in the clouds. 'Good Christ!' she said, over and over again, and then the clouds broke and once more the moon slipped out.

There was no one at the window.

The old woman put her hands over her eyes and ran over to the step that led up to the loft, knocking into a bench at the foot of the steps. But she didn't feel the pain in her hurry to touch the warm and living body of Solly.

Solly didn't feel her crawling in across her either, but she wasn't surprised in the morning when she found her in the bed.

'I often wondered why you didn't sleep up here,' she said. 'It's warmer here than down below. Were you cold? Did you rap on the wall?'

'I didn't rap,' said the old woman. 'I wasn't cold. I was only lonesome thinking of Matty.' She looked at Solly with a sly look, but Solly was drawing on her stockings and didn't notice anything unusual.

'Will I make you a nice cup of tea, Mother, before you put your feet out on the floor?'

'No,' said the mother. 'I'll get up. What time is it by that clock?'

'It's ten minutes past eight.'

'I think I'll go to Mass,' said the old woman. 'The only way you can help the dead is by praying for them.'

Solly looked at her.

'Why are you raising your lips like that, Mother?' she said sharply. 'You look as if you'd seen a ghost!'

'Nobody ever saw a ghost. Stop your nonsense!' said the old woman.

'Last night I was afraid you were going to stay up all night to see Matty,' said Solly.

'What would be the use of that?' said the old woman irritably. 'If he came, I wouldn't see him!'

'How do you know?' said Solly, throwing down the broken comb on the chair. She was thinking more of what she had to do than of what she was saying. She had to go to the well and fill the bucket. She had forgotten to do it the night before. She had to gather a few twigs to blaze up the fire, and she had to put the pig's mash to boil on the fire.

'If Matty came back, and walked in that door,' said the old woman, 'you wouldn't have the strength to lift your eyes to look at him. It isn't that the dead can't come back, but that we haven't the strength to face them. We don't want them to come back!

That's the truth. It all comes to the same thing in the end! They might as well be gone for ever. When they're gone, they're gone.'

'There's no need to shout, Mother, I'm not deaf,' Solly said, and she looked at her mother again, more sharply. 'Didn't I tell you not to drag your lips back across your gums like that, Mother, you look terrible. I don't think you ought to go to Mass this morning. It's quarter past eight already. You wouldn't be down to the chapel before the middle of Mass. Get back into bed and I'll bring you a nice cup of tea.'

When Solly went downstairs there was a sound of sticks breaking and a sound of crockery hitting against crockery and a sound of a door opening and shutting. There was a sound of a pail being left down on the floor with a clatter and a sound of water splashing into an empty vessel. Then there was a sound of voices in the yard. Soon after that Solly came to the foot of the stairs leading up to the loft.

'The kettle is beginning to talk, Mother. The tea will be ready in a minute.' The sound of the cup could be heard wobbling in the saucer as Solly came up to the loft with the tea. The spoon was in the cup, sticking up straight because there was so much sugar in the bottom. 'Here's your tea, Mother, the way you like it, boiling hot with plenty of sugar, and the top off the milk.' The old woman put out her hand and took the cup. She began to drink.

'Don't get the spoon in your eye, Mother,' Solly said, looking nervously at the shaking hand.

'Give me the saucer so,' said the old woman, and she poured a thin stream of the tea into the saucer and held it to her lips, holding it with both hands and tilting it like a shallow goblet. 'Who was that I heard talking to you below?' she asked,

'It was Packy Reilly. He stepped across the fields to tell me that he was passing here late last night and the cottage was so bright he looked in the window. There was a fire on the hearth big enough to roast an ox, he said. He thought surely there was something wrong. He tried the latch but the door was bolted. He looked in the window a second time, but he could see nothing. I said we didn't hear him. At least, I didn't hear him. Did you hear anything, Mother?' The old woman stared into the pool of tea in the bottom of the saucer. 'Did you hear me asking you a question, Mother?' Solly asked sharply.

'Go down and drink your own tea. It's getting cold while you're standing there talking.'

Solly went to go down but she didn't. 'Is there anything wrong with you, Mother?' she said, standing over the ladder-hole and looking back at the old woman. She got no answer. She was no sooner at the foot of the ladder though than she came running up it again.

'Mother, Mother! Look what I found in the ashes when I was throwing them out in the ash pit.' She held out the steel picture frame. It was blackened and twisted from the heat of the fire. 'The wind must have blown it off the mantelpiece,' she said.

'It will shine up again,' said the old woman, and she reached out her hand for it.

'But the photo of Matty is burnt out of it!' Solly said. The old woman took the frame, She stared at it and Solly stared at her. Then Solly stamped her foot.

'Mother! will you stop drawing back your lips from your gums like that? If you could only see how awful you look!'

The old woman's face returned to normal at once, but when Solly went downstairs the corners of the mouth lifted and the face became a mask again.